PNEUMASPHERE

PNEUMASPHERE

The Next Phase of Human Evolution

PAM BISSONNETTE

For my daughters Danielle and Nicole Bissonnette,
fibers of my heart

ACKNOWLEDGMENTS

Pierre Teilhard de Chardin's life, philosophy, and science provided the fertile soil that inspired and nurtured this story. To make his genius known to a wider audience through an entertaining story was my purpose. I was helped by Scott Driscoll and Pam Binder, who taught me the craft of writing. Also, by friends and professionals who checked my truth: Father Paul Fitterer, SJ; Imam Jamal Rahman; Karin Kalff, MD; and Carolyn Duncan. Denise Spalding, Ann McCurdy, Kristin Strout, and the many beta readers who provided feedback and encouragement were invaluable. I am particularly indebted to Nicole Bissonnette and Danielle Bissonnette who patiently listened and provided wise guidance during the story's development; John White, my agent who had unflagging faith in the book; and my editor James Thayer who honed the book to become ready for publication. All their support on my journey to publication was a gift.

"When goodness grows weak
When evil increases,
I make myself a body.
In every age I come back.
To deliver the holy,
To destroy the sin of the sinner,
To establish righteousness." Bhagavad Gita

Prologue

The Vatican, Rome, September 29, 1978

Pope *John Paul I, Dead.* The headline leaped out at Bishop Marcel. He bought a copy of the Corriere della Sera at a sidewalk stand and sat in a café near the Spanish Steps to read it. The sixty-six-year-old pontiff, after only thirty-three days in office, had been found dead of unknown cause in the papal apartments.

Marcel, a broad square man with heavy-lidded dark eyes and straight silvery hair that framed a face severe in its lines, folded the paper and ordered a macchiato.

So soon. So quickly.

Pope John Paul I had summoned him only last week to a hoped-for reconciliation. The interview had disturbed Marcel in the extreme. He had rejected the Vatican II policies of the prior two popes that had ceded the supremacy of the Catholic Church over other religions and degraded the liturgy with a vernacular mass. John Paul's attempts at persuasion had failed. Marcel had repeated, with considerable heat, that the church's ancient laws, traditions and decrees were eternal, unchanging. Modernizing the church was leading the faithful down a path to perdition.

John Paul had then asked that they pray together for guidance. Kneeling, facing each other with closed eyes, they'd prayed silently. Marcel still shivered at what happened next.

A static charge prickled his skin. Opening his eyes, he saw a faint shimmering light emanate from John Paul's head and then grow to encompass them both.

What was this devilry?

Fear constricted his throat. Froze his limbs. Something – a light, a force, a presence – penetrated his eyes and followed the optic nerve into his brain. He grabbed the sides of his head. Tried to move, to shout, but felt trapped in a lucid nightmare. Emotions intruded: cloying, feminine, a maudlin miasma, corrosion.

He staggered as he pushed himself to his feet. Balled his hands into fists to keep them from shaking. Stood over John Paul. The shimmer vanished. Repugnance replaced fear.

"Get out of my head. You're profane, possessed. The prophecies are true. You are the Anti-Christ in St. Peter's Chair."

"No, my son," said John Paul.

Marcel shouted down at him. "You pollute me." He whirled around, his cassock flapping, and strode forcefully from the room.

And now, John Paul I was dead.

Marcel finished his coffee and ordered another.

The fledgling organization had acted quickly and competently. Now I must move faster. How many votes do we have? We must prevail this time. He mentally compiled a list matched against available leverage. His tight lips eased into a thin smile.

1

"It happened that while he was traveling to Damascus and approaching the city, suddenly a light from heaven shone all round him. He fell to the ground ..."
Acts 9:3

* * *

Ignatius of Loyola University, Seattle, October 5, 2042

Walking to early morning mass Father Paul Pennington breathed deeply of the crisp air to tamp down his irritation. He tilted forward giving the impression that his head towed his modest frame. His stride was quiet, soft, as though not wishing to draw attention or expend unnecessary energy. Gray had advanced from his temples into his thick black hair, except for the sable forelock that rose and then curled over his prominent forehead to touch his right eyebrow. It resembled a question mark which gave him a quizzical look. Beneath dark brows pinched with purpose restless blue-gray eyes observed and recorded the world. High cheek bones overshadowed triangular hollows descending to an angular jaw in a clean-shaven face with a nose and mouth of no particular note. It was as if the upper half of his face contained who he was, and below the eyes neglected shadow.

Mauve, rose and salmon pigments in the dawn sky softened the angular outlines of the edifices that made up Ignatius University. Paul avoided the manicured rose, azalea and rhododendron gardens, and aimed for the patches of native western hemlock, Douglas fir, and dogwood. A blood-orange fly agaric mushroom-cluster pushed up through a patch of kinnikinnick and salal, netted over by a web glittering with dew. A pupa, tucked under a leaf, hibernated for winter. Within its bronze armor-carapace miracles of transformation were taking place, a humble earthbound caterpillar morphing into a moth. If the caterpillar were conscious, would it perceive the moth it is to become? Or would the moth recall the caterpillar it once was? Why, dear God, did you subject the universe to such a long blind evolutionary metamorphosis?

Entering the church sacristy, Paul introduced himself to a visiting short portly priest from Montreal fussing into vestments. Monsignor Lavaliere's black satin hair might have been dyed or a toupee. Close-set eyes, a stubby nose, and a receding chin formed his face into a permanent pout. With a curt nerve-grating high-pitched greeting he extended to Paul pudgy fingers bearing a flashy ring on each hand. Paul prepared communion vessels, donned his surplice and stole, and together they processed to the altar.

A Benedictine nun and seven balding or white-haired campus neighbors sat in the pews. Lavaliere's words crackled over the sound system: "In the name of the Father, and of the Son and of the Holy Spirit ... confess to Almighty God ... sinned through my own fault ... Lord have mercy...."

Paul's irritation peaked. Why do we dwell so much on guilt? Will the mass ever evolve from the stern Old Testament?

Lavaliere whined on. Paul had said these same words thousands of times since his ordination twenty years ago. Then the mass had filled him with exhilaration and hope. But that had been lost over the years from lack of nurturing by an increasingly conservative church, by a cerebral and repressed order, and – he had to admit it – by his growing resentment at God's silence.

The tall angular church reflected the strident accusing voice of Lavaliere and swallowed up the feeble responses of the small congregation. The 'Alleluia', which should have been an expression of joy, was sung like a dirge. The scriptures from St. Paul and St. John were read in a rapid monotone that squandered

4

their beauty and transformative power. Lavaliere returned to the presider's chair, leaving his flock to ponder the readings rather than trouble them with a homily.

Paul glanced around at the tableau for any spark of spirit. They might as well be attending a funeral. Is anyone truly alive here? More like mannequins. Are we a priesthood of a dead religion?

Mass resumed. Hands purified. Gifts blessed and consecrated in swift order. "Do this in memory of me," intoned Lavaliere.

Paul wondered whether Jesus would have left any ritual so stripped of feeling as a remembrance. Would he recognize it? The last meal among his closest friends before he died celebrated the last great divine intervention. God incarnated to become human, one of us. It would have been deeply moving. Not this hollow husk.

Communion was distributed followed by a quiet period. Then a final blessing from Lavaliere, who droned: "Go in peace. The mass is ended."

"Thanks be to God," responded the congregation.

Did liturgists get the irony in these words?

Paul preceded Lavaliere into the sacristy. After hanging his surplice and stole, and cleaning and storing the communion vessels, he took a shortcut back to his residence through the woods, clearing his mind of sepulchral cobwebs and briefly restoring his equanimity. A Bewick's wren trilled at him from the branches of a magnificent Douglas fir that was littering the ground with its ridiculously small cones. The tree took him back to the lonely little boy that Father John had introduced to God's great outdoor cathedrals of towering craggy peaks clad in snowy-white robes and tall pillars of evergreen fir. The small patches of native trees on campus, sadly hemmed in like zoo specimens, reminded him starkly of how much he missed John, followed by a guilty pledge to visit him. Paul pressed his palm against the largest Douglas fir. Under his touch its deeply grooved brown bark held a spirit, John would say. Within its weathered folds he imagined John's old face. Paul smiled. Could be there's more druid than priest in me.

He spent most of the day tutoring students and preparing his next two lectures. Teaching was the one aspect of his life where he felt freedom and authenticity. Physics and theology complemented each other, and in his most popular classes he integrated them. But it was also where he drew the most criticism for skirting, if not flouting, orthodoxy.

Jesuits had a long history of challenging the status quo and defying it when justified, like Father Daniel Berrigan in the 1960s. Paul entered the lecture hall named after the famous Jesuit Vietnam War protestor and recipient of honorary membership on the FBI's roll of most wanted. Tonight, Paul's lecture would introduce the works of another challenging Jesuit.

Night blacked out the lecture hall windows as if they had been covered with tarpaper. The tables were filled with earnest students tapping notes on tablets.

"...Teilhard de Chardin's theology of evolution resulted in a ban on his theological teaching, the quashing of his writings, and exile from France for the remainder of his life. He believed Christ to be the force of evolution, pulling the universe into the future to what he termed the Omega Point ... cited increasing complexity ... cephalization ... development of the noosphere ... predicted the future evolution toward a pneumasphere ..."

While Paul proceeded with his lecture, the other half of his attention watched Father Tom Bradbury, university chancellor, sitting still and expressionless in the back of the room. He'd quietly slipped in shortly after Paul had begun his lecture, leaned back stretching out his long legs under the table, and folded lanky arms across his chest.

Paul felt light-headed. The room seemed to brighten and then waver before his eyes. His lecture notes fluttered to the floor. He stooped to collect them. Shook his head and pulled out a handkerchief, unnecessarily blowing his nose to provide a moment to recover. When he focused again, the room was normal, the dizziness gone. The class stared at him. Tom was sitting up straight.

"Any questions? Yes, Jesse."

"Why did the church suppress his work?"

Jesse, a wiry dark-haired and bearded young man with a colorful yarmulke, reminded Paul of his younger self.

6

"Teilhard rejected creationism over a 100 years ago when it was still mainstream religious belief. He held we're all a part of a continuum of divinely driven evolutionary progress from simple matter and energy toward higher orders of complexity and consciousness. There was no original sin or fall of man. Genesis was a myth to explain mankind becoming conscious of suffering and death. He paid a high price for his beliefs."

"Do you agree with him?" Jesse asked.

Paul glanced toward the back of the room. Tom's piercing gray eyes watched him keenly.

"Both beliefs wind up at the same place."

Several hands shot into the air. Paul ignored them. "The assignment for next class is to come prepared to debate your view of the next step in human evolution. Or if you believe mankind is no longer evolving, then your arguments why. In either case include circumstances and consequences."

The students filed out with an undercurrent of mumbling while Paul packed papers, texts, tablet and notebook into his backpack. Tom waited until Paul locked the lecture room and then fell in with him as they walked to the priest residence hall across campus.

"Interesting assignment you gave them." Tom pulled up the collar of his jacket to shield his neck from water droplets falling from skeletal maples that were collecting the evening's drizzle on their limbs.

"I try to challenge them to think, like we were taught," Paul said.

"Do you like evening classes?" Tom asked.

"I get a wider diversity of students in the evenings. Some are young ideological firebrands. Others maturing philosophers. They come from all faiths and no faith – the curious, seekers, scholars. I like them."

Tom and Paul walked through puddles that nurtured the ubiquitous moss. One cone of luminescence after another, cast by the lamplights, backlit the Brownian motion of the mist dampening their coats.

"Why'd you attend my class tonight?"

Tom took a couple more steps and then glanced sidelong at Paul. "One of your young ideological firebrands, the seminarian, complained to me about your unorthodox lectures. He says you're heretical."

Paul stiffened. "That's a harsh word. So much blood and suffering in it. He can't really mean that?"

Tom strode along, his fringe of dank hair glistening. "The young use labels carelessly. I've talked to our seminarian and made it clear we don't use such words lightly. But we have to be careful. Archbishop Bauer is trying to undermine the independence of Ignatius U. Exert control over our curriculum. According to him we're a hotbed of 'liberation theology and modernism'."

"But in complete alignment with Pope Francis's papacy," Paul said.

"That was a while back. Jesuits who were close to him were evicted from the Vatican and we've been in disfavor ever since. Times and church culture have changed. And while we may not change totally with it, we shouldn't openly flout it."

Paul kicked a stone off the path. "We're a rational order."

"Yet many would say faith itself isn't rational," said Tom.

They climbed the steep worn stone steps to the residence and entered the hall permeated with the scent of wood polish and mellowing leather. It was just 10:00 in the evening. The heavy mist had turned to rain. Tom shook the moisture from his jacket and brushed the droplets from his head.

Paul sighed. "What do you want me to do?"

Tom's gaze bored into Paul. "As your conscience guides you. But you've got to be discrete. Don't give Bauer any reason to take an interest in us." Then Tom walked away through a side wing off the main hall, his footsteps and shadow receding through the corridor.

Paul scaled the stairs to his room. The walls of orthodoxy were closing in. Hopefully just one more blip in the centuries of oscillations between progressive and conservative leadership. Sticking it out would require creative integrity.

The architect who had designed the hall of the priest residence must have been a disciple of Gaudi, Spain's architectural master.

From a floor of natural stone, the mahogany staircase spiraled up a wide shaft through three floors. A long crystal chandelier suggestive of a bright waterfall suspended down through the stairwell. The walls of glossy sky-blue tiles inlaid with occasional green swirls, sprays and fronds reflected the chandelier's light, simulating dappled sunlight under water. The crystals reacted to the slightest air movement, making the walls appear to waver. It was like ascending from the bottom of a deep, cool, grotto.

Paul paused midway up the stairs. In some way the illusion of suspension in water, the wavering walls, the shimmering light, evoked the light-dizzy experience he'd felt in the classroom. He stopped and closed his eyes until it passed. What's going on with me tonight?

Presumed to have healthy heart, hips and knees, Paul was housed with the few younger priests on the top floor. Most of the adjacent cells were vacant. Tucked under the eaves, Paul's chamber consisted of a bed, a roll-top desk, two mismatched chairs, a wardrobe, a sisal rug, and sink with a mirror. Tonight, his east facing dormer window framed a dark portrait of rain tears.

He set his wet shoes on the dormer ledge above the radiator to dry, leaned on the window frame and gazed out over the campus. A depressing day. One of many. Dead liturgy, petrified dogma, straight-jacketed rationality and Tom's warning made it inescapable to conclude that the church was other than mummified bones and dust.

Why do I stay?

The answer was always the same. Because the church raised me. Because the only place I feel I belong is within the order and at the university. Because I love the challenges of teaching.

And God?

Out of the window the drizzle had stopped, and the clouds were dissipating.

How can I love a silent God? About whom I have no experience? If I were honest, I'd admit I'm an imposter. Just going through the motions.

The spike of the church bell tower, campus edifices dedicated to various dead patrons, the compact boxy chapel, and the distant commercial neon lights were faintly visible in the night.

For a moment the bell tower seemed to sway to the right. Then its middle bulged. Chartreuse luminescence outlined the trees below. Moist patches on the ground left by the rain reflected an unnatural sheen. A zigzag of blue light flashed across the lawn below then vanished. Sweet Jesus. What...?

A wave of vertigo and nausea hit Paul. Then pain as sharp as a skewer lanced into his skull. Incandescent light blinded him. His eyes shut but the light was still there. He collapsed to the floor holding his head, teeth clenched. Curled up in a fetal ball. Retched. The piercing pain swelled from an acute point to a distended bubble, then expanded like a balloon in his right temple.

He heard himself groan. Then the pain blinked out. He was suspended in brilliant light. The light pulsed and flowed and shifted from pure white to the full spectrum of colors. Light upon light – and ecstasy. The light contained joy of such overwhelming magnitude that he felt shrunken to a point too insignificant to absorb even a scintilla of it.

At what seemed a far distance the light coalesced into a dense center. Paul's desire and curiosity drew him toward it. He felt the sensation of movement, but the center – the presence – never got any closer. It shimmered and then receded like a vanishing comet.

Paul found himself prone on the floor. He rocked forward onto knees and hands, and then stood, grabbing the bedpost for balance. The clock on his desk glowed 12:53.

Over an hour gone. Sweet Jesus, what just happened?

Drained, disoriented, Paul lay on the bed without bothering to remove his clothes.

Whip-sawed between excruciating pain and unimaginable euphoria made it impossible to think rationally. Sleep, I need sleep. My brain feels bruised.

* * *

The alarm clock jarred Paul into somnolent confusion. Light seeped through the dormer window. He noticed his rumpled clothes, his aching head. Then sat up with a start. Last evening's ordeal flooded his bleary mind, pumping a spike of adrenaline up his spine. What happened to me?

10

Paul's hand shook as he shaved, and he nicked his chin. The mirror traced the ruby blood as it snaked down his throat to lodge in the hairs of his chest. He splashed cold water over his face. Grabbed both sides of the sink. Inspected his face. His blue-gray eyes stared back at him, dusky with anxiety and defiance. Saliva oozed into his mouth. He swallowed. Ran both hands through his thatch of hair.

His thoughts swirled in a kaleidoscope of anxious questions and reactions. What was it? What happened? Did something precipitate it? Should I see a doctor? Tell my superior?

Paul's stomach twisted. Tom is already concerned about my teaching. How would he feel about me collapsing in pain, seeing lights, losing a sense of time? The twist in his stomach tightened.

Maybe it was a fluke. Won't happen again. He glanced at the clock. No time to think about it now. He took some ibuprofen, grabbed his materials, and left for class.

Over the next few days worry over the possible return of the episode kept him continually on edge. He avoided unnecessary contacts. Consulted the library and internet. Decided what he had had was a severe migraine. While debilitating, migraines were not serious enough to seek medical attention or to keep him from teaching. After a week without a re-occurrence he relaxed a little.

His theology class was studying the lost gospels discovered at Nag Hammadi that were rejected from the Christian canon. In the last century some of these texts caused scholars to re-open debates about Gnosticism, long since thought to be discredited and dead. Paul cautioned the class they may find some Gnostic beliefs about the value of the physical world untenable, "…but consider whether the Gnostics held a kernel of truth. They believed one could achieve direct knowledge and experience of the divine during one's lifetime."

Paul assigned them to read the rejected Gospel of St. Thomas Didymus, the famous Doubting Thomas, and compare it to the accepted Gospel of St. John.

He closed his lecture notes and wondered, while waiting for the students to talk and jostle their way out, whether we would be closer to experiencing the mystery of God and the universe by now if the Gnostics hadn't been suppressed. He turned out the lights, locked up the empty room, and walked out into the rainy night.

A figure stepping from the shadows startled Paul.

"You're out late." Ambrose shortened his stride to match Paul's and offered the cover of his large black golf umbrella. Ambrose wore his usual tentative smile on a placid face. The big fleshy man, with pale wispy hair framing a baby face in which small blue eyes were almost lost, was a fish out of water as a diocesan priest among the Jesuits. Paul had recognized and befriended a fellow loner.

"So are you. Got behind at the library?" Paul tripped on a rough stone and barely caught himself from falling.

"You okay?"

"I'm okay." Tiredness in his voice belied Paul's words.

"Bet you'd like a nightcap," Ambrose said. "I've got a nice aged scotch in my room."

Ambrose could be counted on to be uncomplicated. He didn't seem to have the qualms of faith and conflict of doctrine that haunted Paul. And Ambrose had the best-stocked liquor cabinet on campus.

"That'd be nice."

They walked along in silence through the droopy, dead and dying landscape. Slippery leaves squished under foot.

Near the entrance to the priest residence Ambrose halted, "Something on your mind? You seem withdrawn lately."

"Last week Tom monitored my class," said Paul. "He warned me that a student complained my lectures were heretical. Can you believe it? He said Bauer is looking for reasons to interfere here at Ignatius and he didn't want me to provide any."

Rain dripped around the umbrella. At such close range the pupils of Ambrose's eyes looked dark and dilated in the dim porch light. Pursed lips replaced his usual Mona Lisa smile.

Ambrose dropped eye contact. "What'll you do?"

"I'll be careful. The problem is I find it difficult to conceal my views. The church has been regressing since the death of Pope Francis. Taking us back to the static faith of a hundred years ago. Emphasizing blind obedience to rules rather than exercise of conscience."

12

Ambrose looked away into the distance. "I don't understand you Jesuits. You're never content with the way things are. Always pushing." He turned back toward Paul. "Surely you can find a way to represent the views of the church even if you can't make them your own? That's how to survive around here."

Honestly? Paul looked up expecting to see a sign of this revelation. But Ambrose's face wore its usual mask. This was not a good time or place to explore this side of Ambrose. Paul stepped out from under the umbrella.

"I think I'll visit the chapel before turning in. Rain-check on the nightcap?" He turned up his collar and watched Ambrose's broad back as he lumbered up the stairs into the residence hall.

The interchange disturbed him. Tonight was the first time Ambrose hinted at some fissure in the facade of his placid persona. Maybe he's an oyster without appearing to be one? How many of us are covering up secrets here?

Paul reached the reflection pool at the entrance to the St. Ignatius Chapel. Raindrops formed a pattern of small dimples radiating across its surface merging one into the other in a tessellating pattern. The chapel behind the pool rested like a rock butte on a land-bench. Less used and smaller than the main church, its austere lines, soft lighting and intimate atmosphere soothed, especially when Paul needed solitude from communal life.

The floor-to-ceiling wooden doors of the chapel swung silently inward. The plain hand-hewn stone altar soaked in the burgundy glow of the suspended sanctuary lamp that threw a mottled pink shadow. The lamp's octagonal leaded glass housing fractured the flame, projecting a flickering shadowy duet onto the wall.

Paul knelt in the sanctuary. A two-pronged Madrona branch, the size of a small tree, reached from the floor flagstones to a stucco ceiling. It flanked the tabernacle, a solitary receptacle, an unadorned stone crypt perched on a pedestal. The sacred space with its single kneeler conducted Paul to deep prayer.

Head bowed, he recited the Profundis: "Out of the depths I cry to you, O Lord; Lord, hear my voice..."

After twenty years as a priest, why have I never felt your presence? How many times have I consecrated bread and wine to you? Held you in my hands? Touched you with my lips – and felt nothing. All I've ever wanted is to know you – feel you're there – understand your will.

But the only response was the beating of his heart marking precious finite time.

What kind of father ignores his children?

Silence.

He rose to leave. Dizzy, he stumbled and gripped the kneeler. Something funny about the light. Objects were rimmed in a faint glow. Then tingling behind his right eye grew to an irritation he recognized.

No.

Pain struck. Stabbed his right temple. Proliferated in pulses through his head in a crescendo to agony. He dropped to the floor. Grasped his skull. His stomach heaved. The sharp bitter taste of bile fouled his mouth. He felt and heard the pulse in his neck.

Jesus, what is this? His defensive instincts took over. Muscles tightened to maintain control. Fight the pain. Please – stop. Dear God. He writhed on the floor until he became rigid.

2

"Allah is the Light of the heavens and the earth...
Light upon light.
Allah guides to His light whom He wills."
Excerpt, 35th verse of the 24th Sura of the Quran, Sura an-Nur.

* * *

Harborview, a massive block of bricks perched on the west side of First Hill sloping down toward the heart of Seattle's central business district, boasted the busiest emergency room in Washington State. The most acute cases were flown in by helicopter. But most were local from the night streets and port quays of Seattle: homicides, drug overdoses, attempted suicides, mental patients off their meds, extraordinary injuries.

Dr. Rabia Habib reported to emergency. Her stature was such that she could have passed for a girl. But her deep brown eyes were wary, reflecting life experience and past trauma that she had tucked away behind a soft smile. Milk chocolate skin contrasted with her white coat. Her long jet-black hair was pulled back to fit like a cap, from which dangled a thick braid that swung in time with her quick steps.

A white male with salt and pepper hair, about forty to forty-five, of average height and moderate build, lay on a gurney.

Dr. O'Neil, a wiry young man who exuded energy that appeared to escape through his undisciplined curly hair, addressed her without looking up from his tablet. "His name's

15

Father Paul Pennington, a professor and resident priest at Ignatius University. He was found on the floor of their university's chapel this morning. No one knows how long he'd been lying there. At most it might've been six hours. His vital signs are elevated. We can't find any obvious cause for his unconscious state. Someone from the university came with him. He's in the waiting room. Can't tell us much."

"Has he talked? Moved voluntarily or involuntarily to stimulus? Opened his eyes?" Rabia asked. Something was odd about him. A faint filminess seemed to glisten on the surface of his pale skin.

"He's been unresponsive since he arrived," said Dr. O'Neil. "The medics said he didn't move or make a sound en route. No symptom of stroke or heart attack. His pallor could indicate internal bleeding or shock. I'm admitting him and scheduling a toxicology scan. Check out his neurological function." He handed her the tablet and left the room without mentioning the odd look of the patient. It was more than pallor. Did he not see it?

The blink and glow of the ER monitors recorded Paul's heart rate, blood pressure, oxygen saturation levels and EEG activity. Normal temperature. Infection unlikely. She checked his chart. Examined his head, ears, and gently lifted his eyelids. His pupils were unresponsive to light and looked like pinheads. She palpated his abdomen. His limbs were rigid, and his skin clammy to the touch and unusually pale.

Though the room was cool, perspiration beaded his upper lip, forehead, the sides of his nose sloping down toward his cheeks, and the smooth triangle of skin between his nipples and sternum. His legs, arms, face, and throat muscles had a tone of rigidity to them – jaw taut, hands clenched – uncharacteristic of sleep or coma, more like a seizure or pain response.

She took his hands, uncurled the fingers, and held them. Tense and slippery. His heart monitor beeped, beeped. She let go. Walked around behind him. Placed both hands along his temples, felt around to his frontal lobe. No obvious anomalies.

She flicked off the lights. The windowless room – except for the small window in the door to the corridor – darkened. Rabia caught her breath. His skin faintly shone. An indistinct luminous sheen encased his body but was strongest around his head.

Rabia cupped her hands around his cranium and closed her eyes. Concentrated on the tips of her fingers. Sensed suppressed energy like a low-level static charge just beneath the scalp that prickled her fingertips.

He stirred. Murmured.

Her eyes shot open. Merciful Allah.

Rabia withdrew her hands, pulled the privacy screen around the bed, and sat close to Paul's head. She laid a hand on his forehead and shut her eyes. Not in thirty years had she sensed this. Energy bled from him, as it bled from another long ago....

She was crying and kneeling beside her father as he lay bleeding and broken in the wreckage of a Sufi shrine that was now a pile of rubble and smoke. She cradled his head in her small hands. His vital energy seeped away with the blood that pooled around his body. With his last breath his inner light emerged, flowed into her, and awakened her own. Then it dissipated like vapor in wind – and he was gone.

The intervening decades of horror, pain, and sorrow had stripped Rabia to spiritual solitude except for her own spark of light. The joy of the discovery of someone else who was awakened washed through her.

I'm not alone.

She peered at his face, pinched with pain and tension. He's fighting it. Why? She leaned down and whispered in his ear, "Father Pennington let go. Don't fight it. Don't fear it. Let go."

She chafed his hands. Heat radiated from his skin. Softly, she called his name several times until he shuddered and uttered a cry. A light as delicate as the glow of a firefly emerged from his right frontal cortex and expanded to envelop his full head. It was as though his skull was permeable to light shining through from the inside. A few inches of shimmering luminous blue-gold feathered into the darkened room. His facial muscles flinched then softened. His body eased its rigidity but seemed poised as if for action. The monitors around the wall like a cockpit reflected his experience in lights and sounds and numbers. Amplitudes and frequencies in greens, blues and reds peaked, beeped and flowed with his release. His body trembled. She covered him with a light blanket.

She replaced her hands around his head within the corona and closed her eyes again. The light of the corona flowed up from his head through her hands and arms to her temples. She caught a glimpse of his state.

He's being drawn in. But doesn't understand.

She leaned down next to his ear and whispered, "You're not ready. Come back."

The light faded. His eyes opened. He stared at her for several heart beats and then heavy eyelids closed.

"Sleep."

She sat at his bedside, in wonder. Here was objective medical evidence of another's aura experience. She stayed with him until his breathing relaxed and deepened. The monitors on the wall recorded vital signs returning to normal. Heartbeat slowed, blood pressure dropped, and oxygen saturation levels returned to within range. The capillary return flow in his extremities was good.

The discovery flooded her with hope, after she had given up hoping. Other than her father, she'd never experienced the inner light of another. But this man – a Christian priest – his aura was very different from her father's and her own. How did he awaken? Why did the light cause him fear and pain? Questions that had no answers yet. But I've found another. I must know this man.

She brushed damp hair from his brow. Then she reluctantly left to attend other patients.

3

"The sleeper must awaken!" Frank Herbert's Dune

* * *

Paul's awareness grew in stages. Blood throbbed in his ears. His diaphragm worked the bellows in his chest pumping warm air that carried the astringent scent of antiseptic through his nostrils. A light weight of cloth rested on his feet, knees, stomach. An itching, pins-and-needles sensation made his hands restless. His muscles were as sore as if he'd worked out hard. Sensitive to the bright lights, he kept his eyes closed.

People came and went. They seemed far away, except one. A woman with small cool hands. With a long thick black braid. She'd helped me. Who?

A door opened and closed. Footsteps approached. A hand touched his shoulder. He raised his arm awkwardly and tangled his IV.

"Father Paul? Paul Pennington, can you hear me?"

"Yes," Paul managed with a nearly inaudible sigh. It was hard to open his eyes. Focus his thoughts.

"Please look at me. I'm Dr. O'Neil. Open your eyes."

Paul pushed open eyelids that felt as heavy as silver dollars. He winced at the harsh light. Sweet Jesus, what happened to me? How did I come to be in a hospital?

But the doctor had many questions of his own. "What's your name? What year is it? When were you born? How do you feel?

Are you in pain? Watch my light." The interrogation went on. "What do you hear when I do this? Look at this chart and tell me what you see."

Dr. O'Neil proceeded with the physical examination aided by a nurse: limbs pricked, tendons thumped, temperature recorded, blood pressure measured, blood samples taken.

"How did I get here?"

Dr. O'Neil continued with his examination. "You were found on the floor of your chapel early this morning. Do you recall anything of this?"

"I remember visiting the chapel last night."

"You lost consciousness."

Did I? Paul eyed the room. Looked for something or someone missing but saw just beige walls and monitors. He hung on to one thing from the fog. Someone he remembered. Someone who'd helped him.

"There was someone here, a woman. Had long dark hair in a braid. Who was she?"

"You must mean Dr. Rabia Habib." He said something to the nurse who then left, and then he turned back to Paul. "Soon someone will take you for an MRI. Shouldn't take long. Then I'll be back later with the results."

Alone, Paul turned his face toward the wall. His heart and the blip – blip on the monitor beat in time. The IV drip – drip hypnotized. Lying there he sank down into the space between the subconscious and conscious, and tried to remember.

I was in pain. Someone was here. Her voice. Gentle. Saying something about letting go of fear. Her hands. I felt cool hands. Then the pain stopped, and I was flooded with brilliant light – and euphoria – like before.

Memory moved through him of a panoply of colors, as though cast through a prism: blues, golden yellows, greens, violets, reds; in sparks and waves. Now opaque. Now transparent. The light in its variations extended beyond sight in every direction. Yet there were no bearings where a compass could point. The colors swirled, funneled, magnified and spiraled off; toward something, into something dense and fluid. A center that drew everything to

20

it. What was it? A light – hole? Paul moved toward it but felt pulled back.

"You're not ready," said the voice.

Not ready? No. I want to know.

The light receded, thinned, faded. He opened his eyes. A young woman sat beside him in the dimness, petite with long dark hair in a braid.

So tired. He closed his eyes.

"Sleep."

He felt cool fingers brush damp hair from his brow.

* * *

Over the following day Paul endured a series of tests to pinpoint or rule out one ailment after another. Every time his door opened, he feared bad news: brain tumor, epilepsy, aneurism, trauma, infection, toxic reaction. But what he was hoping for was to see the woman again with the long dark braid. What did she know? How had she known?

Clinical tests revealed nothing. No tumors, no epilepsy, no aneurism, no blood chemistry or neurologic abnormalities, or things he'd never heard of like inflammation of the transverse mandibular joint. Physical causes of his episode had so far been ruled out. The hospital discharged him with several prescriptions for pain and dizziness should it happen again and lined up additional appointments, including one with a psychiatrist.

As Paul was leaving the hospital a petite woman in a white coat approached him breathlessly. A thick black braid swung over her shoulder. Startled, he stopped. She's the one.

"Fr. Pennington, please, I would like to talk with you about your – experience. Would you be willing to meet with me?" She pressed a business card into his hand.

Caught off guard, he stood mute in awkward silence. He read the card she'd placed in his hand: Dr. Rabia Habib, Neurologist, with her contact information. Then he looked at her face. She stared at him, unwavering, with the slightest of smiles.

She was younger than he remembered but with the same rope of black braid down her back.

Paul extended his hand. "Dr. Habib, I very much would like to talk with you. When? Where? You've only to name it."

"I'd prefer not here. I'm free most early mornings. Please pick a place and text me."

She retreated down the corridor. Paul watched her disappear to become another anonymous white coat.

4

No one has greater love than this, to lay down one's life for one's friends. John 15:12

* * *

Father Eduardo squirmed his numb buttocks on the wooden stool in the cramped stuffy confessional. Hearing confessions was a hopeless job yet endeared parishioners to him. The majority were hard working, hard living people trying to survive, trying to find a little pleasure in a harsh life. He loved them. Twice a week he listened for hours to streams of misery and suffering and doled out forgiveness and penances – three Hail Marys for petty theft and up to a month of rosaries for adultery. For egregious violence, murders for passion, or for hire from drug deals gone wrong, he required confession to civil authority, but he knew they never did.

The church squatted in the midst of a sprawling favela on the outskirts of Sao Paulo amid the rest of the squatters and squalor, except it was constructed out of brick and mortar instead of salvaged plywood, plastic tarps, and rusted corrugated sheet metal. Eduardo had been assigned here to lie low when the Jesuits were expelled from the Vatican after the sudden death of Pope Francis. But he didn't mind. He was a tall spare man of kindly face in the last third of a full life who approached the world with a long view through clear eyes.

The interior of the church reflected its community: folding chairs and threadbare dirty cushions for kneeling; a wooden table for an altar with an embroidered bed sheet for a covering; crude wooden plaques of the stations of the cross carved by a parishioner hung around the sides; a small wall safe made shift as a tabernacle that housed the plate gold communion vessels for mass. But the cross and Madonna that Eduardo had brought from Rome were the glory of the congregation who left simple offerings at their feet.

The dark confessional expanded one's sensory faculties. Eduardo could tell the penitent's age by the sound of shuffle, heavy tread, or patter of feet; creaking of the kneeler; wheezing; or the occasional grunt due to reluctant knees. Their voices signaled fear, shame, resignation, sorrow, despair. Odors wafted through the thin porous partition: tobacco, body odor, cheap perfume, alcohol, chewing gum, wet dog, urine, vomit.

Today's parade of sadness ended. He closed the partition panel and waited in silence to give time for those praying penances in the church to maintain their anonymity. He reflected on the mystery of why in the divine design there needed to be so many poor. As he rose from the stool and stretched another penitent entered. With a sigh Eduardo took his seat, opened the slide on the partition, and waited for the "Bless me father for I have sinned...." None came.

It was a big man, breathing heavily. He smelled of cologne and cigars.

"How can I help you?" Eduardo asked.

"You have something I want." The man's voice was gravelly, deep, threatening.

"What might that be?"

"A memory stick you stole from the Vatican," the voice said.

Eduardo's head snapped up. "I stole nothing from the Vatican."

Silence. Then the door of the penitent's side of the confessional banged and Eduardo's door jerked open. A man about forty, with a shock of shiny black hair and full mustache grabbed Eduardo by the arm and pulled him out. The man was fleshy but strong with a grip like a tourniquet. Gold chains dangled out of his open neck shirt. His puffy pocked and scarred face smiled with a curled upper lip. Eyes confident and mocking

24

scanned Eduardo as though sizing up what it would take to get the job done.

Eduardo noticed a thin man in the background in cargo pants and jean jacket with greasy long hair. He had a pistol aimed at three parishioners. Julio sang in the choir and eked out a living delivering packages. His wife Maria cleaned houses and the church. They huddled together with their three-year-old daughter Lucia. Maria was on her knees comforting Lucia who wailed into her mother's hair clutched in her baby fists. Julio stood in front of them both, arms spread wide with a wild look on his face.

Julio pleaded. "Please..."

"Shut up," barked the accomplice.

"I'll let them go if you give us the memory stick," said the first man. "I'm in a hurry."

"Please let them go," Eduardo said. "It's me you want."

"Wrong answer." He nodded.

The accomplice shot Julio in the stomach.

Julio fell backwards over Maria spraying her with blood. Lucia screamed. Maria crawled from under Julio and pushed Lucia to the floor. She covered the child's body with her own and implored the Madonna for protection. The accomplice laughed.

"Get it now or the next one dies," the first man said.

"It's in the tabernacle," Eduardo said. He trembled violently. "I'll get it. Please let them go."

The first man released him and pulled out his own gun to prod Eduardo up the aisle toward the altar.

Eduardo's mind raced. What can I do to save these poor souls? I need to make myself the sole target, eliminate leverage. No Vatican secret is worth their lives. Why do they want it? The memory stick can't have any intrinsic value to these thugs. What might? Maybe – it might be enough – an instant of distraction.

He reached the wall safe, worked the combination, and opened the door. Inside were the gold ciborium and chalice. He threw them on the floor and they rolled away. As his captor lurched for the gold, Eduardo grabbed the memory stick, thrust it down his throat, and swallowed as fast as he could. He gagged, coughed, and tasted blood; dropped to his knees and fell over.

"Yeoul," yelled the thug. He grabbed Eduardo by the neck and squeezed. "Give."

Constriction of Eduardo's throat after choking down the stick brought him close to losing consciousness.

The thug called the accomplice. "We'll have to cut him open to get it."

Two pairs of eyes stared down at Eduardo. He remained lucid long enough to sense Maria running with Lucia out of the church. Then his shirt was ripped open and a knife moved to his throat.

5

"The work of the devil will infiltrate even into the church in such a way that one will see cardinals opposing cardinals, and bishops against other bishops." Excerpt from the Third Akita Prophecy, 1973

* * *

"Satan, the Father of Lies, the Anti-Christ, will seize the throne of St. Peter. Spirit of Wisdom will awaken the righteous to despoil the Anti-Christ and empower the Spirit within all who follow Her." Excerpt from the Huaraz Prophecy, 2039.

* * *

Archbishop Bauer's taxi crawled through Chicago's morning traffic. Winter snow crouched in building corners and floated down gutters in a brownish-gray sludge punctuated with cigarette butts, used condoms, plastic wrappers, and all manner of sordid urban flotsam and jetsam.

Bauer was nearing sixty, balding, of stout stature, and dour. The heavy folds of his face made his arrogant eyes appear to squint from under ponderous brows and eyelids. His cheeks were furrowed in lines descending around a fleshy nose to a frowning mouth in a perpetual pout. He cocked his head to the left when addressing people implying distrust or condescension. His plump fingers sported a gold ring on his right hand, and a large ruby ring on his left. For being well over five feet tall, his gait was short as though his hips were inflexible and his buttocks frozen. It gave him a prissy demeanor.

He had flown out a day early to enjoy a meal at his former club, and a comfortable stay at his favorite hotel. Even Chicago snow was preferable to dreary rainy Seattle. But his mood hadn't improved. *I'd still be here and probably in a red hat if I hadn't trusted the wrong person.* As he taxied to the meeting, the unfairness of it all tasted sour.

He took the private lift to the penthouse of the building where they were to meet and adjusted his collar and attitude in anticipation of the conclave. The summons had been secret and cryptic. Leadership of the three most conservative Catholic clerical societies were to convene in Chicago. Bauer guessed that the conclave would be about preparing for the election of the next pope. Pope Pius XIII couldn't last much longer. Bauer mentally rubbed his hands together. *Now may be my opportunity.*

A young man with the posture and manner of a Marine in a black suit and white bowtie met him as he stepped off the elevator. "Archbishop Bauer, this way please."

The conference room into which he was escorted could have seated more than a score. The long ebony table gleamed, reflecting the broken gray clouds from the windows on three sides of the room. Plush burgundy chairs, a credenza, and a high-tech wall completed the room arranged on a floor of black and green chevron tiles.

Nice. Corelli obviously has friends in high places.

Bauer was not the first to arrive. Already conversing at the far end of the table were four others unknown to him. He brushed an imaginary speck off his PXII insignia of two overlapping red hearts crowned in gold – emblem of the Society of Pope Pius XII – and approached wearing a winning smile.

One of the quartet, a lanky sandy-haired man with a weasel face addressed him. "We're waiting for the others. Best to leave introductions until they arrive," and then turned back to the conversation.

Snubbed. Bauer snorted and moved to the far end of the table. The subtle insignias of the Society of Saint Pius V and Opus Dei were unmistakable. Bauer wasn't accustomed to being treated so coolly. He turned his back on them and looked out over the Chicago skyline.

The bright morning sunlight penetrated the thin clouds but not the chilliness of the room. Who do these people think they are? It was PXII who masterminded the navigation of Pope Pius XIII onto the Chair of St. Peter. It's to PXII he owes his allegiance, not these zealots. Where are my own confreres?

A flurry of activity at the door heralded the arrival of coffee, croissants, and PXII leadership, the last seven attendees led by Cardinal Corelli of Chicago. They clearly had been at a pre-meeting somewhere. Why wasn't I invited?

Corelli strode into the room, his robes swishing like a lady's ball gown. Grizzled hair poked out from under his red zucchetto. Behind a frozen smile, Bauer smoldered. You'd think Corelli wore a crown the way he had flounced in and ensconced himself at the head of the table.

"Welcome distinguished members. I have the authority of Pope Pius XIII to convene this conclave. But before we begin... In the name of the Father, the Son ...."

Then they went around the table for introductions. Of the group's dozen, cardinals and bishops all, PXII had eight members. The other four were evenly divided between the Society of St. Pius V and Opus Dei members. Together the three societies covered the landscape from Washington DC and New York, to New Orleans and Dallas, to Chicago and St. Louis, to Seattle and L.A., and the heartland.

Cardinal Corelli had the keen eyes, quick movements and pointed features of a hawk, and at times preened his robes for effect. The rest of them impressed Bauer more by temperaments stamped on their features, than their names. The catfish with a broad mouth, dull eyes and full lips used his hands like sensitive feelers. To his right the red satin-haired tiger with a smooth voice implied sheathed danger. At the far end of the table perched the praying mantis, tall and gaunt with cruel glittering eyes. The rest were a motley menagerie of predators including the weasel who had affronted him earlier. A treacherous arena. Undercurrents here. Uneasy alliances. Be careful.

"Our purpose here is to assure papal succession sympathetic … return the church to a righteous course … back to its roots … oppose modernism…"

Bauer internally groaned at having to endure another of Corelli's fatuous speeches. He took out a handkerchief and blew his nose in salute. Can't we just get on with business? We all know this. Who's he practicing for? He can't seriously think he could be a papal candidate? By God, he does. Bauer's mind raced down one avenue of possibility after another of how he could use this to his advantage, until Corelli approached the important points.

"We're called by his Holiness Pope Pius XIII to provide a list of candidates for him to appoint the next cadre of cardinals for the papal consistory," Corelli said. "Since he's expanded the number from 120 to 170, there are eighteen existing vacancies to fill plus the additional fifty. Given the current count of College of Cardinal members loyal to us, this will give us a firm majority and assure complete control of the selection of Pius XIII's successor. Sixteen of these vacant cardinalates have been allotted to the U.S. The men selected are to have credentials as traditional conservatives, preferably no older than fifty-five." He looked down the table at Bauer. "They must be beyond reproach, and loyal." Corelli handed out a list for consideration.

Bauer ignored Corelli. A bubble of glee floated up from his gut and expanded into his chest. I fit the criteria.

Bauer claimed his copy and scanned for his name among the two-dozen listed. Yes, there it was. What's this? 'Potential risk'? His cheeks flushed.

They discussed each candidate. When they came to Bauer, he strained to keep the hostility out of his voice. "What do you mean by showing me as a 'Potential Risk?"

Corelli trained his hawk eyes on Bauer. "I would've thought that was obvious. The unfortunate incident when you returned to Chicago from Rome. Public memories are long. We can't have the consistory and the new College of Cardinals tainted by public scandal. It will be left to the Curia to make the final determination for papal appointments. Your candidacy will be forwarded."

"I've been a loyal PXII member for twenty years and risked a lot during Francis's papacy. The risk didn't pay off, for Rome or for me. But he who risks nothing gains nothing."

"Gains are rewarded, not failures." Corelli returned to the list.

Bauer silently fulminated over the reproof. I've got friends in the Curia. I'll go around Corelli. Suppressed rage made him perspire.

At the end of two hours the list was confirmed with one deletion, no additions, and no further changes. The group rubber-stamped Corelli's selections. How did he get this powerful in so short a time?

Corelli adjusted himself in his seat, straightened his shoulders, cleared his throat, gathered all their eyes. "We have another problem to address. We've only just learned that when the Jesuits left the Vatican after the death of Francis, they took several documents with them. Documents that don't belong to them and are very important to us and Pius XIII. It is of the utmost urgency and criticality that we retrieve these documents and suppress any knowledge of their content."

"What's in them?" asked the smooth-tongued tiger.

Corelli frowned. Opus Dei always liked knowing the risks before committing. And if they declined, PXII would already be exposed.

"You can't expect us in on this if we don't understand what we're getting involved in," said the weasel.

"What you're about to hear would be damning if ever publicly disclosed." He tapped his finger on the table, glared around at each face and continued in terse, clipped words. "To all of us."

Bauer thought it good theater.

"The lost Vatican documents contain financial information from the Vatican Bank that if disclosed would be ruinous. They also contain evidence of how Pope John Paul 1 died, and his private diary." Corelli took out a large white handkerchief, daubed his brow and lips, then continued. "John Paul I visited Sister Lucia dos Santos before she died, the last surviving visionary of the three who received the prophecies at Fatima in 1917. The full prophecy about the coming of the Anti-Christ to usurp the papal chair was never published. We were certain the prophecy referred to John Paul I himself. We know from his diary and from Bishop Marcell, PXII's founder, that John Paul I had a supernatural power that could only come from the Anti-Christ. It justified his . . . removal. But the Huaraz prophecy reveals this threat has returned. John Paul's diary contains information about a 'catalyst' who will transmit the power of the Anti-Christ to others."

Murmurs circulated around the room. Bauer was well-aware of the defalcations of the Vatican Bank having had a close hand in them himself. But this other information was wholly new.

"So I hope you appreciate how critically important it is to retrieve these documents quickly, and to heighten our vigilance. We have to find this 'catalyst' and purge him from our midst, as we have prior catalysts."

"What are the Jesuits intending to do with the documents? Why haven't they disclosed or used them?" asked the catfish.

"We can't be sure. Any disclosure would bring down the papacy. The ignorant would not understand the risk or necessity of our actions. It may be the Jesuits think exposure would be a critical blow to the survival of the church. Or they intend to use the documents as leverage at some future point," said Corelli. "But we can't take the chance that they'll continue to suppress them."

Bauer, behind his somber façade, felt a cold chill. If his involvement with the Vatican Bank came out, he'd be finished, prosecuted, imprisoned. For once he hoped Corelli had a plan that would succeed.

"Do you have a plan?" probed the praying mantis.

Corelli polished his glasses and readjusted them on his face. "We know there were two copies made of the Vatican documents on memory sticks stolen by the Jesuits closest to Pope Francis. One we've traced to a Jesuit in Sao Paulo, Brazil. He's been dealt with." Corelli looked at Bauer. "The second we believe to be in the possession of Tom Bradbury, Chancellor of Ignatius University in Seattle."

Bauer sucked in his breath. There was no mistaking Corelli's drift. The entire table was staring at him. No one spoke.

Corelli smiled narrowly. "Bauer, I want you to locate the Vatican documents and inform me where they are. Just that. They should have the Vatican trace on them. Don't do anything to retrieve them." Corelli's exaggerated emphasis made it clear that Bauer reported to him and no one else.

Corelli held his gaze until Bauer nodded, dropped eye contact, and sunk back in his chair, his jaw clamped tightly. Bastard. I get all the dirty, high-risk work. He never lifts a finger. Keeps his hands clean. But he can't afford to have me fail. Not like last time. He'll have to help me.

Then an unnerving thought intruded. He won't allow failure. He'll have me watched, monitored. Bauer surveyed the flinty faces around the table. They'll take me out like an expendable pawn if I fail.

The tiger disrupted the uncomfortable silence. "What of the catalyst?"

"Based on what we know from both John Paul I and Bishop Marcel, the catalyst will be someone who can project visible luminosity that can penetrate, read and possibly control the consciousness of another. Our entire worldwide organization and sympathetic governments are on high alert to detect the emergence of such a one. We would all do well to be vigilant in our own spheres."

The prelates glanced at one another with suspicion and distaste. Corelli grimaced as though he had a bad smell under his nose.

"The church is at a critical point. We can't go down in history as having allowed the largest, longest-lived, farthest-reaching organization in the world to collapse. We've risked much to get here and will need to risk more to succeed. When the survival of the church – the divine presence on earth – is at stake, the ends justify the means. The church, as in the past, must be cleansed of corruption."

Corelli rose. They all followed him across the hall to a gallery with walls swathed in chintz between portraits of distinguished men, each with a brass engraved pedigree that Bauer was too distracted to read. Down the middle of the room a long table covered with a white linen cloth edged in eyelet lay before them, set with gilded china, etched crystal and cast silver. Menus embellished with each of their names listed sumptuous fare and epicurean wines.

Bauer's place was set at the far end of the table from Corelli's. At least I can avoid those piercing eyes of his and think. He just wants me to find the documents. I don't have to retrieve them. That can't be too risky. Doesn't trust me. I'll get Geoffrey's help, and that man I put in Ignatius. What's his name? But if I can get my hands on the memory stick, I'll have real leverage. Bauer's face relaxed as he began to scheme and plan.

During the meal the catfish remarked, between slurping oysters from their shells, "Have you read today's BBC headlines? That crazy Japanese priest continues to claim that the prophecies of La Salette, Fatima, Akita and Huaraz are about to come true. His claims of apocalypse, apostasy, and satanic infiltration of the church are beginning to gain traction. He calls for the complete publication of the prophecies. It's execrable that John Paul II published a portion of the Fatima secret to aggrandize himself as the subject of the assassination attempt."

The prelates debated whether suppressing the troublesome priest would only draw more attention to the prophecies and give him credibility. Conversation shifted to the growing calamities around the world purported to accompany the advent of the Anti-Christ: war, religious terrorism, famine, pandemics, destruction of the earth's biosphere. The doomsday discussion intensified until the wine and luncheon over-rode intellectual discourse that capitulated to indulgence.

The tiger raised his glass to the light for a swirl, sipped generously, aerated and rolled the excellent H. Boillot Montrachet Grand Cru around in his mouth to caress his tongue. Bauer could almost hear him purr. The mantis ate and drank abstemiously. The archbishop from Dallas who resembled a shaggy gruff bear had already finished, leaving no trace of the Boeuf Bourguignon, or the bottle of Ausone Bordeaux he had consumed entirely by himself. He tapped the table with his fingers. "Are we to deal with financing the Vatican or not? Let's get on with the job. I need to get back tonight."

Corelli dabbed a dollop of béarnaise sauce from his cassock with a napkin and took the reins of the conversation again. He ordered them a round of brandies and opened up the last subject of the conclave. "We need the Vatican Bank back completely under our control ...."

Bauer now saw how Corelli had risen to power so quickly – money. And Chicago's the center of the U.S. financial partnership with the Vatican Bank. He'll have to remove the current director and dismantle his organization. Let's see how he plans to perform that miracle.

Corelli wrapped up. The luncheon broke up. Taxis came to whisk the prelates away to the airport.

The conclave had left a bad taste in Bauer's mouth. Corelli had too much power. And now I have to do his bidding. Damn Jesuits.

* * *

The next afternoon without rising or looking up, Bauer motioned Father Herst, who was filling most of his office doorframe, to a seat. Bauer rocked back in his chair, elbows on its broad arms, and placed fingertip to fingertip. Peered over his hands. "How're you getting along at Ignatius?"

"Fine, sir." Herst, though a large man, slumped in his seat as if trying to shrink into insignificance. His moon face, with watery blue eyes framed with wispy strawberry blond hair, focused on his lap where he rubbed large clammy hands on his thighs.

"Good. A safe environment for you." Bauer's eyes gleamed in satisfaction at the discomfort this caused.

"Thank you, sir."

"And how is Ignatius?" Bauer asked. "I hear it's a little radical in its viewpoints."

"They're Jesuits."

"Got a little arrogant under Francis. Do you agree with them?"

"No."

"How do you do 'fine' there?" Bauer leaned forward over his desk, grinning directly into the priest's eyes.

"I keep my head down, sir. Do what I'm told."

"Obedience. It's a fine virtue." Bauer enjoyed the impact he was having. "I need your obedience. Ignatius is a problem for me

– and for PXII. You remember?" Bauer watched Herst's head jerk up and eyes widen. "You're still loyal?"

Herst swallowed and whispered. "Yes, sir."

"Good. I – we need you to do something. We need information from Ignatius."

Herst swallowed again. "What sort of information?"

"Ignatius has become troublesome. I need to know who is financing them, its wealthy patrons and supporters."

"Yes sir."

"And when the Jesuits were evicted from the Vatican after the death of Francis, they took many important documents and items that didn't belong to them. Chancellor Bradbury was one of the Vatican Jesuits closest to Francis. It's likely he brought some of these with him. I need them."

"Sir, I have no access to such things."

Herst repelled Bauer with his pathetic round sweaty face. Disgusted and tired of the conversation Bauer wanted it concluded. "I put you there not just to keep me informed about what goes on at Ignatius, but also because you have skill with information: document files, manipulation, control and retrieval. Locate the information but make no move to read or remove it. It's a memory stick you're looking for. It should have the Vatican trace on it. I need results quickly. Are you clear on this point?"

No response.

"Are you clear?"

Herst shrunk his large frame further, if possible, into the seat. "Yes, sir."

"You understand, loyalty to PXII is paramount. Serious consequences happen to those who let them down."

Herst looked away, gripped the seat's armrests, and took a deep breath.

Bauer buzzed for Geoffrey. "You'll not report to me."

Geoffrey entered.

"You'll report your findings to Geoffrey, my assistant." He turned to Geoffrey. "Show him out and then return."

Bauer leaned back and contemplated his opportunities. I doubt Corelli disclosed all the documents contain. They're leverage I can use with him, or members of the Curia.

Geoffrey re-entered. Closed the door. Of medium height, lithe and wiry, he moved quietly, smoothly, efficiently. Brown straight hair pulled back in a short ponytail emphasized thin eyebrows that set off hazel eyes with nearly invisible lashes. Narrow pale lips contrasted little with his sandy complexion. It was as though he was designed to blend in, be unremarked, yet contained the veiled strength and agility of a jaguar.

Bauer studied his face. How much can I trust him? Not too far at this point. "Geoffrey, I want you to closely monitor Herst's progress. In fact, back him up without him or anyone else knowing. He's looking for some Vatican documents – a memory stick with the trace – at Ignatius that we must find quickly. It will be held in a secure place known only to Tom Bradbury. If you find out where, confer with me before retrieving it. You understand your actions must not be traced back to me or the church."

Geoffrey nodded.

Bauer relaxed back into his chair. "And book me a massage." As Geoffrey left, in his mind's eye Bauer tried on a red zucchetto.

6

Deep in the human unconscious is a pervasive need for a logical universe that makes sense. But the real universe is always one step beyond logic.   Frank Herbert

* * *

Coffee houses on Capitol Hill were as thick as fleas on a stray cat. Décor ranged from homespun to chic. Stumptown on Pine was of the industrial smart sort, with concrete floors, metal bar and furnishings, and high windows looking out at road and sidewalk traffic. Paul had arranged to meet Dr. Habib there at 7:30 in the morning after she got off an on-call night shift. He was surprised she didn't offer to meet in her office.

Paul had not seen her since the brief encounters at Harborview. While he badly wanted to meet her and find out what she knew about his condition, he also approached the meeting with apprehension. There were two kinds of news one gets from a doctor. What if she told him something he didn't want to hear?

As the time approached Paul started to sweat. He was already on his second cup when she arrived.

"Good morning, Father Pennington." She approached and held out her hand. "Dr. Rabia Habib."

He rose to greet her and pulled out a chair. "Thanks for coming."

She had small, almost childlike hands, elfin nose and lips, dark chocolate eyes, lashes as fine as hummingbird feathers, smooth mocha skin, and a long black braided plait of hair like a thick tail down her back. He had to acknowledge that her youth, stature and appearance clashed, in his own mind, with his stereotype of a neurologist.

"Sorry I'm late. We had a psychotic patient come in just as I was leaving." She hung her bag on the back of the chair. Took out her cell and placed it on the table.

"I'm sorry to take you away from going home to sleep."

She smiled. "I can't sleep for several hours after night work anyway, until I unwind."

"Please let me get you some coffee – or tea?" Paul rose to stand in line. Then glanced back at her a couple of times. Now that she's here, how to ask? I must know what she knows of these mental attacks. She's my best hope for figuring out what's going on with me. But she's so young. What could she possibly know that all the other docs don't? He bumped the table as he set down a cup in front of her, slopping tea into the saucer.

"Sorry." He recovered his seat. The silence grew awkward.

He grasped his coffee mug to anchor his hands. "Thanks for helping me that night in the ER. You were the only one I have any memory of that night – you seemed to have an understanding of what was happening to me."

Rabia's eyes locked onto his with a fierceness that clashed with her soft demeanor. She put down her cup.

Paul went on, "I've been through one test after another and a string of doctors who can't find a cause."

"What course of treatment have they prescribed?"

"A psychiatrist." Paul's eyes dropped, fixed on his coffee. "I guess that means they think it could be a mental illness. I just can't accept that. It's true I lost track of time and saw, well, visions of light. But it was all so real. I don't think a hallucination would be like that."

He hesitated. The pedestrian atmosphere in the café contrasted with the recollection of his dramatic experience.

"It was as though you knew," continued Paul. "You talked to me. Brought me out of it. How?"

Rabia brushed away a few loose strands of her hair then folded her hands in her lap. "I sensed feelings you were experiencing. And observed some signs."

How could she sense my feelings? The pain. The light. She wouldn't know about those. Paul vacillated between shame of disclosure and the need to know. He blushed as she studied his face. "Please, I need to know."

She resumed sipping her tea, peering at him over the rim of her cup. "It's happened again, has it?"

Reddening, Paul kept his eyes down. "No. But it happened once before the incident that put me in the hospital. In my room at the university."

"The same experience?"

"As far as I can tell – visual distortion, disorientation, objects rimmed in greenish-yellow light. Then stabbing pain, here, in my temple and fanning out through my head. Then brilliant light that I saw even with my eyes closed. When I came around over an hour had passed. I thought it was a migraine."

Rabia's face showed no surprise. "Did you feel anything besides pain?"

"In the light I felt – it's hard to describe – the pain went away, and I felt expansive, tranquil, drawn toward something. What is it? What do you know about – about it?"

"Father Pennington ..."

"Please call me Paul."

"Then you may call me Rabia."

She rested her elbows on the table, her chin on clasped hands, leaned forward, said in a low, almost whisper, "I think you're experiencing something mystical."

He sat back in his chair. Couldn't help a nervous laugh. This was ludicrous. She's a doctor. "You can't seriously believe that."

Rabia remained still.

"Sorry." Paul felt ashamed at his outburst. "Why would you think that?"

"That night in the hospital you emitted a light."

"What?"

Her eyes didn't waver. "Once you stopped resisting and let go, your head emitted light. Names for it are aura, nimbus, gloriole, tongues of fire, halo."

Stunned, Paul inhaled sharply and looked away. His attention veered to the clatter and chatter of the cafe. He watched a young man walk to the bar to claim two coffees. Walk to the counter that held napkins, stir sticks, creamers, and canisters of sugar, vanilla and cinnamon. He sprinkled cinnamon. The cinder powder puffed into a micro brown cloud as it hit the hot liquid. Paul's frozen thoughts thawed.

A light. I emitted a light. Impossible. Incredible. But she's a doctor. Why would she make such a thing up? No, no. This can't be. There has to be some other explanation. He refocused. Leaned forward. Whispered. "Impossible. I don't believe it," he said.

"When someone is touched by Allah – God – they at times channel divine light," Rabia whispered.

Divine light. How many more weird theories would he have to listen to before someone actually knew something, told him something rational.

"God doesn't 'touch' people like me. It wouldn't feel like this. There must be some other explanation. I've never heard of such a thing."

Rabia said, "But you must have. I've seen great paintings of Christ and Christian saints surrounded by light. Tradition tells us that Muhammad and Buddha had flaming auras."

Paul crossed his arms over his chest and gazed off in the distance, frowning. A dead end, like the sucked dry insect carapace in a spider's web. I guess I never really believed in tongues of fire, haloes or transfigurations. How much of what I think I believe – what I'm supposed to believe – I really don't?

"Why would I have one? I'm no saint."

Rabia whispered, "Who can comprehend the ways of Allah?"

Paul shook his head. He wanted her to leave so he could be alone. Ashamed of his ingratitude he said, "Thanks for meeting with me. I should let you go."

She didn't move. "Please. I know this must be difficult. I'd like to help you if you'll let me."

"How can you help me? Even if what you say is true, what could you do? Can you rid me of this thing? Or teach me to control it? I don't want whatever it is."

"I could teach you how not to fight it. How to embrace it."

"And why would I want to do that?"

She looked intense. "To experience Allah – God."

"How do you know so much about this phenomenon?"

She inhaled deeply followed by a long sigh. "Because I too have the awakened light."

Paul pulled his hands off the table into his lap. *She's trying to get me caught up in her fantasy and giving me the fantods.* "I'm sorry, but you can't help me."

He read desperation in her face, then discouragement.

She placed her hands palms up on the table. "Please."

Paul shook his head. "I'm sorry."

She fumbled with her cellphone. Stowed it in her bag. Thanked him for the tea. Turned away to leave. Then turned back. "There may come a time when you have no choice but to embrace the light. When that day comes please contact me. I can help you. And you can help me." She walked toward the door. Stopped. Turned toward Paul again, hesitated, then left.

Once she was gone, he sat in the café swirling his cold coffee, watching the dark creamy vortex as though it would deliver some direction, some insight on where to go from here. Though the café was noisy and crowded, he felt alone, embarrassed, disappointed.

The specter of mental instability reared in his mind. *What would it be like not to teach? To have pastoral duties rescinded. What would I do? I've no other skills or abilities.* He glanced at the baristas harried by a long line of waiting patrons and shook his head.

As he finished the dregs of his coffee, he resigned himself to his upcoming appointment with the psychiatrist referred by Harborview. Any rational answer, no matter how difficult, would be better than not knowing.

* * *

MEDIA HEADLINE: Life on earth not worth living?

We are killing ourselves at historic rates worldwide.

The World Health Organization (WHO) today reported the number of documented suicides worldwide has reached epidemic proportions. They fear that the actual count could be as much as 20% higher due to unreported or misreported incidents. The highest rates are in developed countries in Europe, Asia, and the United States....

7

"Mad Hatter: 'Why is a raven like a writing desk?'
'...I give it up,' Alice replied. 'What's the answer?'
'I haven't the slightest idea,' said the Hatter."
Lewis Carroll, Alice in Wonderland

* * *

After his recent experiences with doctors Paul noticed that waiting rooms all looked the same: tropical fish swimming lethargically in a tank; beige walls hung with prints of geraniums, dahlias, daisies; thumbed and out of date magazines strewn around side tables advertising vacation spots, haute cuisine, and dog training. Dr. Haukenstad's office continued the theme: bland colors of cream, buff, and mauve blended into each other, masked contrasts, blurred definition.

Dr. Haukenstad introduced himself and shook Paul's hand with the suggestion of a slight bow, sat down and consulted his tablet for a few moments. He gave a fair imitation of Lenin replete with mustache and goatee. The caricature was underscored by the hint of an eastern European accent spoken in a stiff manner.

"How have you been?"

"Okay."

Haukenstad looked at his notes then back at Paul. "I'm here to help you. Together we will – hmm – find out what happened. What caused the – hmm – event. For that I need some background information for a start. You are a priest I see. Can you tell me more about yourself?"

Haukenstad's thick glasses magnified his eyes to the size of a great horned owl's and looked just as fierce, which conflicted with the pablum tone of his voice. The discord made it difficult to trust him. And listening to his irritating speech felt like cotton balls, insulators between words, being stuffed into Paul's brain.

"What do you want to know?"

"Please tell me about your – hmm – profession."

"I'm a professor. I teach at Ignatius University. I teach physics and theology."

"For how long?"

"About fifteen years."

The interrogation proceeded, probe and parry. Paul didn't like being exposed, and Haukenstad's job was to do just that. Paul's irritation rose as Haukenstad bored more deeply.

"Please tell me about your family."

"I don't have a family."

"Can you please expand on that? It's important that I get a family history."

Haukenstad apparently was trying to look kindly but it came off as creepy. Lips in a big smile but the eyes piercing, determined, as though Paul was an interesting bug under a microscope.

Paul squirmed to get comfortable in the over-stuffed chair in the overly warm room. The vinyl made his shirt stick to his back.

"I was abandoned at age four."

"And your parents? Can you tell me about them?"

Paul swallowed, gazed at a wall poster about hand washing. Wished there was a window. "I never knew my father."

Haukenstad peered over his glasses at Paul. "And your mother?"

"She left me at a convent. I grew up in foster homes. Never adopted."

"Do you remember your mother?"

"No," Paul lied. Her image floated up out of his memory to foreground stage, especially her hands, the only human warmth he'd ever known. Why did she leave me? Is it easier to think she died than she never came back for me?

"How did you feel as a child?"

What kind of question was that? How is a child supposed to feel when abandoned by parents? Paul wondered what Haukenstad would do if he just got up and walked out. He looked at his watch. "Growing up I wanted to be part of a family."

"The foster families did not provide this?"

"I was always an outsider, never a part. Don't get me wrong. The people who took care of me were nice, kind. But I was more like a pet than a person. I lived in three different foster homes until I entered the seminary."

"Have you maintained a – hmm – relationship with any of your foster families? "

"They had lives to get on with. It wasn't like they'd adopted me. They had their own children."

"What about your needs? Did you feel – hmm – loved?"

How to answer that? Paul noticed a large Pholcus phalangioides spider on the wall behind Haukenstad's head. It carried a small gauzy bundle and was missing a leg. The spider picked her stately way toward the ceiling corner.

"Father Pennington?"

"If you mean in the way my foster parents loved their own children, no."

"Have you ever tried to find your own parents?"

"No." The spider lodged the egg sac in a cloudy web in the corner and then dropped down out of sight.

"Why not?"

Paul's tone sharpened, and words came out in a rush. "I guess I was afraid of the kind of people they might be. Why does it matter now?"

Haukenstad put his tablet aside, sat back in his chair. "May I call you Paul? I understand these disclosures are – hmm – private and painful. To help you I need your candor."

Paul sat up straight; tamped down his belligerence. He usually didn't resent anyone calling him by his first name. Preferred it. But he didn't like this guy being so familiar. "What else do you need to know?"

"And the seminary? How did you come to be there?"

"Why's that relevant?" Paul's voice prickled.

"We have not been able to find an organic cause for what happened to you. So, we must look for a psychological one. Sometimes things buried in the past can much later exhibit in unusual ways. I need to understand you to help you. To prescribe a course of treatment."

Paul could imagine what treatment might entail: hours baring my soul to this guy, or drugs, group therapy, or all of them together. Can't see how any of this is going to address the attacks. Paul resolved to try again to cooperate. But it was getting harder. Haukenstad dug into all his vulnerable spots.

"I was too old for more foster care and needed a place to go. A priest helped me. He suggested the seminary would be a good next step and I could get a scholarship. I wanted to study science and philosophy. This was a way."

"Did belief in – hmm – God have to do with your choice?"

"Yes, of course," Paul snapped. He didn't even bother to disguise consulting his watch again.

"Are you content with your choice?"

"Look, can't we leave this? I don't see how my career choice or my childhood can have anything to do with these mental attacks. Isn't that what we're here to discuss?"

Haukenstad sat back in his chair. Consulted his tablet. Adjusted his glasses again. Folded his hands on his desk. "Have you had any more episodes?"

"No."

"Please describe your last episode." He favored Paul with a wooden smile then directed his attention to his tablet.

Paul obliged but by this time he was getting irritated having to repeat the 'episode' over and over again of disorientation, pain and light. Why don't these docs communicate? They're supposed to be in a single clinic. And all they wanted were his answers. They didn't give any.

Haukenstad leaned back in his chair again and made more notes. Paul unstuck his shirt from his back and stared around the walls of the office. Framed certificates acclaimed Haukenstad's research in chemical dependency, drug therapy and schizophrenia.

"Hmm." He made some notes on his tablet. "Was there any precipitating event?"

"Not that I know of."

"What were you thinking or feeling or doing just prior to the event?"

"I was praying."

"And then what happened?"

"It just happened."

"Were you aware when it happened?"

"I don't know. Unaware I guess. Just getting up to leave." There were coffee stains on the desk. Paul counted them.

"Going forward I want you to record even the smallest symptoms, precipitating events, dates and time of day, and your reactions." Haukenstad made more notes on his tablet. "And I am prescribing a drug to help with your symptoms."

Paul looked up. "What?"

"Incubatol. It's useful reducing severe headaches that contribute to hallucinations. We'll talk again next week to see how you are doing."

So, he's decided my experience was a hallucination. Drugs. Is that all these Leary types can come up with?

Paul leaned forward. "I'd like to get some answers. What's your theory about how this could be psychologically based? Do you know of prior cases like mine? You haven't offered any explanation, or even a theory, about how my condition could be caused psychologically."

"I am sorry you feel this way. Our time today is up but at our next session we will discuss the relevance you are seeking."

I doubt it. Paul stood, shook Haukenstad's hand and left. Another dead end. On his way out, he cancelled the remainder of his sessions. At least I won't have to put up with that anymore.

As Paul walked toward campus he turned over in his mind the situation. What if it gets more severe and I lose control again? He'd read everything he could find on his symptoms. Found nothing technical or clinical. Only some mystical stuff about transcendental states, drug induced ecstasies, and near-death experiences. He watched a video course – 18 hours' worth – on brain anatomy and chemistry. Fascinating but unhelpful.

Tom had been solicitous. Offered Paul a sabbatical from teaching. Possibly a stay at the Western Province Center. Clearly, I'm a problem. Send me to headquarters to become their problem.

He stopped for a beer at Sophia's Pub. The converted 1940s house of generous proportion perched on the west side of steep-sloped Yesler Street, where in the old days logs skidded down to the wharf on Puget Sound for milling, earning itself the title of Skid Road.

Sophi, the proprietress, used the place as her museum for period artifacts: Ma Bell dial phones; Remington and Selectra typewriters; an RCA stereo that still played LPs; and even an old jukebox. Her memorabilia littered every space and surface not dedicated to the serving of spirits and bar food.

It was nearly empty of the habitués who crowded the popular eclectic pub at night. Paul swirled his glass and pushed the hair back from his brow. A shadow fell over him.

"What're you doing over here in the corner alone?"

"Hi Sophi. Just thinking."

Sophi's roundness, brown soft skin, black dreds tied back in a colorful bandana, and apron pockets stuffed with bar towels, coasters, and tips exuded safety and sanity.

She patiently wiped his table even though it didn't need it. "Things not going well? You look down." She nodded at his near empty glass. "Want another?"

"No thanks."

She plopped down with a smile. "What's up?"

Paul sighed. "A conflict over my teaching. And bad headaches."

"One could cause the other."

Sophi was a more real confessor than his priestly brethren at Ignatius. Her absolutions were from the heart accompanied with wise words instead of criticisms and penances. She listened. Didn't interrupt.

"I guess I'm tired of unanswered prayers." He swirled the beer around in this glass. "And I've had some serious – I don't know what to call them – incidents, where I experience painful

49

headaches followed by something beautiful – and frightening. I've been to a bunch of docs, but they can't tell me what it is." He splayed his hands out on the table and gazed out the window. "I'm worried."

Sophi covered his right hand with her own. "You're a good man, a good priest. Bad things happen to good people. Sometimes it's for a good reason. Now's not the time to lose faith in yourself or your God. It's in times like these we lean on God." She patted his hand, rose and returned to the bar to serve others.

8

"Do you wrestle with dreams?
Do you contend with shadows?
Do you move in a kind of sleep?
Time has slipped away,
Your life is stolen." Dune by Frank Herbert

* * *

Traffic clogged the highway out of town for the first hour before it broke loose in the foothills, with their bare bone trees, sodden fields, and mountains emerging in the background. Paul had little daylight left to reach the cabin but wanted to savor every mile of return to his childhood retreat. Small towns, with their gas stations and roadside cafes, forced their presence on drivers by reducing the highway speed limit to a crawl, and in case you weren't noticing enough, peppered them with unnecessary traffic lights and roundabouts.

As the white-capped mountains grew nearer, it began to snow. Large flakes see-saw-swirled before hitting the windshield. The maelstrom matched his thoughts. Phrases and words floated up out of his subconscious to accuse him – keep your head down – use discretion – heresy – aura. I'm running to John like I did as a boy. But what can he do now?

Father John O'Malley, SJ, was the closest thing to a father Paul had ever had. John had been 'retired' by the church for his activism against the unjust wars in the Middle East, against sexual predation by the clergy, against the sale of assault weapons, against the death penalty. He'd been a vocal advocate for women clergy, homosexual marriage, making clerical celibacy optional. Far from a firebrand he was a gentle but persistent soul. The church found him too controversial and persuaded the Jesuit Order to silence the inconvenient priest.

For a decade the mountains had been John's home. He lived in a cabin he and his brother Bob had built by hand when they were young men. Paul had been invited to spend summers and the occasional winter break there, where he imbibed a deep love of mountains and trees, rivers, and solitude.

Paul wondered how John got along up here all alone now that Bob was dead. How would I? I could be following in John's footsteps, another Jesuit pariah.

A narrow corridor of trees hemmed in the highway. Evergreens, standing strong against the cold, wind, and snows at these higher elevations, shouldered aside the weaker alder and maple that abandoned their leaves to earth during the hard times and retreated into hibernation. Evergreen? Alder? Which am I?

The snow accumulated on the road, erasing and blurring its hard edges into the woods, as though the forest was reclaiming its own. By the time he reached Stevens Pass he was in full blizzard, exhilarating, a veritable baptism of snow. Always it had this effect on him, like stepping into another world more expansive, forgiving and liberating than the one he knew.

The Cascades were well named. Storms that formed over the ocean just to the west blew in over the mountains delivering their heavy load of moisture in snow, rain, mist, or fog. Thousands of crystalline waterfalls and frothy streams etched the rugged mountains, softening their profile and carrying them away grain by grain to a distant sea. Just like the human race. We're being eroded, honed, and swept on to our divine home. Will we dissolve in God like salt in the sea?

He reached the pass and headed down. The highway east of the summit was deserted. Stormy weather had a habit of breaking up just a few miles to the east of the pass. The snow thinned and eventually petered out. Billowing gray clouds frayed into broken white wisps. Nason Ridge to the north and McCue Ridge to the south reared a couple thousand feet above the highway creating a narrow defile.

Paul reached the turn-off. The tall, slim cabin with green roof and cedar siding was easy to miss among the Douglas fir and Ponderosa pine. The side road had been plowed and was drivable but John's driveway was deep in fresh snow. Paul's old Subaru got stuck about ten yards up the driveway. He halted and flashed his brights a few times to let John know of his arrival. Shouldering his backpack, he pushed through snow to his knees, post-holing the rest of the driveway toward the cabin lights flickering in the early dusk. Wings of joy unfurled in his chest. Why have I left it so long to come back here?

The entryway started outside where skis, snowshoes, poles and boots were discarded, the first stage of the disrobing process before entering through the heavy door into the warm inner sanctum. The door opened, and the firelight beamed out backlighting a compact figure, a little bent, head rimmed in a fuzzy halo of silver hair.

"Paul." John beamed at him. "Hope the road wasn't too bad. Sorry about the driveway. Good to see you. Come in. Get warm."

John's lined and smiling face was all the warmth Paul needed. He crossed the threshold and hugged his friend. Peeling off gloves, hat, scarf, backpack, coat, boots, Paul felt he was molting a carapace in a stage of metamorphosis like some out-of-season nymph.

The well-remembered cabin enfolded him as if no time had passed, except for John. In a faded flannel shirt, patched jeans and big dog-paw scuff slippers John shuffled inside. Vigor had left him. The lines on his face were etched by pain. His chalky hands trembled. But his eyes were as bright and kind as ever. He eased himself into a rocker by the fire.

The fireplace and stone chimney with a split log mantel held mementos of John's lifetime: pictures of his brother Bob, an engraved gavel from his time as order president, a box of fishing flies, a tattered Audubon book of birds next to an equally tattered Bible, and a picture of young Paul in the river. The natural incense of fir and alder smoke; the scarred wood floor; the kerosene lamps and Coleman lanterns; the old Monarch wood cook stove; the large windows that tonight framed a giant snow globe – all brought back Paul's vivid memories of visits here as a boy. His breathing deepened and slowed. This was more sanctuary than any church. To stay here again, no conflicts of conscience, nature for company, maybe the headaches and light shows would cease.

With their hands wrapped around steaming mugs of tea spiked with a dram of whiskey, they recounted old times late into the evening. Paul repeated his trick of balancing the saltshaker on its edge. He forgot his troubles for a while until John dug into them.

"Something's clearly on your mind. You carry a weight."

The saltshaker fell over spilling grains of salt over the table. Paul swept them into his hand and threw them into the fire. Splayed his hands out on the table. "I've been warned that my teaching is unorthodox, even been deemed heretical. If I don't tow the line, I'm afraid I could be barred from teaching," he said with some bitterness. "Isn't this how it started with you?"

John took out his pipe. Knocked the spent ash into the fireplace. Carefully cleaned it. Refilled it with tobacco from a dented cookie tin. Used a spill to relight it from the fireplace. A thin blue ribbon of smoke curled from its bowl. "What exactly got you into trouble?"

Paul rose from the table, moved to the fireplace, leaned on the mantelpiece, and stared into the flames. Then turned to face John and warm his back. "I can't conceal my conviction that God is the force of evolution. That much of the bible is myth. That great minds like de Chardin, de Mello, Rahner, and others have been marginalized or outright discredited by an ultra-conservative church. I'm coming to believe Catholicism is dead or dying and doesn't provide any real experience of God."

John nodded in time with his rocking. "You always did push the limits, even as a boy."

Paul sat in the armchair that shared the fire with John's rocker. Stared into the flames.

"Have you ever experienced God?"

"What do you mean?" John asked.

"I mean have you ever felt God's presence? I don't mean intellectual knowledge, but actual experience. Something true – real – that comes from beyond yourself. Not just imagined."

54

John peered at Paul through smudged glasses. Then took them off and cleaned them with the sleeve of his shirt. "The church left that path almost 2000 years ago with rejection of the Gnostics. What we're left with is an intellectual knowledge and faith. Only rare mystics ever get a glimpse of anything more."

"Is it wrong to want more?"

John smiled. "No. But prepare yourself for life-long disappointment and censure."

He refilled their teas and doctored with another shot of whisky. His palsied hands slopped a bit on the table. "What'll you do?"

"I don't know." Paul picked up his mug. "Maybe it's time I give up on the church."

"You were never one to give up or give in."

Paul rose and placed his mug on the mantel. He straightened John's trinkets one by one, while his mind just as carefully arranged words to tell say what he really came for. Then realizing what he was doing he shoved his hands in his pockets, licked his lips and faced John.

"There's something else. The past couple of months I've been having headaches, seeing lights. I go into something like euphoric trances. I lose track of time." He searched John's face for a reaction but saw none.

John just sat there looking at him with kind eyes.

"The worst time put me in the hospital. Doctors couldn't find a cause – except for one person. She's a neurologist. Says what I'm experiencing is mystical, not physical or mental. When I'm in this state she says I produce a visible light – an aura. I've no evidence myself that it's true. She assures me she witnessed it."

John drew on his pipe. Exhaled a long aromatic plume of smoke into the rafters. "There're descriptions, sometimes detailed, of auras in all the great religions. Of a nimbus, tongues of fire, halos, transfigurations – they go back thousands of years to the time of Moses. Rare I grant you." John resumed puffing on his pipe.

Paul laughed. "I'm no Moses."

The snow was falling again. It muffled the cabin into deep silence. John gazed into the fire. "At the time of their calling there was nothing special about Abraham, King David, or Peter. Or

Moses for that matter. St. Paul was the last person you would have thought would be called by God."

John hitched his chair closer to the fire, turning the soles of his feet to the flames. He rocked back and forth several times before speaking again. "What do you feel deep down when you're in this state?"

Paul chewed his lip. "After the pain I feel peace, joy. I want to stay with it. Then I'm drawn toward something dense that's both awe-filled and beautiful. But I pull out, or get pulled out, before I can get there. It leaves me feeling – I don't know – bittersweet, but that really doesn't describe it. It's like a combination of both joy and sadness."

"*Charmolypi*" John smoked and rocked. "It's a Greek word for what you describe. Seems like you've no choice but to explore it. Samuel was called by God three times before he finally got it."

Paul stared into the fire, watching the tongues of flame lick the sides of the fire brick. What if this is the spiritual experience I've prayed for? Why can't I believe it? What was I expecting? To hear a voice? To see celestial visions? Now examined by his rational mind he had to admit these were as fantastic as the 'light' events he'd experienced. Do I really believe, deep down, in divine experience? Or God? The thought of being anchorless, nothing but energy and matter to be redistributed into a godless finite universe, frightened him.

"Father, do you think there could be a spiritual cause for what's happening to me?"

John smiled. "You haven't called me 'father' in years. I'm not saying that it is but that it could be. You've criticized the church for being closed to new ideas and experiences. Don't you be." John put down his pipe and scratched his head.

"But it's so hard to believe. And it's more than that. I want to control my life. Instead it controls me. I don't want that. It scares me."

John stopped rocking. Studied Paul. "Son, the most authentic sign I know of that one has been chosen by God for a purpose is that they don't want it, like Jonah. We don't get to decide these things. We only get to decide what we do with them when they confront us."

56

Paul drained his mug. The tealeaf residue formed a pattern like black ice crystals. He shook his head. "I don't see a path."

John ruminated a bit and drained his whiskey-tea. "When you find life buffeting you about, confusion all around and even fear, it usually means you're in a period of transition. Your path is there, it just hasn't yet become clear. The only guide to steer by at such times is within you, your good conscience. That's faith, not just in God but in yourself. Sometimes we only see our path clearly after we've traversed it, and see it looking back from where we are."

John picked up their empty mugs and took them to the sink. "I think we've talked long enough for one night. You look tired. See you in the morning."

Paul carried his sleeping bag to the loft. The rungs didn't seem as far apart or as big as he remembered. As a boy he could stand upright in the loft, but now he had to stoop. He rummaged around a pile of rugs to arrange a make-shift mattress, then smiled. Good God. My Jiminy Cricket pillow is still here: "Always let your conscience be your guide."

My problems back then were boy-sized. Limited. Well-defined. Do this. Don't do that. Now it's all blurry. I can't find the end of the ball of twine to begin to unravel it.

Wrapped in his sleeping bag in this place of childhood security, in the warm darkness and absolute silence, was like being in a womb.

Or a tomb....

Paul entered a door into a spherical room with rough brown walls, ceiling and floor. Light was dim and diffuse. A door at the opposite end opened to green and sunlight and tall trees. He walked toward the door, but it kept receding. Looking back, Paul saw the way shut behind him. Then forward a large wasp appeared blocking the entrance to the doorway with its glittering eyes and long waving antennae rotating its large triangular head from side to side. There was no way around it. I've got to get through the doorway....

Paul woke. The dream faded into his subconscious but left him with a feeling of disquiet and a tight knot in his chest. It was still ink-dark, but he sensed dawn not far off. The banked fire had kept the loft warm. He lay there for some time before sitting up and lighting a small candle. This place of solace invited him to profound prayer. He searched his memory for an appropriate psalm.

"To you O Lord, I lift up my soul; my God, I put my trust in you."

He focused his mind deep within his consciousness. First his thoughts flowed in language, until finally his mind just rested, wordless in silence.

Then it came.

This time he could feel the beginnings of the familiar disorientation followed by tingling. He prepared himself for the inevitable pain by breathing deeply and relaxing, letting go, letting it come. This time the pain was something objective, happening to some part of him, but didn't claim the whole center of focus. Then the pain extinguished, and the ecstasy of the radiant light engulfed him.

9

"There is in me a radiance that never ceases,
And if I had eyes to see into the darkest depths of my heart
I would know ...this inner spark...." Meister Eckhart

* * *

The fire had subsided into ashes. The cabin cold woke John. His joints ached. There would be no more sleep tonight. It was near enough to dawn to make up the fire and put on the coffee. Padding out in his threadbare robe and slippers, he was quiet to not awaken his guest. He collected kindling from the wood box just outside the door. The frigid air made his eyes water. Returning inside the loft was in full view.

John looked up, dumbstruck.

Paul was sitting up straight on his sleeping bag, eyes closed, arms resting on his legs, his body outlined in a faint shimmering light visible in the darkness. Transfixed, John cycled from fear to incredulity. His legs trembled, so he laid aside the kindling and sat down. He couldn't think, his mind in the grip of a conflict between the rational and the mystical.

Deus meus.

As he stared memories flowed through him of Paul as a boy, introverted and deep with the sad-happy face of a clown. Curious and questioning, spiritual rather than religious, lonely, never getting enough love.

Then Paul's account of last night. What is he experiencing? An overwhelming desire to touch Paul seized John. He sat still, arguing with himself. I shouldn't disturb him. I won't disturb him. But I must get closer. See closer. Before the light vanishes. Eventually, John climbed the rungs to the loft.

To reach him John had to crawl along the floor under the eaves. Paul's breathing was easy, a hint of a smile on his lips, lids softly resting on his eyes. He appeared completely reposed within light of blue-gold that projected from his body several inches into the dimness. A burnt-out candle made John wonder how long Paul had been in this state. He knelt facing Paul shivering with suppressed tension. He couldn't help himself. He hesitantly touched Paul's hand as early man would have reached out to touch fire.

Paul opened his eyes. Then he raised both his hands and placed one on each side of John's head. John felt a slight tingling or low-level charge come through Paul's fingers. Then he felt jarred by a mental spasm followed by suffusion with radiant light.

Jesu Maria.

The bright light eclipsed Paul's form into a pale shadow. John floated in a cloud of light, smooth and crystalline, active with shooting and swirling glints, like subatomic particles. A section of the light-cloud formed a tourbillion center. He couldn't be sure if it emerged in the foreground or background. Tendrils of light spiraled out and touched him. Pierced him with a joy so intense that he wondered his body could bear it. Then John realized, with complete absence of fear, he had no body....

Dawn streamed in the windows. The ethereal light faded. Awareness of the physical world returned. John was sitting opposite Paul. Paul had dropped his hands and his eyes were open. Neither moved nor spoke as the sun rose.

10

"There is no fear in love, but perfect love casts out fear." 1 John 4:18

* * *

By the time Paul and John descended from the loft, the sun had climbed high enough to beam shafts down into John's dell and reflect off the fresh snow through the cabin windows. Snow crystals, like prisms, converted the sun's rays into specks of red, yellow, green, and blue that twinkled and glinted from bent branches. Occasionally the sun loosened a suspended tuft that cascaded in a small avalanche to the ground.

Paul and John were absorbed in their own thoughts until the oatmeal and coffee were consumed. Now they sat by the fire watching its flames. John rocked and smoked his pipe. Paul turned his coffee mug round and round. The atmosphere was gravid with unexpressed thoughts until John broke the silence.

"Paul, it's true."

The only response was the crackle of the fire.

"You not only emitted light – an aura – you shared it with me. I've never experienced anything so sublime."

Paul just gazed down into his coffee mug. The dark brew mirrored his feeling of foreboding. Having John experience and authenticate his secret – of having it known as something objective and not just a malady of his mind – was a relief. He should have been elated. But it rocked the rational foundation of his life.

Touched by God she'd said.

Now he understood in his gut all the references in scripture to holy fear. He felt like a ship released from its moorings in surrender to the pull of the moon, the cycle of tides, the restless waves on a dark sea.

He rose and walked to the window. Stared out into the woods shrouded in snow that reflected the bright sun, but pale against the incomparable light of the aura that was now impossible to deny. Consequences raced through his mind. There'll be those who think me a hoax, a freak, a saint, a demon. The order will want to claim me or shun me. The church will want to use me or expel me. There's no place for me in a rationally based university.

And I can't control it. Can't explain it. It's not subject to the kind of proof required to make it believable. Worse, I don't know what it wants of me. Rabia said someday I would be forced to embrace it. Well, the day has come.

Paul asked John, "Can you describe it? I can't see it. Or what I see is from the inside out. I see brilliant light even with my eyes closed."

"You looked as if your whole body was encased in a cloud with an indistinct edge. It shone with its own light. Not reflected light you understand. It was strongest around your head. The color, hard to describe. It seemed to shift or pulse between warm white and cold blue. When you touched me, I felt a jolt like an electric shock. Then I lost track of everything except the light. Well not everything. I experienced immense joy. After all these years I think I finally understand the term 'glory'. That's what I felt. You can't deny or demean this experience. It's real. And sacred. It eclipses the pinnacle of my spiritual experience at ordination. It's the closest to a beatific state I could ever imagine this side of death."

Paul gazed out at the snow. "I've prayed a long time for direct experience of God. I guess I never really believed my prayers would be answered. Why now? And why in this dramatic fashion?"

John joined him at the window, looking out at the white world. "You may not get answers to such questions. The point is what're you going to do with this great gift? Such gifts aren't given for our private gratification. A charism like this is for a significant purpose. 'No one lights a lamp and puts it under a bushel but puts it on a lamp stand'."

There's a scriptural quote for every occasion, Paul thought, like Shakespeare. "But to what purpose? What I experience is personal. I'm drawn toward a dense center of light, but I can't get there – or afraid to go there. Is this what I'm supposed to do? Get to the center?"

Paul turned to John. "And now I discover I can share this aura with another. Is this my purpose? To do that wouldn't I need to control it? But I can't. It's like being struck by lightning. Or am I simply to be a channel? My only talent is teaching. How can I teach what I don't understand myself?"

John poured more coffee and sat down again. "You are at a beginning. Beginnings are fragile, vulnerable times. You can't expect to comprehend it or its purpose all at once. Let it teach you. What you have is a great blessing. If you can facilitate that in others you will literally be a godsend."

"I can't imagine the church is going to welcome it. Most likely fear it."

"They will. They oppose what they don't understand or control. But you can't let that stop you. You must delve into the experience, learn from it, you'll find its purpose. And didn't you tell me there's a person, a neurologist, who told you about this aura? Knows something about it? Offered to help you? Find her."

"I'll need to apologize to her. I blew her off."

John shook his head, then reached to the mantel. Took down a plain wooden box. "When I knew you were coming, I searched for this. You left it here many years ago."

Paul found inside three objects from his past: a magnifying glass, a prism, and a gall the size of a large walnut.

"You were always drawn to light, concentrating it with the magnifying glass, disaggregating it with the prism. I figured you'd go into physics. I never knew the story behind the gall."

Paul took the gall, polished from riding around in his pockets for many years. Cupped it in his hand. "Your brother explained to me that a gall was formed when a kind of wasp implants an egg in tree bark. The tree reacts by encasing the wound to protect itself. The egg hatches into a larva, which eats of the tree until metamorphosis. When it's time to emerge, the young wasp chews its way out. If the tree had grown too thick and strong a casing the wasp couldn't get out. That made me sad. I looked for galls that had no exit holes such as this one with the idea of breaking or sawing them open to find the wasp."

Paul rolled the gall between his palms. Fancy John keeping these things all these years. I always liked playing with light. But the gall? I was the wasp, am the wasp. Paul put the prism and magnifying glass back into the box and replaced it on the mantel. The gall he slipped into his pocket.

Paul's backpack lay ready in the corner. He laced up his boots, pulled on his coat and gloves, and pushed outside through the drifts to grab a snow shovel. They shoveled snow together in silence, their breaths wreathing them in crystalline fog. The hard exercise and burning muscles felt good. After unburying Paul's Subaru, they cleared a rough path down the driveway to the road. Time to go.

John hugged long and hard as though he didn't know if he would see Paul again. "Go in peace, my son."

Paul said good-by with a promise to come again soon. He drove away leaving John waving in the mounds of fresh snow.

Paul had a lot to think about. Why did John immediately recognize the sacred nature of the aura and I didn't? I've prayed for divine experience all my life. Then when it comes, I don't recognize it. Is that true? Or did I not want to see it for what it was?

Ambrose says I'm arrogant, wedded to my own notions of truth, and he's right. John is a humble, open, selfless man. Detached from the world. Without expectations. Just grateful for what comes. God knows I'm not open, nor particularly selfless. Where's my gratitude for this divine gift? Sweet Jesus, I should be in a transport of thanksgiving, but I all feel is anxiety.

I need to see Rabia. She has knowledge I was too arrogant and too closed to appreciate. I was rude. Ungrateful. Didn't believe her when she risked disclosing something so deeply personal to a virtual stranger. A stab of compunction reminded him of how he felt in the same situation. The taste of blood in his mouth didn't stop him from continuing to bite the inside of his lip.

11

"Light is the left hand of darkness"
Ursula K. le Guin

* * *

Rabia drove down Pacific Highway South to a hotel near SeaTac Airport. Windshield wipers, swishing on intermittent, smeared the street grime gifted by a passing semi. The highway was encrusted with seedy dives populated with defeated people. Men and women loitered on its broken sidewalks, or waited at graffitied bus stops, dressed in incongruous Value Village or Goodwill attire. No children. No one in a hurry.

Rabia's Uncle Fakhruddin, her oldest surviving relative, had finally managed to obtain a visa to the U.S. after the long war in Syria had resolved into a hard won and shaky peace. The motel where her uncle was staying blended in with the line of sketchy establishments: pot shops, used car lots, fast food joints, laundromats. The Imperial Motel belied its name: a two-story affair with rooms opening to an outdoor chipped and stained walkway with concrete block walls that once must have been painted beige but were now blotched with mold and moss. A faint hint of urine wrinkled her nose. But she thought it better to meet him here than have him come to the hospital and create a scene.

During the drive she'd prepared herself for what she knew would be a difficult conversation. Fakhruddin was extremely conservative, not used to being thwarted, and certainly never by a woman of his own family. Unruly women and children in one's family were shameful. Ever since she was nine years old her uncle held it his right and duty to control her or risk dishonor. He'd already ruined her girlhood. He wasn't going to destroy the rest of her life. Her polite but firm long-distance refusals to return to her husband had gone unheeded. Distance had precluded a face-to-face confrontation. But now that her uncle was here she had no choice. There must be some way I can get him to understand I'm never going back to Ibrahim.

She scaled the flight of outdoor stairs. The thock-thock reverberation of her shoes on the metal grate reminded her of jails and mental institutions. Why would he stay in such a place? She found his door, took a calming breath, and knocked.

Her uncle opened the chained door a crack and peered through before letting her in. She entered the stuffy space leaving the door ajar. The small room had the standard-issue hotel bed and video screen on a table that also served as a desk with chair and minibar. The fake plant, mottled rug, and institutional wall art with table lamp could be Anywhere, USA. At least it looked clean.

Uncle had changed. His face was puffy and scored with deep lines that lead down to full lips turned down at the corners. The whites of his eyes were tinged yellow. His once shiny black hair had thinned, dulled and grayed. Veins were prominent even through his dark skin; his paunchy belly sagged and hinted to be due to more than just fat. He was not healthy, if not actually unwell. She wished she could take his blood pressure.

There was no second chair to sit on, so she remained standing near the door rather than sit on the bed. Standing helped her maintain some semblance of control.

"Uncle, how good and unexpected of you to come and see me."

"I come for your good," replied Fakhruddin.

As anticipated, steering him away would not be possible, but she could perhaps turn down the volume with friendliness. "How is Fayah?"

"She is well."

"And how is Muhammad? He must have his degree by now?"

"He is graduated."

"You must be very proud of him."

"But not of you. You shame me and yourself. A good Muslim woman does not leave her husband. You will go back to Ibrahim."

There was no other way than to be direct with him. "We have been over this before. I will not return, now or ever."

Standing up with force Fakhruddin shouted at her, sprays of spittle escaping his lips. "You will. You belong to him."

"I'm not Ibrahim's property. I didn't come to this country, study hard, work hard to become a doctor, to be anyone's property. I never wanted to marry him. You forced me to when I was too young to resist. But I'm not now. My father would not have wished this."

Fakhruddin's hands balled into fists. "Kabir was an infidel. It was the will of Allah that he died and you became my responsibility." He beat his right fist into his left hand, a staccato of ominous sounds.

Rabia dropped her eyes to pray for strength then faced her uncle. "In this country you have no rights over me. No responsibility for me. I'm sad, Uncle, that it's come to this. My father didn't die, he was murdered by his own countrymen because he was Sufi. I too am Sufi. I'm threatened even here in the U.S. But the biggest threat I fear is from my own family. I know you believe you're doing the right thing, but you're wrong."

Trembling, he grabbed her by the shoulders and shook her. "You will do what I say," he shouted through curled back lips that exposed crooked dingy teeth. His breath was hot and sour. Strong fingers dug into her flesh, hurting her.

Rabia's memory flashed back to being beaten as a young girl. For the first time since she was a child she feared him. Twisting out of his grasp, she flung open the door and backed out. "Goodbye." It seemed a ludicrous understatement, but she couldn't think of anything else to say. She left him with his fists clenched sputtering in a paroxysm of rage and powerlessness as she fled down the stairs to her car.

Driving back to the hospital, Rabia didn't kid herself that anything had been accomplished other than hardening of positions. Uncle would be back. He was intractable in matters of family honor. Why was he so unlike Kabir, his brother? Why did Kabir have to die? Life would have been so different.

Every day that passed she had thought of her father, Kabir, a selfless gentle loving Sufi mystic. He'd left her with a great gift. Gratitude and grief spilled out in tears. Merciful Allah.

She wiped her eyes and struggled to calm and clear her mind in anticipation of patient rounds when she returned. By the time she pulled into the Harborview garage she had put the difficult encounter behind her, at least for the moment. A resolution would have to be found later.

After uneventful rounds, Rabia headed for the hospital's quiet, non-denominational room that could be a chapel, temple, or mosque depending on the imagination and fervor of the inhabitant. It was for relatives and friends of patients but rarely used. Rabia found it a reflective space for meditation and peace. In the darkened room she stretched, then sat on the carpet and arranged her arms and legs. Closed her eyes. Drew several deep calming breaths then relaxed into a pattern of breathing: three counts to inhale, seven to exhale.

Merciful Allah. She repeated this in her mind as a mantra to center her concentration. Her respiration deepened. Pulse slowed. Her consciousness narrowed to a point within her heart and then expanded to encompass a locus behind and between her eyebrows. The point became a light. From it flowed energy and warmth. But the point of light flickered against a backdrop of darkness, sorrow, regret, and shame. Will I ever be free of it?

MEDIA HEADLINE: Last Inhabitants Abandon Marshall Islands
It was a sad day today as the last of the population living in the Marshall Islands boarded ships for new homes scattered around the world. They join climate change refugees from ....

12

"We must have bloody noses and crack'd crowns…"
Shakespeare's Henry IV, Park I

* * *

S everal tries of the starter and pumpings of the accelerator
failed to produce ignition.
    "Damn."
Tom reconciled to a dead battery. Irritation mellowed into a
smile at fate. A cancelled meeting meant a couple of free hours in
an overly scheduled day. He pulled down his watch cap, turned
up his collar against the chill, and enjoyed the stroll back to his
chambers under a wan winter sun. Global warming had caused
Seattle weather to become erratic. Too often it was wet and warm
even in winter. But occasional artic blasts returned the city to the
cold he remembered as a boy, with dependable snow and ice that
sometimes cancelled school.

The priests' residence was empty, quiet, peaceful. At
midafternoon all were out. Tom walked to his room reaching for
his keys grateful for the gift of time. At a glance he frowned. The
door was slightly ajar. I'm sure I left it locked. He slowly and
quietly pushed the door open. Saw no one. Stepped inside.

The room was in shambles. The floor was strewn with papers
and files, upended boxes, books heaved from shelves, desk
drawers pulled out and dumped. The contents of his wardrobe,
some with pockets turned out, lay in a floor pile. Furniture had

been moved away from walls. Area rugs were bunched in the middle of the room along with the window curtains. A lamp had been dismantled and his wall clock smashed.

His initial shock subsided into anger. Who would do this? He threw aside his hat and coat as he strode into the room. He started at a slight movement behind him. Then a heavy blow struck the back of his head.

He perceived the next few instants in slow motion: a metallic taste on the back of his tongue; dizziness; ringing in his ears; buckling knees; his body collapsing onto the floor. Then he lost consciousness.

When Tom came to he was alone. He revived enough to sit up causing a wave a nausea. Blood on his collar had dried. His head ached and throbbed. He tenderly felt around for the impact point.

Too shaky to stand he dug for his cellphone and called for help.

Later when Tom read the police report, nothing in it or from his spotty memory helped in determining who had done this. He kept nothing of value, except one important document which was too important to keep in his chamber. Who would know that he had it? Only one organization would dare such an attack.

13

"The teacher kindles the light.
The oil is already in the lamp."
Hadith of the Prophet Muhammad

* * *

A watery sun shone through gray clouds that blew in from Puget Sound. They billowed their way east to the Cascades where the peaks caught them and extracted their moisture.

In the brisk breeze, Paul walked down Yesler and considered what he'd say to her. Not a very auspicious beginning. Hope I didn't sound too desperate on the phone. Wonder what she thinks of me?

He'd arranged to meet Rabia at Sophia's. Sophia's Pub was favored by denizens of the university, students and faculty alike. The eclectic pub was reasonably quiet in the midafternoon, and close to both Harborview and the university. He selected an isolated small table away from the bar, ordered and waited.

Sophi brought him a beer and perched on the edge of the opposite chair. "Haven't seen you in a while. How you doing? Things any better?"

"Hard to say. I've had to swallow some inexplicable things about myself."

She grinned. "We've all had to do that many times in life. As we get older it doesn't even astonish anymore." She wended her way through the tables back to the bar, stopping for a short chat or a hug with regulars, and welcomes for strangers.

Rabia entered a few minutes later. Paul stood, waved her over, and pulled out a chair.

"Thanks for meeting me. Especially after I wasn't very congenial at our last meeting."

"I understand." Rabia sat down, settled in, and glanced around at the unusual array of gadgets. Then she returned her attention to Paul. "I'm glad you contacted me. I've often thought about you. I've never met anyone else like you. I can appreciate how hard it must be to believe me."

"May I get you something?" Paul asked.

He was struck anew by her birdlike physique, petite but not fragile, with smooth fawn skin. Her movements see-sawed between sprightliness and stillness that reminded him of the juncos that fed on the ground around the campus. And she had a soft enthralling accent from the Arabian Nights. Iranian? Egyptian?

She smiled. "I don't visit taverns much since Muslims don't drink alcohol. But I would enjoy some tea."

Paul finished his beer and ordered tea. "Do you ever get tired of night work?"

"That's when we get the best cases, or the worst depending on your point of view. Neurologists have a difficult time with research since we can't experiment on people. Animal models don't always work. So we study patients who have clinical abnormalities or injuries to understand the brain."

She stopped. Paul wondered if she was embarrassed implying that he might be such a subject.

"Are you well?" she asked. "You look strained. Have you had more aura episodes?"

Strange putting a real name to it. Mental attack, aura episode, gift. Depends on your point of view.

"Yes, and when it happens, I try to follow the guidance you gave me in the ER. The painful headaches have been getting shorter and less intense."

Sophi delivered an ample teapot. Rabia filled both mugs. The aroma of orange and cinnamon wafted around the table.

"What changed your mind about me?"

Paul put his mug down. Sat back in his chair. "John – a fellow priest – witnessed the light, my aura. In fact, he shared it. Confirmed it. I guess I can't avoid facing it. Believing doesn't make it any easier. I need to understand it. Why I have it? What it demands of me? You told me the last time we met that you also have an aura. How'd it happen to you?"

"My father, Kabir, was a holy man, a Sufi sheikh. He called me Rabia, after Rabia of Basri, the first and greatest woman Sufi saint. All Muslims revere her. My father taught me about Sufism, and about my namesake. Rabia was a slave. When her master saw her praying enveloped in light, he freed her. She performed miracles, left us beautiful sayings and poetry, and at times emitted a light, an aura. So did my father. When he died, I was with him. He awakened my aura. I was only nine."

Paul didn't know how to respond, with sympathy at her loss or wonder at her ability. "What happened to you then?"

Rabia blinked. "My mother was already dead. My brothers also. I was taken in by – my uncle." She dropped her eyes to the table, drew her hands in to her lap.

"I didn't mean to pry."

Rabia sipped her tea. "I want to help you. You're the only person I've met other than my father who emits an aura."

"These aura incidents or trance states …."

"Call it an aura state."

"They come when I least expect but thankfully so far when I've been alone except for John. I'm afraid that disclosing it to my Jesuit community may bring serious negative consequences unless I can explain what it is and prepare them. I've so many questions. To start with, what is the aura?"

Rabia poured them both more tea. "Everyone has an aura residing deep within. We aren't sure exactly where but within the brain as a component of consciousness. In most people it's dormant or ignored. In rare cases the aura emits under certain circumstances visible light, even though we've determined it has no light signature, no frequency, phase or amplitude. But so far we have only one sample to study. Me."

"Who are the 'we' doing the studies?"

"Dr. Nic Novgorod, and a neurologist and psychologist who work together. Study is difficult because one doesn't control the aura. It's like the wind. We can only be open and remove obstacles to it."

"But how to control it is what I most need to know," Paul said. "I can't afford its emergence at the wrong time. But mostly I need to understand the purpose for having it."

Rabia searched Paul's face as she continued to drink her tea. "I can help you access it. Learn its properties. Teach you what I know. But I've never had an incident as you describe when it happens without, well, sort of calling it, even if it doesn't always come."

Paul pushed his hair back from his forehead. "The witness I told you about, John, I shared my aura with him. We underwent a common ecstatic experience. A sacred experience. Is this your experience?"

Rabia's seemed to withdraw into herself. Then in a low voice, "We call the divine light *tajalli*. It's experienced when the individual ego surrenders completely to Allah. The heart is unveiled – *kashf,* which is knowledge of the heart rather than intellectual knowledge. The human becomes a pure receptor of divine light and achieves pure consciousness. Great Sufi masters teach and guide seekers to achieve *kashf.*"

"But I have none of this training or ability."

"As a priest you must have a strong dedication to God. Unveiling only happens through the grace of Allah. He must have a great purpose for you. The manifestation of the divine light is a great blessing, but unusual in you because so painful. Forgive me, but the pain may come from your ignorance and fear."

Fear. Yes. Fear of alien painful territory. Intellect is my strength. But a journey of the heart? A heart that's been rejected, wounded, scarred, starved. A heart I've veiled, encased, fortified, muted.

"Your father evidently awakened your aura. How?"

"I don't know how he did it. It's something I've wanted to understand. And yours awakened in a different way. Evidently without the help of another." She looked into Paul's eyes. "Please. We could learn from each other. I will help you, teach you what

I know. And I'd like your help. I've had no one to practice with – share with for the past thirty years since my father died."

Paul withdrew into his thoughts. This was a choice to move out of his world of physics, scholastic theology, rationality. A choice that might involve exposing his inner self, his vulnerability. The gift had brought with it responsibilities. Expectations. How naïve of me to think divine experience would make no demands? I have to discover what those are with whatever help is offered. Rabia was looking at him, her eyes hopeful.

"Do you trust me?" she asked.

Paul felt like he was leaping off a cliff into an ocean of the unknown. His rational mind baulked, but he overrode the resistance.

"I need to know."

14

"...Sophia, the divine wisdom of the feminine ... brings the meaning of the Self into consciousness. Sophia connects us with the center and so allows us to see the inner purpose hidden within everything." Sufism, by Llewellyn Vaughan-Lee.

* * *

The winter solstice was just days away. A hard freeze had left its mark on wilted and collapsed geraniums and nasturtiums, and had administered the coup de grace` to the university pea patch. Tall bean and pea vines hung on their trellises like tattered and bare ship rigging.

Paul walked down Yesler to Sophia's to meet a few of his students. The night-lights of Seattle's high-rises sparkled in the distance. Already dusk, Venus shone brightly, and stars were faint but visible. It would be a cold walk home.

Sophia's eclectic clientele matched its eclectic décor. It was a haven for scholars to argue metaphysical points, challenge equations, propound theories. Artists sketched outlines, debated musical styles. Writers critiqued the latest books and shows. Dozens of dialogues created a more or less uniform buzz, punctuated by the occasional strident voice. Ubiquitous tablets and notebooks were consulted as reference libraries to make a point. Fines were levied for talking on a cellphone, and no one sat alone or disengaged. Sophia's was a place for face-to-face discourse, usually polite, often animated.

Paul wove his way between tables and around chairs to the Rotunda, a circular side room next to the bar with windows on three sides overlooking a small urban garden. It might at one time have been a conservatory. It contained a sizable round oak table with a lazy-susan in the middle.

Paul recognized Jesse's yarmulke and two other students: Ali in a hijab with deep-set brown eyes, and David with curly long brown hair, John Lennon glasses, and a mustache.

David continued his conversation with Ali. "Explain how suffering and evil is necessary for evolution."

"Evolution doesn't happen in stasis," said Ali. "It requires disequilibrium or backpressure. If we're to evolve spiritually or morally, then suffering and evil must provide backpressure, just like the environment provides challenges for physical evolution. All evolution is achieved in struggle and learning. The old evolutionary theories of random beneficial mutations have been replaced by epigenetics."

"Do we know the laws of evolution apply to the spiritual development of man?" Jesse asked Paul.

"Our experience of evolution is movement toward greater organization, unity, complexity," Paul said. "Entropy is the counter force: dissipation of energy, breakdown of complexity, disorganization, division. To explain evolution there must be a force in opposition to entropy. We might think of evolution as the product of creative tension between entropy and spirit."

A physical presence breathing heavily overshadowed Paul.

"Ambrose. Please, pull up a seat."

Ambrose nodded. His blond hair stuck out from under his wool cap like a pallid fringe. He struggled out of his coat while the group shuffled to make room as he was introduced and poured a beer.

"If God created everything and is pulling mankind toward the omega point of evolution, then God must have created evil if it's necessary for evolution," pressed David. "How do you explain that?"

Paul munched some popcorn and sipped his beer. "Your question has been debated for centuries. There are about as many theories of evil as there are of God."

David looked mulish. "But I want to know what you think."

"If evolution requires back-pressure, such as suffering and evil, then in a sense one can say God allows evil. But I see it more like a parent raising a child. As the child grows and learns it suffers and may do evil things as it matures. A child must learn from its suffering and mistakes. If a parent never allows a child the freedom to make mistakes and shields it from all suffering, it never learns or matures, never evolves. We are as a species still children evolutionarily speaking."

"But your religion believes that children are born evil and need saving," David said.

"I don't believe human beings are born evil – but incomplete as we all are. Genesis, in my opinion, is a mythology to explain evil, suffering and physical death. Genesis is more appropriately a story of mankind becoming conscious of evil, suffering, death, and of God. But I do believe we need 'saving' in that we were not created perfect and complete because creation isn't complete. It's still ongoing. We still need to evolve toward higher consciousness by opposing entropy and following the 'pull' of the spirit toward the omega point.

"Then shouldn't there be some experience of this spirit?" asked Jesse.

Paul emptied the pitcher and paid for another. "Can there be an inner spirit of which we have no sensation or experience?"

"Maybe we aren't yet evolved sufficiently to perceive it," said Jesse. "I mean, think about it. Can an amoeba hear or appreciate a Beethoven concerto?"

"If you remember the Gospel of Thomas, he held that direct divine knowledge is possible in the here and now," Paul said.

"Do you believe that?" Ali asked.

"I think it's rare but possible. What do you think Ambrose?" Paul asked.

Ambrose frowned and shook his head.

"Seems the Thomas gospel should be added to the canon," Jesse said. "After all he was an apostle."

Paul turned his glass round and round on the stained table. "I can't see that happening. That'd be turning back the clock two millennia."

David gulped his beer then frowned. "The Catholic Church is the longest surviving largest NGO in the world. But glaciers move faster. It might disappear along with the glaciers at the rate it's going. I can't understand how you can still be a part of the church given their past and present crimes. And their ultra-conservatism is completely contrary to what you teach."

It was hard for Paul to defend the indefensible. "Tension between religion and spirituality has existed from the early temple priests and prophets down to the present."

"What about all the ritual, dogma, sacraments? Where do they come in?" Ali asked.

"Forms to tether people to the institutions. Every hierarchical religion has them whether it's the Jewish Torah, Islamic Sharia, or the Christian Canon. Christ never mentioned original sin, nor any sacrament except what has become the mass. All the rest were established by religious institutions to substitute for direct spiritual experience," Paul said. "Whenever religion organizes as an institution, the side of the spiritualists – the mystics – usually lose out because they can't be controlled."

"So which side are you on? You're part of the institution but sound like a spiritualist," David said.

All eyes were on Paul. "Both sides contain truth."

David snorted. "Where does your heart and conscience lie?"

Paul felt Ambrose's glare. "Spirituality. That's what the coming of the Paraclete, the Holy Spirit, is about."

From there the conversation wandered on to what various religions had to say about the divine spirit until they pushed back their chairs, stood, and said good-byes.

Wrapped in their coats they emerged from the warmth of the pub into the night and scattered. The stars shone sharp and blue. Paul and Ambrose walked up the freeway overpass toward campus. The updraft from the freeway blew around bits of paper and grit. Moisture from the recent rain had already frozen in the gutters. Despite the late hour, streams of bright headlights headed north on I-5, and red taillights headed south like an endless crimson centipede. The roar from below made talk difficult until the two of them hiked up Yesler a block or two. Their breaths puffed small clouds of fog into the frigid air.

Paul glanced sidelong at Ambrose whose face looked as frozen as the air. "You're unhappy with me."

Ambrose continued puffing up Yesler. "I'm concerned about you. What you're doing with your students. You said you already got a warning." Ambrose looked straight up the hill and kept going. He pulled his hat down tighter over his ears and jammed his hands in his pockets.

"It wasn't my session. I was invited. They're explorers, seekers. We're training them not just in the subject matter but in critical thinking and judgment. Besides, none of them are Catholic."

"I thought you were going to be careful. Secular teachers can clock out. A priest can't."

Paul grimaced. "Nothing I said tonight violates the Creed, or the Beatitudes, or the two greatest commandments. Or the ten commandments for that matter. I choose not to be a blind guide."

Ambrose whirled on Paul. "We can't have personal beliefs," he said tersely. Ambrose strode up the hill again for several paces then turned to loom over Paul again. "Why're you a priest? You don't believe what we're required to believe. Worse, you're compelled to teach these errors. Why? Arrogance?"

Paul reeled back from Ambrose's vehemence. He's really upset. This can't be only about me. "What about you? Do you take everything we're given as gospel to be the actual truth? We're supposed to continue to seek truth."

Ambrose resumed walking up Yesler. "That's what you Jesuits do. Gets your order in trouble. You don't have Pope Francis to protect you anymore."

Ambrose's surprising testiness muted Paul. Why is Ambrose bitter?

"Ambrose, I'm sorry. I don't mean to be arrogant."

Ambrose scowled, quickened his pace. "Please quit swimming upstream. Just do what's expected and avoid crossing the hierarchy. Think of the trouble if you don't."

Paul watched Ambrose's back as he pumped uphill. His shoulders were slumped. Was that due to a lifetime of trying to shrink his large frame or because he carried a burden? He pulled level with Ambrose.

But when he spoke again Ambrose abruptly changed the subject. "How are the headaches?"

"I'm okay." It was difficult to be open about it, even with Ambrose.

"You sure scared the hell out of me that day I found you in the chapel."

"And I never thanked you. But you didn't tell me what I was like when you found me?"

Ambrose continued lumbering uphill to the crest then slowed and caught his breath. "You were cold. I thought at first you were dead. Your breathing was faint, and your eyes fixed and staring. You were lying there like you'd been sitting on the floor and just fell over backwards."

"Did you notice anything odd about the way I looked?" Paul's curiosity over-rode his caution.

"You mean being pale? I don't know that I've ever seen anyone so pale and still alive. It was like something bleached you out. Ghostly to tell the truth. Never seen anything like it."

Tired and back in his room, Paul readied for bed. But his mind reflected over the evening with the students and the walk with Ambrose. Am I underestimating the risks? For that someone would have to take me seriously. He recalled Tom's warning about Bauer a few weeks back. Discretion, use discretion.

He pulled out his worn volume of the Psalms. It opened at Psalm 51. "Have mercy on me O God in your kindness. In your compassion blot out my offenses...."

He tried to put his heart in it, but it was hard to concentrate. His mind cycled again through the parade of horribles. What if his superiors learned of his aura attacks before he could control or even explain them? Despite his work with Rabia, he didn't think he'd made much progress on understanding it. In fact, if anything, the aura attacks had ceased. I should be glad I'm back to normal. But I'm not."

He started the psalm again with determination: "Have mercy on me O God ...."

Then the words on the page bobbed and weaved. Itching-tingling sensations budded in his brain. Greenish-yellow light rimmed his bed and bookcase. The crucifix over the door bent and swayed.

Oh, God.

Pain burned. Blistered.

Don't fight it. Breathe. Let go.

He willed himself to let the stabs of pain and surges of nausea pass through him unresisted. Then the pain extinguished like the blowing out of a candle and left him suspended within the warm embrace of radiant euphoric light.

Floating. No time. No spatial reference points. Surrounded by an infinity of waves of light. Far on the horizon he felt a gentle and persistent tug. A center of gravity pulled him like the moon pulling the tide. Buoyed on light waves he was being carried out on a luminous sea. Abyss below. Abyss above. He drew nearer to a center, a presence, but could see nothing. What is it? What's there?

He felt an alarming thinning. I'm dissolving. I'm becoming one of these waves. Terror of absorption, of dissolution, overwhelmed him.

Pull back.

He found himself back in his chair in his room, the book of psalms spread-eagle on the floor. The clock read 3:34. He was shaking. Adrenaline coursed through his body. His heart hammered in his chest. Good God. Over two hours gone.

Sleep was impossible. He sat in the chair breathing deeply and rhythmically. Tried to still his heart. What did it mean? What is the center that attracts but also repels? I felt I'd lose myself – my identity – if I didn't pull back. But it felt like for the first time in my life I'd be complete, whole, if I could only join with it. Is there a price? A sacrifice for joining?

All his priestly life he'd been taught the necessity of 'dying to self'. He thought this meant not being self-centered. But this experience demanded more. A complete surrender of self to the point of dissolution. Is that what it takes? What does it feel like – the death of the ego? How can one be whole and complete – and empty?

After a long while, he picked up his Book of Psalms. Found a calming one. "The Lord is my shepherd...."

Pam Bissonnette

15

"Yesterday this day's madness did prepare;
tomorrow's silence, triumph, or despair."
Rubaiyat of Omar Khayyam

* * *

Ice on the pool at the entrance to the Ignatius Chapel reflected wan light from a sun low on the horizon. Students hurried to morning classes with heads down muffled in scarves and stocking caps or hoodies. Several clutched insulated coffee cups from Starbuck's. Tom, in sympathy with them, sipped his own brew and tried to stay warm as he walked and waited. A gray trench coat cloaked his lanky frame. He adjusted his muffler higher around the back of his neck to fill the gap up to his watch cap. The cold hurt his sore head which caused a pinched look to his aquiline face. Fog from his breath preceded him as he circled the frozen reflection pool and rose garden to keep warm.

The rose garden was nothing but thorny clipped canes that pointed accusingly at the sky within a bed of shriveled and curled rusty leaves and petals. The grass coated in rime at a crossroad of walkways staged a sorry little drama: small spikey footprints of a bird who braved the winter were followed by the rounded paws of one of the university's stray cats that had left behind a dismembered bloody wing. A few dun-colored feathers on the turf waved in the light breeze as though in parting. Tom turned back to walk widdershins around the pool, confronting the cold air current. He blew warmth into his hands. What was I thinking meeting outside?

His friend finally approached, her gait slow and cautious as though she was walking on the frozen reflecting pool. Her walking stick afforded a third leg of purchase on the hard ground. An odd friendship they had had over the years. More than a principal benefactress to the university, she had reached the stage of his personal sage dispensing wisdom when Tom needed someone safe to confide in.

She looked like a piece of night walking toward him: a long black wool coat and black boots, her head swathed in a combination jet wool hat and scarf, and warm soft black gloves covered her hands. Only her eyes behind gold wire-rimmed glasses could be seen glittering like crystal. She nodded in greeting.

Tom led her from the walking paths to a stone bench. Behind it a stand of cedars that formed a bower for statues of St. Francis with his birds and St. Dominic with his dog. Tom brushed off the detritus from the seat and offered a hand. She eschewed his hand and, hinging slightly at her hips, leaned on her walking stick and lowered herself onto the bench. She laid aside her stick, arranged her coat about her, and sat up straight as a rod, regal, despite the arthritis and austere garb. She drew down the scarf from her lips and tucked it under her chin.

"You wished to see me." She stated it as a fact, not a question. Her voice was deep, mellow, and gave nothing away.

"Are you warm enough?"

She nodded.

"I'm sorry about meeting here," Tom said. "I thought it best to make sure we're alone and won't be overheard."

She turned toward Tom. Her finely striated lips smiled at him along with her eyes. Both had pain lines radiating from their corners. "Then let's get on with it before we freeze into statues like the ones behind us."

Tom looked at his feet and rubbed his hands together between his knees. "You may not have heard. My chambers were broken into and I was attacked."

She sucked in her breath and lifted her chin. Her eye lids rose exposing fierce pupils trained on him.

"And I just heard that Fr. Eduardo Garcia of Sao Paulo has been murdered," Tom said. "We served together in the Vatican. When Francis was installed, he took along several Jesuits to support him. We were two of the closest to him."

"What is behind this violence?" she asked.

Tom looked side-long at her. "There was a lot of opposition to his progressive policies. He found out things – things the Vatican wanted to keep hidden. Just before he died, he made copies of what he found on memory sticks and gave them to Eduardo and me to keep safe. He told us not to publish them until the proper time and it would be evident when that was. Then he died, some believe murdered. We were evicted from the Vatican. And now Eduardo has been found tortured and murdered. I have to assume they retrieved his memory stick." Tom drew a deep breath and exhaled mist.

"And now they're after you, after these incriminating documents. Who are they?" she asked.

"The Society of Pope Pius XII. Do you know them?"

"Unfortunately, I do," she said. "Archbishop Bauer is one of them. What's in these documents?"

"Evidence that Pope John Paul I was murdered and who's responsible. Even though John Paul is long dead, the murderer was part of PXII, and they'll be implicated. There's also material implicating people both inside and outside the Vatican who were engaged in the Vatican Bank fraud that resulted in Roberto Calvi's murder."

"Why didn't Francis disclose them? Why don't you now? I realize it would cause a firestorm but why else did Francis dig up all this evidence if it wasn't to use?" she asked.

"Good question. All I know is that he said it would be needed 'at the proper time', and we would know when that is. Maybe some time when we need leverage or defense?"

"Seems vague for something so critical."

"It might be related to another record included in the documents, a part of a curious diary of Pope John Paul's. It's cryptic. It's been a while since I read it. He described a mysterious phenomenon associated with human consciousness, and a catalyst. Usually catalysts are chemicals, like a reagent in a chemical reaction. But John Paul made it clear the catalyst is a person. If we had more of the diary, we might've been able to find out. It's a puzzle. And I'm not really sure why Francis included it with the criminal evidence unless he felt it's somehow related to John Paul I's murder."

She wrapped her coat around her legs more tightly.

"I need someone to know and take action in case something happens to me," Tom said looking away and shivering. "Someone I trust. Not a Jesuit since we're all suspect. And not someone beholden to the church."

"What about Bauer? He must be involved somehow. You'll need protection."

Tom sighed. "Don't worry about me. Seattle is not Sao Paulo. I'm grateful I can be frank with you. Bauer's been looking for anything he can find to exert influence at Ignatius or gain leverage for control. He placed one of his minions here a while back to spy on us. Bauer complains about our 'radical' teaching. Calls us heretical. Probably using this as an excuse to interfere here so he can search for the documents. A university is such an open access place. That's why I couldn't hide the documents here."

She peered through her spectacles studying him. "How can I help?"

Tom gave her a note that she read, folded, and stowed within her coat.

"But how will I know when it's the proper time?" she asked.

"I know no more than you," Tom said as he muffled up.

She placed her hand on his shoulder and nodded, retrieved her walking stick and they both rose. She took his arm as they walked out of the wood into the cold morning sunshine.

16

"To attempt an understanding of Paul Muad'Dib without understanding his mortal enemies, the Harkonnens, is to attempt seeing Truth without knowing Falsehood. It is the attempt to see the Light without knowing Darkness. It cannot be. "
Dune, by Frank Herbert

* * *

The double bell towers of St. Luke's cathedral rose up above its lofty position atop Capitol Hill. It was only a twenty-minute walk from the Ignatius campus, but the two priests decided they would drive and stay dry. Archbishop Bauer would enjoy confronting a couple of drenched and wind-whipped Jesuits.

It was New Year's Eve, and Christmas lights still festooned trees and house eaves, a reminder that the light cycle was on the rise again until its apogee in June. But the cathedral and the bishop's residence next door, that should have represented light in the world, were dark.

Tom and Paul sat in Bauer's anteroom waiting for the audience that he had demanded. The mint spiritual tomes encased in glass along the wall were meant to impress. The heavy furnishings, burgundy plush carpet, and wine damask curtains were meant to intimidate. Images of the Madonna in her various roles as virgin, mother, and queen, cluttered the room like so much bric-a-brac, and hinted at a prurient rather than pious interest.

A withered elderly woman also sat in the anteroom turning over and over in her hands the strap of a purse. Her sunken eyes glanced around anxiously. Gray hair, gray eyes, gray personality. Her recessed lips quivered occasionally as though she wished to speak but thought better of it. Whenever the archbishop's door opened to his inner office she looked up, hopeful, only to be dashed when Bauer's assistant walked in or out, ignoring her, closing the door firmly behind him.

Behind the door Archbishop Bauer frowned and his eyes narrowed in impatience listening to Geoffrey recite his daily appointments: requested visitations of small delegations, representatives of poor congregations, an appointment with the Chancellor of Ignatius U, and worse an unannounced visit of his mother. Geoffrey, a sinewy man who padded about like a puma, moved on to cover the briefing book and calendar. Bauer listened with half an ear while surveying his office, a dependable source of diversion and satisfaction.

The walls paneled in black walnut; the cherry wood conference table and high-backed chairs; his ponderous baroque desk with an ornately carved swiveling chair; the carpet so lush it allowed him despite his girth to walk in silence; a picture of His Holiness Pius XIII signed "In gratitude for your work at the Curia" mounted behind his desk combined to imply visitors were in the presence of royalty. Bauer had wrapped himself in the accouterments of power. It made up in some measure for being assigned to this backwater.

"Cancel these appointments, except the one with Ignatius U."

"They're already outside."

"Good. Have them wait. I'm expecting a call from the papal nuncio that I must prepare for."

"What about your mother? She's sitting outside."

Damn. "Make a short appointment for her later this week and make sure there's another engagement waiting."

With the merest suggestion of a bow, Geoffrey glided from the room, closing the door silently behind him. Geoffrey's unctuous presence made Bauer feel self-assured. Good man that.

Impeccable. Competent. Never gets on my nerves like other ex-military types. Keeps his counsel. Understands his place. Not like women. Just emotion and babble.

Bauer rifled through the papers in his inbox while playing back his private phone messages on a speaker. He eventually found the *Bene Placitum* document for Ignatius University dating back to 1902 denying him direct control of the property. He didn't like any independence in his bishopric. Exasperating. I need leverage. Would it be possible to get the *Placitum* nullified, or subordinated? At least initiate proceedings as a threat?

Bauer shuffled through more papers and signed documents as he listened. He hated the tedious details of running a backward archdiocese. I should be in Rome helping secure suitable papal succession.

He slouched back in his chair and brooded how he'd handle the growing crisis. That bad bit in Chicago had flung him off the trajectory to a cardinalate. Confined him to this heathen backwood. Maybe it's resurrection time. Get out of soggy Seattle. The Vatican documents would be his ticket. How to get Bradbury to reveal where they are? If he could be alarmed into retrieving them ….

He buzzed Geoffrey.

A discrete knock at the door and Geoffrey ushered in and announced Fr. Thomas Bradbury, Chancellor of Ignatius University, and Fr. Paul Pennington to the two seats facing Bauer's desk.

Bauer had his back turned, fussed with files while eating a chocolate truffle. Let them sweat. Let the room's atmosphere do its job. These two aren't going to ruin my chances.

Rounding on them, Bauer confronted his nemesis in battles with the university. Tom Bradbury's aristocratic stature and aloof bearing peeved Bauer. And Bradbury had brought with him an insignificant looking priest Bauer had never met. Dark hair with gray at the temples, deep penetrating eyes, a sense of defeat about him.

Bauer leaned forward in his chair, rested his arms on the desk, glared over his bifocals, and opened on the offense, as though his time was too valuable to waste on customary opening pleasantries. "I'm hearing disturbing complaints about some of your lectures. Ignatius University stands for the highest in orthodox erudition. Helps prepare scores of young men for the priesthood. A seminarian complained recently that foundational precepts of the church are being called into question. And I've heard from some quarters what amounts to heretical positions. What's your explanation?"

Tom crossed his legs, folded hands in his lap, and sat back in the chair. "Fr. Pennington has been teaching a class on modern religious theories, not to be confused with established Catholic doctrine."

Bauer snorted. "Why is it necessary to have lectures on modern religious theories? You know Pope Pius XIII has condemned modernism. The university should concentrate on what is doctrine rather than what is not." This was all necessary theater, an obligatory warning, part of his case against Ignatius and Bradbury. Bauer didn't expect them to reform and didn't want them to.

Paul explained. "Students today come from all over the world and many different cultures and religions. They're not just Catholic, or even Christian. They're well read and expect to study and understand the current frontiers in theology. As for seminarians, they need to understand heresies if they're to be able to refute them."

Bauer tapped a long fingernail on his desk for emphasis. "We cannot afford any ambiguity about church doctrine, and certainly not because of outside influences and challenges. I strongly suggest you change the curriculum to avoid further possibility that radical theories be given any credence whatsoever."

"I can't do that," Paul said. "It would be disingenuous to teach a class on comparative contemporary theology and present only the currently accepted version of Catholicism."

This priest isn't as weak as he looks. Bauer turned a ring around on his hand. His eyes narrowed. "Then cancel the class."

"You have no authority to direct our curriculum," Tom said quietly.

Tom's professional rebuttal enraged Bauer. No one talks to me that way. I may not have the authority, but I have the power. He rose. Placed both fists on his desk. Leaned forward on his arms speaking in a crescendo mounting to a diatribe.

"While I can't direct you, should I continue to get complaints about the content of your lectures I'll be forced to take it up with your Order Provincial and have you barred from teaching in my diocese. We've enough problems already counteracting the Seattle liberal agenda. We can't have you providing reasons to attack the foundations of our theology."

Bauer plumped down and swiveled about in his chair, pretending to consult a stack of documents, exercising the power of rudeness to end the interview. In the awkward silence Tom and Paul stared at his back until Geoffrey slipped through the door to show the two priests out.

Bauer whirled around in his chair. "Bradbury, stay for a moment. We have something further to discuss."

Paul continued out. Once Geoffrey had closed the door behind them, Bauer motioned for Tom to be reseated. He glared at Tom for several seconds. "I have a directive from the papacy to retrieve something. Something that you Jesuits took when you left the Vatican, something that doesn't belong to you."

Silence.

"Did you take any Vatican documents with you when you left?"

The silence in the room had substance, felt thick. Tom crossed his legs "I took nothing from the Vatican that wasn't mine to take."

Bauer leaned back in his chair and folded his arms over his ample belly. "That's not what I understand from those now in the Vatican. They're quite sure that some of you Jesuits – let's be more forthright – specifically you, took documents that belong to the Vatican and must be returned."

"I've already told you that I didn't take anything that didn't belong to me," Tom said.

Bauer's eyes glittered. "You realize that one of your number, Fr. Garcia, did take documents, unlawfully, when he returned to South America. These have been retrieved. Unfortunately, Fr. Garcia had an . . . accident."

Silence.

"We know that there is at least one more copy. We intend to find it. Just like we found Fr. Garcia's."

"I can't help you I'm afraid," Tom said.

Stalemate for the moment. Bauer hadn't expected anything else, except it might propel Bradbury to make some kind of move. Bauer buzzed for Geoffrey. He must have been virtually standing at the door as he popped in like a jack-in-the-box and waved Tom out.

Once Bradbury was gone Bauer buzzed Geoffrey again.

"Yes, sir?"

"I want you to closely observe Fr. Bradbury. See if he makes any unusual moves for the Vatican documents. Have we got anything yet from that idiot we placed at Ignatius? Get him in here. See if he's found out anything."

Geoffrey nodded and left.

Pressure Bradbury. Make him understand he could lose Ignatius. Or take him out like Garcia. That's the way to handle things. Cut out the rot like amputating a gangrenous limb. He reached into his desk drawer and poured himself a brandy.

17

"I shall know you, secrets,
by the litter you have left,
and by your bloody footprints." Lola Ridge, Secrets

* * *

As university chancellor, Tom's quarters were larger than others. They included an office and small sitting area for visits from the priests and professors under his charge. The sleeping area was in an alcove discrete behind a partition. The main room was appointed with a couple of comfortable leather club chairs set around a low oak table on an oriental carpet of subdued pattern and colors.

It was the comfortable chamber of a scholar. A bookcase filled an entire wall with works of Greek philosophers; prominent theologians; Hindu, Sufi and Buddhist masters; and mystical poetry of Rumi, Rilke and Eckhart. Apart from a plain small wooden crucifix over the door, there was no other obvious sign of the religious profession of the chamber's occupant.

Paul accepted a glass of wine from Tom and they both settled into chairs.

"I'm sorry to have let you in on a reprimand for my actions. I've tried to be careful."

"You're only one of many causes for Bauer's anger at us," Tom said. "Ignatius has had both positive and negative relationships with the many archbishops in our nearly hundred and fifty years of existence. The exempt status of the Jesuit Order is a constant source of friction with most non-ordered bishops. But with Bauer, the relationship has been particularly difficult.

"Any man who aspires to be a bishop has enough ego to want to be in control of his domain. But none have been so blatant as Bauer in trying to exert authority over Ignatius. His last diocesan seat was in Chicago. He had hopes of a cardinalate but got in trouble. His re-assignment here was a great disappointment, a blow to his career. The archdiocese here is considered a backwater. A place from which to retire rather than advance. Bauer hasn't made many friends here except a few arch conservatives. The archdiocese is hurting. Bauer must be pretty desperate. And Ignatius is just one more thorn in his side."

"Is he just taking out his frustrations on us or is he serious about his threats?" Paul asked.

Tom raised his glass. Swirled and examined the glycerin rivulets running down its sides. "Bauer is a member of PXII. You've heard of it?

"Some kind of reactionary Catholic organization. I've never paid much attention to it," Paul said.

"PXII stands for the Society of St. Pius XII. They hold that Pius XII was the last legitimate pope. Since his death in 1958 all the popes that followed until Pius 13 are considered anti-popes."

"Seriously?"

Tom refilled his glass and settled back into the leather. "The conclave at the death of Pius XII in 1958 was unusual. There's more than just rumor that an early ballot elected Cardinal Giuseppe Siri. He took the name Gregory XVII. It's a fact that white smoke appeared from the Sistine Chapel. A huge crowd waited for a new pope's appearance on the balcony. Instead, after a long while, black smoke re-appeared. It took another two days for a pope to be elected, John XXIII. Cardinal Siri was a staunch conservative and implacable enemy of communism. There was a lot of speculation about what happened. Some involved threats from the Kremlin and others threats from the far left. According to Canon Law, '...resignation out of grave danger...' is invalid, making Siri if he had been eleced, even if he resigned, the rightful pope."

96

"How'd this get out?" Paul asked.

"Someone talked. It happens. But usually only harmless anecdotes. Not something so serious as to undermine papal succession. As you know John XXIII immediately initiated the Second Vatican Council. His sweeping liberal reforms were anathema to conservative Siri supporters. Clergy who didn't like the reforms founded societies to uphold the 'true pope' and 'true' Catholic tradition. PXII is the most powerful of these societies. They've publicly skated so close to the edge criticizing former pontificates that they've risked excommunication. Other groups have gone over the edge and elected their own popes. It has taken the better part of a century for PXII to infiltrate and manipulate the ecclesiastical hierarchy to succeed in returning a 'legitimate' pope to the throne in Pius 13."

"I always thought these fringe clerics were a sideshow," Paul said. "How'd they get so powerful? Who're these other groups?"

Tom swirled the golden wine in his glass. "The Society of St. Pius the V is one, more conservative than PXII. Opus Dei you know, one of the wealthiest conservative sects in the U.S. And the Palmarian Church in Spain, to name the most prominent."

"How'd they manage getting P13 elected? They would've needed many sitting cardinals as members."

Tom set down his glass. "They did. And P13 was well camouflaged in the Curia. Even at that he barely had enough votes to win the election."

Paul chewed his lip. "There've been worse papal successions going back over the centuries to Borgia and Avignon. Even more than one sitting pope at times. We survived. P13 is eighty-eight. In poor health. Can't last long. We'll have another shot soon."

Tom stood up and walked the short distance to the window, stretched his back and gazed out over the campus. "Maybe not. Think back over the popes since 1958: Pope John XXIII, liberal, lived barely five years; Paul VI liberal, believed by some to have been martyred; John Paul I, liberal, murdered after only thirty-three days; John Paul II, conservative, long reign; Benedict XVI, split politics, after a short reign the first 'retired' pope in 600 years; Francis I, first Jesuit pope, liberal. There are suspicions about how he died. It's taken nine decades of intrigue to get to this point.

PXII's next move I'd guess will be to consolidate their hold. I shouldn't be surprised if P13 calls a consistory to expand the membership of the College of Cardinals. Pack it with conservatives. That'll allow them to regain control of the Vatican Bank. It'll also assure the next pope will be of the same conservative stripe."

Paul smacked down his glass slopping drops of wine on the table, stood up, addressed Tom's back. "This is hard to believe. You're actually telling me that forces inside the Vatican murdered a pope."

Paul found these revelations too bizarre to assimilate. We're a thinking, conscience-based order. Where does one – can one – make a stand? Is there a place for intellectual honesty in the church anymore? Moral courage? "If this is the future, where does that leave us?"

Tom walked to his seat and sank down, rested his forehead in his hand, and spoke into his lap. "They'll purge the church of threats. Ignatius is one of those threats. I'm one of those threats."

"How can you be a threat?"

Tom turned a somber face to Paul. "I was close to Francis. Jesuits were supposed to protect him. We failed. Then all the Jesuits were evicted from the Vatican. PXII suspected us of taking things with us. Risky things. Things they want."

Tom rubbed his forehead. Looked at Paul. Started to go on and then stopped. Got up and turned back to the window. Put his hands in his pockets.

"What things?"

Tom didn't respond.

"Did you?"

Tom remained gazing out at the campus twinkling lights. "It's what they believe that matters."

"Is that why your chambers were broken into? Why you were attacked?" asked Paul

"I can't think that Bauer has sufficient gumption to have arranged such a thing. It'd give the assailant a hold over him," Tom said.

"If Bauer means to ingratiate himself into a cardinalate, Ignatius is either his biggest liability or his means to advance,"

Paul said. "If he thinks you have something that could help him do that, you're a target."

Anxiety rose in the back of Paul's mind about his aura experiences. If Bauer knew, he would take extreme measures against Paul and Ignatius. And Tom? Would this be a good time to tell him? What would Tom's reaction be? Not good. Another serious problem for him. It would escalate. He'd have to bring in the Provincial.

Tom broke into Paul's thoughts. "Not everyone at Ignatius can be trusted. I notice you're friends with Ambrose."

Paul said, "I've wondered how Ambrose, a secular priest, came to be the librarian of Ignatius."

Tom glanced sidelong at Paul. "He's never told you?"

"He didn't offer to explain, and I never asked. Didn't want to embarrass him in case there was a story behind it."

"How did the two of you become friends?" Tom asked. "You're so different."

"I was drawn to his uncomplicated nature. I enjoy his simplicity. His views on life and faith are so certain, unlike mine."

"Are you sure he's so uncomplicated and certain?" Tom asked. "Or is it just that he believes what he's told? I find he's ill equipped to defend his beliefs. Falls back into dogma and rhetoric if the least challenged."

"I've never really pushed him. He veers off like he doesn't want to talk to me about himself. Often cautions me though. Warns me to stay out of trouble."

"Probably a good idea." Tom smiled. "But if there're no doubts then where's the faith? I find people who're very certain either have no faith or have given their conscience over to the custody of another. While the first case is sad, the second is dangerous."

"You think Ambrose has done that?"

Tom took off his glasses. Carefully cleaned them. "Bauer recommended Ambrose to me when we had a vacancy for a librarian. He has a degree in computer science. We had no one else to assign so I took him on. I couldn't think of a good reason to refuse. He'd been a chaplain somewhere, a hospital in Chicago I think. Some mystery there. Now he's here I'm not sure he's at peace. Something's causing him deep anxiety, though he covers it well with a veneer of cheerfulness."

"You think he may be a mole for Bauer?" Paul asked.

"Private information from inside Ignatius is getting to Bauer. Someone's passing it."

Sweet Jesus. Paul brushed hair up over his brow. Is this what we've come to? Having to watch our backs with our own?

Tom's wall clock chimed 8:00. Paul made ready to leave.

Tom asked, "How're you feeling? Are you having any more migraines?"

Paul wished that was all they were. "I'm doing better."

"I was concerned."

Paul took himself off with Tom's best wishes in his ears for continued good health. He scaled the blue tiled stairwell to his room with his head full of revolving thoughts. Vatican sins. Underground organizations. Bauer a collaborator. Ambrose a chameleon. Tom with secrets. Me, too.

The Christmas wreath he had placed on his door a few weeks back looked forlorn, its forest green luster gone. Several dried needles scattered on the floor. But it still held its piney scent. Paul lifted it off the door hook and took it inside his room. It deserved a better internment than his wastebasket.

Within minutes a soft knock on the door announced the arrival of Ambrose with a bottle and two glasses clinking.

"I thought we'd herald in the New Year with a toast or two."

His plump presence and moon face beamed in the doorway. Unlike the Jesuits who wore whatever made sense for the occasion, Ambrose stuck to the black diocesan dress code. His thick neck protruded from the tight white Roman collar. Strawberry blond hair contrasted oddly with the austere garb. He smiled broadly with open lips that revealed uneven small teeth and pink gums. For a man so large the whole aspect – Paul was embarrassed to think it – made Ambrose look like an overgrown baby in a costume.

Still feeling the ominous warning from Bauer and revelations from Tom, Paul was not in the mood for celebration. "I don't think so tonight."

"Why not? It's New Year's Eve. Time to bury the old year and toast the new." Ambrose lumbered in and heaved down on the bed. Poured them both stiff shots. Tossed most of his back in a single swig.

Paul accepted his glass, took an abstemious sip, and studied Ambrose.

Ambrose poured himself another shot. "You all right? You look tense."

Could Ambrose really be a spy for Bauer? We should be an open community. We shouldn't need spies.

"Bauer called Tom and me in today. Got a formal warning for my teaching. Implied Tom was harboring a heretic."

Ambrose shrugged. "I told you to be careful. What can Bauer do as long as the order stands behind you? Just keep your head down. Go along to get along."

This was a refrain Paul heard from Ambrose many times. How could he be that naïve? But then Ambrose wasn't a Jesuit, as he often points out.

Ambrose finished his second scotch. "Let's go out and have some fun. Take your mind off your troubles. Be good for you."

Paul, curious now about Ambrose, finished his scotch and muffled up. They walked down Yesler toward Pioneer Square. The boisterous atmosphere of firecrackers, and raucous frivolous fun in the streets seemed fey. It was not yet midnight but out of an open pub door the sound of boozy singing "Auld Lang Sine" was already caroling.

They wove their way through the crowded sidewalks finally arriving at the Pioneer Square Saloon. The Saloon, one of the oldest in Seattle, reprised raucous pioneer days of cards, prostitutes, logging, and gold from the Yukon. Located at the base of Yesler, or Skid Road, near the wharf, streets here were still cobble. Though upgraded to modern standards, some of the seediness of the pioneer days still hung about. The interior boasted a long bar backed by a gigantic mirror, stools, brass rails and gear hooks; on a floor of white, red and black tiles now littered with peanut shells, popcorn, swizzle sticks, and party favors. Booths tucked away mostly in shadow accommodated patrons well on their way to spirited revels.

Ambrose and Paul jostled their way up the upstairs to a loft table where they could overlook the main floor. Paul already regretted coming.

Ambrose took a long pull at his pint and leaned forward across the table to be heard in the din. "Look around. People here are enjoying themselves and you should too. Life's not so serious unless we let it be. Remember 'eat, drink and be merry for tomorrow we may die,' a good ecclesiastical code."

Paul barely touched his beer. Observed Ambrose closely. His baby face must be a camouflage. When Ambrose was confronted with a serious question he would never look at you. After several years Paul knew nothing about Ambrose's past. How he became a priest. Where he was before coming to Ignatius. "Ambrose, are you comfortable at Ignatius? Do you like it there?"

"What makes you ask?"

"You're not a Jesuit. Do you feel part of our community?"

Ambrose drained his beer and signaled for another one. "It's fine."

Paul decided for once to provoke Ambrose out of his complacent shell. "Can't be that easy when we Jesuits have so many liberal ideas. Our independence gives us more freedom. Rankles the diocese. Some of us even think that the Huaraz prophecy about the Anti-Christ applies to P13."

Ambrose's face became a mask of disapproval. "Why're we talking about this? Can't you leave it alone? We're supposed to be here for fun." He turned away from Paul and leaned over the railing toward the revelries on the main floor below, clutching his beer.

Ambrose had turned himself into a balled-up armadillo, nothing but armor showing. "I'm sorry, Ambrose. You're right."

Midnight was minutes away. The denizens of the bar broke out again in "Auld Lang Sine". Ambrose in his deep baritone boomed happily along, waving his empty pint in time. Others in the bar, some of them Paul's students, were doing likewise. It was hard to be depressed in such a place with such people. The atmosphere, scotch, and beer finally permeated him. He drained his pint, smiled, and sang along. "Should auld acquaintance be forgot..." I want to be like all these people here, simply happy in the moment. Why can't I be like that? Going along to get along?

They walked home companionably after the bar closed. Paul forgot for at least a few hours his problems and suspicions. He glanced sideways at Ambrose. "How do you retain your equanimity? You give at least an illusion of contentment and tranquility. Is it real?"

Ambrose walked briskly in the cold. "I walk a fine line between the organization that provides my job, my personal faith, and enjoyment of life. I keep the three separate." He took out his handkerchief and loudly blew his nose, then asked Paul, "Who d'ya think'll win the Super Bowl?"

Paul understood he'd trespassed on personal ground and was being warned off. Tom was right. Ambrose wasn't as simple or content as he seemed.

18

"Let love lead your soul." Attar of Nishapur

* * *

Paul had been working with Rabia on meditation practices for some time. They met three times a week in her small office at Harborview. She had taught Paul how to meditate in the eastern tradition: focus on the breath, clear the mind, correct postures, and use of a mantra or prayer of Paul's choosing. She had given him a long list of books to read, many on Sufi spirituality. She also incorporated special physical exercises and diet designed to calm the body and clarify the mind. And she emphasized the necessity of opening the heart. She'd given him practices such as being mindful of each person he met, even animals and plants, and empathizing with them, projecting compassion.

Paul practiced. When not in her office he trained in his room at Ignatius or around campus.

Rabia began to layer on other techniques: measured breathing, focusing his mind deep into his inner consciousness. Her office at Harborview where she and Paul meditated was small with a single window. But unlike most other medical offices, it was a warm salmon color. Rabia had made it her own. On one wall was a picture of the Mosque of Sufi Saint Abul Hassan Ali Hajweri, Lahore. On her desk was a picture of Kabir, her father, and next to it a framed copy of one of Rabia of Basri's poems:

"Some people make their goals the stars,
They may live and die never reaching them.
But in the darkness of the night,
Those stars will guide them to their destination,
Because they put them in their sights.
How long will you keep pounding on an open door,
Begging for someone to open it?"

His Jesuit training had made Paul a quick learner. A solid foundation of prayer and focused contemplation made grafting on eastern mediation practices relatively easy. Meditating together had become comfortable. But Paul's aura experiences had deserted him in the past months. Now that he accepted the aura, even desired it, he felt dry. Why did you come when I least expected it? Didn't want it? And now leave me? It was frustrating and hard to understand that once he accepted the aura-gift, it withdrew.

During their sessions together Rabia's aura never manifested. Paul felt awkward asking her about it. Or asking why his own was mute. Have I created a barrier?

Tonight, her one window framed stars. They rearranged the desk and two chairs to clear a space on the floor. Each took a small Persian rug from Rabia's stack to sit on. They faced each other on the floor, their knees almost touching.

They started rhythmic breathing exercises. Eyes closed. Paul concentrated his focus within his heart, and then attempted to withdraw deeper into his consciousness. It was hard. He struggled. It wasn't happening. Thoughts intruded, cycled. He pushed them away. Tried counting his breaths, then his heartbeats. He repeated over and over his mantra but it was just words. He found himself clenching his teeth and pinching his eyebrows, as though he could force concentration. Fruitless. He opened his eyes.

Already in deep meditation, Rabia sat cross-legged and still. An arm's distance away, he observed her closely, unnoticed: glossy thick black hair tied back to reveal her classical skull structure; the sylph-like nose and mouth; soft rich flawless complexion; eye lashes like two black goose down feathers resting on her cheeks; muscles relaxed; limbs and body reposed effortlessly on her frame; hands upturned and cupped in her lap.

One of her fingers twitched. Paul flushed with embarrassment, fearing discovery, feeling his scrutiny a violation of her person. Why is she having this effect on me? He closed his eyes again to follow his breath with determination. But he felt blocked from breaking through to his deeper consciousness. He couldn't shift the center of his focus away from Rabia's presence. Confused and unfamiliar feelings roiled up. Then he felt a strange close radiating warmth. He opened his eyes again and gasped.

Rabia's head was in aura, gold shot with azure, shimmering, its edge attenuating into tiny flickering flames. Paul's hair stood up on the back of his arms and neck. He realized he was holding his breath. His senses stilled in inverse proportion to his intensifying internal turbulence and curiosity. So, this is what an aura is like. I want to touch it – touch her. With his fingers spread wide he gently reached into her aura. The air, charged with energy, tingled his fingers.

Rabia stirred, smiled, and raised her hands, placing them on his cheeks. He felt each finger firm and cool, her palms exerting delicate pressure against his jaw. She pulled the two of them together, bowing, until their foreheads touched, setting off a charge of energy coursing through Paul from head to ground.

He became immersed in her light. His consciousness registered being nourished, refreshed, whole, embraced. Is this what it feels like to experience a woman? Ever so lightly he sensed his aura arise as though called, emerge, expand and join with Rabia's effortlessly, without pain, weightless.

Impressions, thoughts, emotions long buried swirled up from the sludge in his subconscious. His mother's hands ... guilt ...why'd she leave me? The loveless foster homes. Rejection and ridicule from his first foray into human love ... bullying from his classmates ... anger at God ... self-hatred ... and ....

No. His consciousness shrank back. I can't. Shame. Too much guilt and need. No one can know this. His breathing constricted. He opened his eyes. His hands shook as he reached for Rabia's to pull them away – but then stopped.

He sensed her coaxing him back with feelings of compassion, understanding and acceptance. Rabia's tenderness and his own fear strove within him. I can't let her in. Then the despairing child within, long buried, awoke, and cried out for release. Keening inside, tears spilled down his cheeks wetting Rabia's hands, but she didn't let go. Continuous rays of empathy penetrated him bearing the blessed balm of a healer. Wavering on the brink of retreat, there came a moment of freedom to choose. Open up or remain in the self-protective encasement so carefully constructed over a lifetime. A choice toward light and life? Or darkness and emotional deadness?

Choose life.

With a firm act of will, Paul quit resisting. He breathed deeply, softened his shoulders, and relaxed the tightness around his heart. He sensed an immediate release of emotional pressure, like a volcanic eruption. Out spurted emotional pain and resentment, anger and guilt, shame and self-hatred. Like black smoke in wind it dissipated and was replaced with clean emptiness.

Rabia dropped her hands away. They were together sharing consciousness, fearless, flying free. Anxiety over exposure of his life's failings – gone. To his surprise in its place – heightened personalization. But like seeing double. He was both uniquely and individually himself but also merged with Rabia. His self-perception refocused from one unworthy of love to gratitude for all the beauty and good in his life: John, nature, the universe, teaching, priesthood, Rabia. He turned his consciousness outward toward her. She was compassionate in spirit and selfless like John. But there was something shielded, an opaque area that didn't yield to aura transparency. Paul didn't pursue it. He didn't want this exhilarating experience tainted by his curiosity.

They sat in mutual stasis until the moon, on its arc through the night sky, glowed through the window. Temporal awareness returned to them simultaneously. Rabia's wall clock read 3:09 in the morning. Paul helped her off the floor and winced at his own stiffness. Despite the late hour he felt excited and wanted to talk. But Rabia forestalled him.

"We'll talk tomorrow. I need to leave," she said.

He couldn't be sure, but Rabia seemed embarrassed. He walked her to her car in silence. Then on foot he returned to campus. The moon was still high, obscuring its neighbor stars. The freezing air felt clean, like all the impurities had been crystallized out of it. He didn't feel good or bad, happy or sad. Just acutely alive.

Paul barely slept. He woke rejuvenated. Ignatius felt vibrant. He placed bare feet on the floor feeling the smooth wood against his soles and toes. He opened the window. Outside the sky was clear and uniformly blue, a backdrop to the sun pinned like a picture on an azure wall. A bracing breeze caressed Paul's nakedness and raised goose-bumps, fluttering the small hairs on his arms and legs. Several deep breaths expanded his ribs. He stretched arms over his head, arched his back, closed the window, and smiled.

The habitual tightness in his chest released into expansive well-being, as though healed of a long debilitating illness. He crossed to the sink and mirror, ran his hands through his tousled hair. The eyes that looked back at him were bright, calm, but something else was there too. A more intense 'seeing'. Detailed tessellations on the scrolled mirror frame he noticed for the first time. His fingerprints that he had never really examined were scrolled like the frame. He dressed and descended through the watery blue stairwell to get outside.

His vibrant mood contrasted with the listless landscape of winter. He anticipated spring: bare dirt that would host crocus, daffodils and tulips; naked brown limbs with pupae-like buds that would burst with the special green of the first leaves; bruised and broken blades of grass that would give way to a fresh green pelt.

Last night he'd cracked open the internal barrier constructed to protect himself from the rejection and pain of a loveless life. What he'd never understood till now – never felt – was that he'd just exchanged one kind of pain for another. Avoiding deep human relationships assured a loveless life.

Paul ambled around the campus taking in every sensation, his antennae turned outward instead of in. During the reshuffling of students between classes he noticed them – really noticed them – as individual people, individual souls milling through paths and corridors. So many future doctors, lawyers, engineers, teachers, artists. Or so many healers, defenders of justice, builders, guides, inspirers, all contributing to the milieu of humanity. Everywhere in the world this was happening in a great genesis. He truly loved them all, not any longer as an intellectual exercise, but in his gut. He took the gall that rode around in his pocket and threw it high in the air. Watched its arc until it disappeared.

His thoughts returned to what happened with Rabia. Tried to critically examine it. It wasn't like it had been when sharing his aura with John. Rabia initiated. He'd felt a power surge when she touched him. Then his aura emerged without effort, without pain. And their merging of auras was very different. They bonded. Communicated. Were one. The fibers of his heart softened at the remembrance. He'd experienced the unknown territory of the sacred feminine and it touched him deeply.

But no dense center reeled him in. No ocean of light. No other entity was present. Only the sharing within their combined auras, intimately joined one to the other.

So, what was the presence in my other experiences?

19

"I must not fear. Fear is the mind-killer. Fear is the little-death …"

Frank Herbert's Dune

* * *

Harborview buzzed with activity after a busy night. Full rooms crowded emergency patients in less critical condition into hallways. Some were strapped on gurneys, and one was handcuffed to the rail. Nurses and doctors moved purposefully through the throng of ill and injured.

"Dr. Habib, please return to Station 8-South," glowed on her cellphone.

Rabia finished with her current patient and returned to the nurses' station. "What's the matter, Ruby?"

"There're two men here asking for you. I told them you were busy, but they refuse to leave until they see you. Said they were relatives. The older one seems wound up. I put them in the conference room so they wouldn't cause a disturbance. Do you want me to call security?"

"Do you know who they are? Did they identify themselves?"

"They declined to give names. The older one has a marked accent, dark complexion, graying hair, I would guess in his sixties. The other man with him probably forty or forty-five, dark, medium height, thin, long black beard."

"It's probably my uncle with someone. I'll just be a minute."

Rabia walked stoically toward the conference room, while her mind raced and her stomach churned. I can't have them here. They've got to leave immediately.

She knocked and entered. It was Uncle and Ibrahim. Ibrahim hadn't changed much in the decades since she'd seen him. His eyes were just as sharp and arrogant; his hair and beard as black; his posture as insolent. But his restless hands alternately squeezed and splayed as though kneading the air, warming up for action. She closed the door. Straightened her shoulders. Turned to face them placing the table in between. Silence pervaded the room for some moments.

"Uncle, Ibrahim, I can't have you here. You must both leave. Immediately."

"Rabia," Fakhruddin said. "Ibrahim has agreed to take you back."

Ibrahim's dark eyes flashed defiance.

"Come. You belong with me," Ibrahim said.

"You mean belong to you. I won't go back. This is my home now. I've built a life without violence and pain."

Ibrahim reached for her but Rabia darted around the conference table and kept it between them. She turned to Fakhruddin. "Uncle, please understand. Our marriage was an unhappy one." She glared at Ibrahim. "You beat me."

The remembrance cascaded fear all through her. Beaten by her Uncle, then by Ibrahim. Force to ... forced to ... Merciful Allah. "I'm not going back." She kept one eye on Ibrahim and prepared for her Uncle's explosion of wrath, but none came, which was even more disturbing.

His eyes were cold, his face quivered.

"If you both don't leave, I'll have to call security," Rabia said.

Fakhruddin didn't even seem to notice her anymore. He said something in Arabic to Ibrahim and turned to leave. Ibrahim clenched both fists. Virulent anger flared on his face as he left. For a moment Rabia thought he was going to spit on her.

She closed the door behind them. Now that they were gone her hands shook. She sat down at the table, her head bowed onto her arms. Her throat constricted. She found herself hyperventilating. All that she had hoped long ago to put behind her had returned.

"Merciful Allah. Please help me. Forgive me."

* * *

MEDIA HEADLINE: Suspected Terrorist Attack Destroys Synagogue

The death toll of 77 is still rising from the bombing earlier today of the Chabad of Bremen-Burg, Germany. No organization has claimed responsibility leaving speculation open to white supremacist or militant Islamic organizations. Police ....

20

"There is a language so beautiful that it is never spoken."
Meister Eckhart

* * *

Sandwiched between Volunteer Park and the Lakeview Cemetery, the Mt. Olives Benedictine Monastery and Hospice commanded a view of both the Cascade Mountains over Lake Washington and the Olympic Mountains over Puget Sound, a fitting view for the dying and the dead. For several years Paul had been their spiritual adviser and had performed pastoral duties for its nuns and patients.

A pathway lined with rosemary, thyme, sage, bay, and lavender lead to the monastery's front door with a sign that read, "Welcome, Come In". Paul rang the bell. A fresh-faced postulant and the aroma of baking cookies greeted him.

"Father Pennington, please come in. Mother Marcellus is expecting you."

Paul nodded shyly and followed her in. For some reason the place had the effect of muting him.

Marcellus was waiting. Like all her nuns she wore the brown habit, and white apron and hair veil that suited well for nursing duties. Tall and slender, with a face neither old nor young but fine featured and reflecting experience of the world, she exuded competence and warmth. Auburn hair that escaped from her veil curled at her temples. A smile animated her face and brightened her eyes.

She sat Paul on a stool at a kitchen island and placed a plate of ginger snaps, a small pot of earl grey, and a mug down in front of him. Patients were at small tables in the dining area just off the kitchen. Some old, some young, all with obvious debilitating conditions. A few had oxygen tubes snaked into their nostrils from bottles strapped to their wheelchairs. Some were fed by nuns. The rest raised palsied or arthritic hands with great determination to their mouths.

The slender prioress strode stately as a crane among her charges. Moving through the tables, she touched a person here, hugged a person there, a kind word to another.

Paul went through the duties of listening to confessions, celebrating mass and anointing the sick. Most of the aspirants and nuns working around him were young nurses, unusual these days when religious vocations of service were dying out.

Toward evening Marcellus led him to the darkened room of an elderly woman. In the dimness a young nun sat by the woman's bedside praying the rosary.

Marcellus excused the nun then said to Paul, "Svetlana may not last the night. Cancer is claiming her. We do our best to keep her pain free. With no Russian speakers here, we can't communicate. I'll leave you to be private with her." Marcellus stepped out and closed the door softly behind her.

Paul pulled up a chair near her head and held one of her hands. Her cool sheer skin revealed purple veins. Cheek bones protruded from her face. Dull eyes peered at him from sockets sunken into her skull. Facial skin sagged in lines from thin bluish lips. She was returning to the earth even before death. Paul began last rites.

As he went through the ritual, her impending death forced him to face this last vulnerability, but with new sensitivity. The final surrender. Is the ego extinguished? Are memories part of who we are, and we go into the beyond burdened with our past? Or are we subsumed into something with a new beginning and clean memory slate? But then do we lose some of who we are?

Paul found himself being drawn into the drama of death. He met her eyes and concentrated his consciousness there, as if his prayer could reach her. "Even though I walk through the valley of darkness, I will fear no evil. Your rod and your staff, they comfort me...."

Warmth as from a low-level current flowed through Paul's hands. The woman's eyes became alert. He became aware of her pain. Her struggle as she clung to life. He realized he was sharing her consciousness. Sensed sorrow and fear – an appeal for help. Snatches of remorse – something about a young girl – regret involving an elderly man – formed in Paul's mind.

He acknowledged with compassion her grief, holding her close in the embrace of their combined consciousness. He absolved her. Then guided her into the diaphanous light that now hovered around her.

The woman faced the final struggle, to let go of physical existence and reach for the ultimate reality. She gradually withdrew from Paul's consciousness, coalesced into a point of fire, and blazed away into the light.

He laid the woman's hand on the bed coverlet. The pain lines of her face eased. He closed her eyes. Gratitude and elation hung with him in the wake of her passing like a scent in the air. I've just witnessed a miracle. An ordinary miracle that happens thousands of times every second throughout the world but misunderstood and feared. He shut the door gently as he left the room and went to find Marcellus.

She sat in the anti-room of her chamber filled with books and pictures of faces. A piebald cat sat on a window ledge licking its fur. Marcellus crocheted an afghan. Her deft fingers elegantly danced with the crochet hook and yarn. In blues, greens and white, the afghan reminded him of the sea near the shore stirring with mysterious restless energy.

Paul sagged, drained of energy. He closed his eyes to block out the discord of Marcellus's cozy atmosphere with the woman's somber death he had just witnessed. In his mind she'd already become 'the woman', her identity fading in the face of the transformation.

"Paul, are you with me? I've been talking to you and you haven't heard a word."

"I'm sorry."

"Are you okay? You're no stranger to last rites. Why has this one so affected you?" Marcellus asked.

The cat left its perch to rub against Paul's leg. He stroked its back as it arched to his fingers. How to describe his experience so that it doesn't sound profane or bizarre? "Remember a while back when I wound up in the hospital? They never found a cause for my collapse, but it turns out the mental disturbance was – is – a mystical gift – caused by divine light. John witnessed it, felt it. A neurologist did too. And just now ...."

Marcellus ceased her needle work. Put aside the yarn.

Paul searched Marcellus's face for a reaction, fearful she'd be skeptical and patronizing. She was neither, only staring at him, still as a statue.

"Just now I had a similar experience with the woman who died. Through this – gift – I entered her consciousness. She was surrounded by light, but she feared it. She suffered not just physically but also from emotional pain. It stood between her and the light. While we didn't communicate with words, I perceived visions of her regrets and sorrows. I responded with – feeling is the only way I can describe it rather than words – that she was forgiven, absolved. I guided her into the light. A spark condensed within her consciousness – into light, her own light. It was then that she was able to let go and die peacefully, even joyfully."

Marcellus didn't make a move. The cat reclined on the floor and sprawled out on its back offering its stomach for attention.

"You don't seem surprised? Do you believe me?" Paul asked.

"When you live continuously around the dying you see and hear unusual things," Marcellus said. "We sit with dying patients as they – well – move on. We don't talk about it with outsiders, but there're rare times when something ethereal leaves a body at death and evaporates like mist in the sun. But please tell me about – what do you call it?"

"Dr. Rabia Habib, my neurologist, calls it an aura state. Her knowledge comes from Islam, not her medical background. I enter an altered conscious state of light and timelessness. Three times now in the light I've been able to share consciousness with another person. But this time with someone who doesn't even share a common language with me. Yet I understood what she

116

needed. I was able to communicate pardon and peace, and she understood me. And I was able to awaken her own aura. Then the light – life – left her body. This light – the aura – must be connected to the life force."

Marcellus remained frozen, just staring at Paul. Her eyes unfocused, as though in realization of a great insight, and then tightened at Paul. She rose, stood for a few moments, then crossed the room to hug him. "To have such an incredible gift. You are blessed."

Paul realized as he relaxed in her grasp how tense he'd been. He hugged her back. "I'm so grateful to share this with you. I've been afraid to tell anyone."

"Which means you haven't told Tom?"

Paul looked away.

"You have to before he finds out some other way. You were able to tell me. Now tell him."

21

"Woe to the conquered." Livy, 59BC-17AD

* * *

While Paul was confessing his secret to Marcellus, Ambrose approached a confession of another kind. He scuttled in a side door of Ignatius's main church, selected a pew in the center of the cavernous empty space so as not to be overheard, and waited.

These enforced confessions were hateful. Instead of feeling liberated by absolution, he felt trapped in a morass of deception. And he couldn't confess everything, not to an emissary from PXII. As he waited, he imagined he heard whispers up in the rafters.

Finally, a tall gaunt priest entered the church, strode up the main aisle, genuflected, and slid in next to Ambrose. He was clean shaven with course hair, rough skin, and shadows under veiled eyes. His beaked nose, small mouth, slight hunch, and spiky hands gave him a predatory appearance. He took a stole out of his pocket, kissed it, and looped it around his neck, crossed himself, and nodded.

Despite the coolness within the vaulted space, Ambrose was already perspiring. "Bless me father for I have sinned."

Silence.

"I've been having doubts lately," Ambrose continued.

"Doubts? About what?" the confessor asked in a raspy voice.

"Are you certain we're right?"

"Of course we're right," he snapped. "Who or what has made you doubt?"

Ambrose rubbed sweaty hands on his thighs. Whispered. "A fellow priest. Fr. Paul Pennington, a Jesuit who teaches here at Ignatius."

The confessor's voice became stern. "What has he said or done to cause you to question?"

Ambrose swallowed. Kept his eyes down. "He says that the prophecies could apply to P13 as the Anti-Christ in the papal chair."

The confessor's eyes flashed. "Blasphemous." The syllables spat out like cobra venom. "Something must be done. This profane pestilence must not spread." A thin scaly hand slapped his leg in emphasizing cadence. "You did right to confess this. Know that we are right. No other thought should enter your mind."

Ambrose endured a diatribe against Paul; against the university and chancellor for harboring him; against church leadership that held liberal and lax views; against Ambrose's weakness in even questioning whether PXII was right.

Ambrose was grateful when the confessor left so that he could say his penitential prayers. The confession left him feeling further entangled in a web of deceit; the absolution hollow as were all the others for the last decade. And his penance. The continued betrayal of Tom, Paul and Ignatius gnawed at him. He bowed his head onto his fists.

God forgive me. How to get away? Get clean? Big tears rolled down his pudgy face.

* * *

MEDIA HEADLINE: Nuclear Deal Causes Nuclear Standoff

U.S. agreement to provide Seoul with nuclear power has Pyongyang threatening South Korea and the U.S. with nuclear strikes. U.S. and Seoul officials reject North Korea's bluster and defend their actions ....

22

"...(B)roadly speaking, we cannot reach our own ultimate without ... uniting ourselves with others in such a way as to develop ... an added measure of consciousness – a process which conforms to the great law of complexity." Teilhard de Chardin

* * *

Paul powered down his window and breathed deeply as he drove to Green Lake in north Seattle. Though still late winter and cold, the scent of spring floated on the air: the 'green' perfume hinting of buds impatient to burst, seeds limbering up to sprout, bulbs thrusting their fingers through the mould of the earth. Limbs on naked majestic maples snapped like cracked knuckles in the breeze. Frayed clouds wafted west across the sky in unison with a regiment of waves rolling over the surface of the slate lake. The usual legion of human foot-traffic, many with canines in lead or in tow, thinned in advance of the freshening weather that prickled Paul's skin.

If it weren't for his trust in Rabia, he wouldn't be here. He'd been practicing with her for months now. She'd taught him everything she knew. But she couldn't answer his questions about what the aura actually was, which he felt he must understand. His several experiences of the aura state confirmed what Rabia had told him, that each person has an aura that's buried deep within. Under certain circumstances it could be stimulated to emerge and emit visible light. The light was somehow connected to the life force. But there was a separate "presence" aura of vast transcendent light that drew individual auras to itself. The presence was the center of bliss. Was this the divine spirit? God? With each successive aura experience he was pulled closer to the presence. But desire and fear strove within him. It was a threshold he could not cross.

In the hope of delving more deeply into the phenomenon, Paul had reluctantly agreed to meet with a few scientists studying Rabia's aura in relationship to consciousness. They met at the abbey, a former Russian Orthodox stone church with a single onion dome bell tower across the street from Green Lake. It emerged from behind two mammoth weeping willows, their barren whips flailing the breeze. Paul shoe-horned his car between a truck and an orange van on the street. He was uncertain whether to approach the church, or what must have once been the rectory. It connected to the church via a short, covered causeway with a roof of uneven slate tiles, punctuated with verdigris appointments and frosted with moss.

Paul sat in his car, hesitant to get out. How much do they know about me? What's Rabia's told them?

At that moment Rabia opened the front door of the rectory, smiled, and walked down the path lined by crocus to greet him. The light breeze ruffled her dark loose hair. Her face shone like an open flower. He got out of the car and approached her.

"I'm so glad you didn't get cold feet. Nic's eager to meet you." She held tangerine slices and offered one to Paul. Taking it from her hand he flushed, frowned, then fumbled, nearly dropping it. The fresh piquant juice charged his saliva glands that complemented a curious sensation in his spine. Mute, he followed her into the rectory.

"Fr. Paul Pennington, please meet Dr. Nicholas Novgorod. Nic bought the abbey when the church closed and now it's his home," said Rabia.

"Welcome to the abbey, Paul." Nic shook Paul's hand with a meaty paw. Nic's overgrown silver eyebrows jutting skyward created the appearance of perpetual astonishment eclipsing his gray beard as the defining facial feature. Full lips and brown eyes surrounded by smile wrinkles helped to dispel Paul's apprehension. He led Paul down a softly lit hallway lined with exquisite miniature icons. His felt slippers shuffling ahead reminded Paul of the grizzled and bent clerics he had encountered in St. Petersburg a few years back.

Through an arched doorway he entered a library. Its inset walnut and glassed casings from floor to clerestory on three walls held books on neuroscience, psychology, poetry, art, music, theology, philosophy, and mysticism. Clearly a scholar's chamber if one were interested in the psychological, artistic, and spiritual state of man. On the fourth wall large rough-cut stones were amassed into an enormous fireplace, its flames adding the scent of pine and a soft warm glow to the room.

Even though all the data and wisdom of the world could be accessed online, books were still revered, achieving nearly the status of incunabula. The library of the abbey smelled of books. The mellow scent of old leather blended with the sharp odors of fresh ink and new paper. Most of the book titles on the spines slanted sideways as though the room was turned on its edge. All that wisdom, resting in pages of tall columns, formed its own weighty walls.

In the afternoon's dying light, other than the fireplace, only a few tapers on the mantle and luminaires tucked under the wall beams that supported the clerestory lit the room. Two brocade and damask upholstered armchairs, a squashy leather couch, and an assortment of wooden straight-backed and rush-bottomed chairs stood on a bare polished hardwood floor. Stacks of Persian area rugs overflowed an open trunk near the doorway. The ebony-beamed and white-stuccoed ceiling displayed a painted mural of a Greek agape feast over a trestle table.

Two men were in the room wearing soft slippers like Nic. They were helping themselves to refreshments: Gorgonzola, figs, dark rye bread. Wine glasses flanked a decanter of H. Boillot Montrachet Grand Cru, 2036.

Nic eased into an armchair and invited Paul to the seat next to him. He introduced Rabbi Isaac Levison, retired professor of Psychology. Isaac looked the part: balding to a tonsure, white bearded, paunchy, with a glint of humor in his hazel eyes.

122

Nic turned to the second man with a prominent cranium, gray clipped mustache, and intense blue eyes, to introduce Dr. Michael Phillips, head of the Department of Neurology at the UW Medical School. He was a fidgeter, as though he had to discharge a surfeit of energy.

Phillips grasped his wine glass as if it might escape and looked at Paul as though straight through him. Here was a zealot-scholar. He interjected, his mustache quivering. "We know new neurons are born throughout life ... centers of high executive function ... seat of consciousness, and the locus of control of the latent expression of genes ... acquired traits through epigenetics ...."

Paul fiddled with the items in his pocket. He didn't follow most of what was said. His face grew hot. How could he discuss his deepest spiritual experiences with these strangers? He glanced aside at Rabia, his nerves keyed to defense. Her expression gave away nothing. No help there.

"Rabia tells us that you seek to understand your aura experience," Nic said.

Paul stared at the two men. He sensed sympathy and support but also hunger for knowledge. He didn't feel capable of satisfying it. Imagined becoming some interesting lab specimen.

"Paul," Nic said, "I understand this must be difficult, a trial for you, sharing something that must be deeply personal when you barely know us. You're clearly experiencing something extraordinary. We're familiar with Rabia's gift. Perhaps we can help you understand yours. Will you let us help you?"

Can I trust them? Can't trust anyone in the church, or the order, or the university. They'd probably assign me to a mental institution. I'm being offered help by professionals who may have some understanding of my condition. Rabia vouches for them. She's helped me so maybe they can. At least they're clinicians who believe it's real, not some hallucination. I need to know. What other choice do I have?

"Yes." It sounded to him like an 'Amen'.

23

"Wild beasts of the desert do hunt there,
Waiting for the innocents to pass.
Oh-h-h, tempt not the gods of the desert.
Lest you seek a lonely epitaph." Dune, by Frank Herbert

* * *

Paul had not been back to the abbey for a few weeks. The equipment was still being assembled and calibrated at the lab. He approached the tests with apprehension.
Meanwhile he had time to appreciate the routine of the university. This evening, he was to celebrate the main mass at Ignatius, something he hadn't done since last year at this time. January 25th was the feast of the conversion of St. Paul of Tarsus. Tom insisted that priests at Ignatius preside at the main mass for their patron saints.

Paul had never liked the formal evening mass. Too much noise and distraction. And, he had to face it, too many people, no contemplative solitude. A January weekday didn't draw much of a crowd beyond the university faculty and a few students. The pomp was kept to a minimum and short.

Vesting felt like girding for a medieval play with layer upon layer of amice, alb, cincture, stole, chasuble. All that was missing was armor and a sword to make him a knight of the Crusades. If there was ever a symbol that the church hadn't progressed out of the dark ages, this was it. He walked out to the altar feeling weighed down by two thousand years of history.

The gothic church felt like a cavern. Candle lights and shadows flickering around the walls and ceiling created an eerie secretive liveliness. The wall figures in the gloom recalled the cave paintings of Lascaux.

The conversion of St. Paul from persecutor to evangelist on the road to Damascus had always fascinated Paul. Its account in scripture was brief, about light and blindness and hearing a voice utter a sentence. But St. Paul somehow came out of the trance-like state with a philosophy of Christology that was still followed two thousand years later. Where did he get it? Inspiration, divination, transcendence?

Paul avoided the eyes of the congregation as he went through the introductory rites. Tom had kindly offered to do the readings, but Paul was expected to provide the homily. Enlightenment was his theme. Why do some have to work at it, and others get it whether they want it or not, like St. Paul? But there seemed to be a price to be paid by those like St. Paul, and all the long line of prophets, apostles and messengers through the ages who were chosen for special tasks. Few died a peaceful death. All were flawed or weak, and most suffered unimaginably. Should we not be grateful God didn't choose us for a special assignment? But we could be surprised. Our own road to Damascus may still be waiting out there for us.

Paul sat down for the period of reflection on the readings and homily. Ruefully, he knew he was preaching to himself.

Glancing out into the congregation he noticed that several of his fellow priests and faculty sat in the first couple of pews. Behind them sat Marcellus. Nice of her to come. She had another nun with her, unrecognizable within her habit and veil but gave the impression of age. Ambrose was in the back with a tall gaunt priest he didn't recognize.

For a moment Paul noticed the lights flicker and pulse. Must be the candles reacting to drafts in this large space.

Paul rose and resumed the mass. He received the gifts of bread and wine. Blessed them. Ritually washed his hands. He was now at the heart of the mass, the consecration. "This is my Body. This is my Blood."

Suddenly the church swam around him and grew indistinct. He felt weightless, as if gravity didn't exist. Where his hands should have been was a pool of light. Warm radiance permeated him. Indescribable peace flooded him. Words that were not his own uttered from his mouth. "I pray they all may be one. Father, may they be in us. Just as I am in you, and you are in me, may they be one in us." And then the moment passed. Paul became aware of his breathing, his hands, his feet and legs.

He breathed deeply. Placed his hands on the altar and stood still. He looked out into the congregation and saw awe, surprise, shock, fright, and elation on their faces. No one moved. It was like looking at a painting.

He scanned down the page of the missal lying open on the altar. Flipped a few pages to find where he thought he should be at this stage. Continued with the mass. As he distributed communion, he saw that his eyes, face and hands were scrutinized by each receiver. Their reception of the host and wine was like nothing he'd ever seen, a greater reverence than he'd ever experienced. Several women knelt, and one young man prostrated himself. Some had tears in their eyes. Tom's hands shook. Marcellus's eyes shone. Ambrose didn't even approach the altar but stayed in his pew toward the back with the gaunt priest.

Once the mass concluded Paul exited to the sacristy, followed by Tom who shut out all others. Paul disrobed, hung his vestments and stored the communion vessels. Tom stood watching him, waiting. Paul finally faced him and leaned back against the sacristy counter.

"What happened out there?" Tom asked.

"I don't know exactly. I had some kind of lapse. It was as though it wasn't me. I felt like I was floating. And light ... I actually don't recall much after the consecration until the distribution of communion. I noticed people acted – well – reverent but very odd. Including you. What did you see happen?"

Tom said, "I can only describe it as your head emitted a light for several minutes during the time you can't recall. You said Christ's words during the last supper in John's Gospel instead of the normal liturgy. Then the light expanded to fill the area around the altar. It only dissipated as you prepared to distribute communion."

Paul folded his arms and stared at the floor. The sublime spirit he had experienced during mass vanished. He was going to have to face what happened, and worse, provide some kind of explanation. And what explanation could he give?

Across from him stood Tom, equally frozen in internal dialogue. Paul imagined what Tom must be thinking. *That I faked it. What does he have on his hands? A fraud? Divine intervention? Ignatius doesn't need this. Bauer will be all over this.*

Paul ran both hands through his hair. *Why didn't I tell him before this happened? Why did I wait so long? He won't trust me now.*

Tom was the first to break the silence. "We must determine how to process what happened. I can't believe it of you, but was this somehow manufactured for effect?"

"No."

"Has this happened before?"

"Never like this."

Tom leaned back against the door, crossed his arms, fixed his eyes on Paul, his face stony, his words clipped. "What do you mean?"

Silence.

Tom wanted answers. "Does this have anything to do with the black-out you had?"

Paul resented the diminishment of his experience to a 'black-out.' "When I was in the hospital, I didn't know what had happened to me. The doctors ruled out physical causes and never discovered what triggered it, except one neurologist. She believed it a – a mystical experience. I didn't believe her. But when I visited John it happened again. He saw it. Felt it. Confirmed it. Since then I've tried to discover what it is and my purpose in having it. I went back to the neurologist who originally identified the phenomenon. She and other doctors have proposed to study me."

Tom shook his head while continuing to stare at Paul. "Why didn't you tell me?"

The sacristy door rattled. Someone called for Tom. He remained silent until they went away.

"I'm shocked that you went to a complete stranger for help rather than come to me," Tom said. "Am I so untrustworthy?"

Paul's frustration with the church, with the university, with Tom, peaked. "Can't you guess? I've already caused you problems. You're struggling with bigger issues. I didn't understand anything about this experience. I didn't want to give you another problem without a solution. I wanted to have something concrete, a plan of action. I've neither. And what was your first reaction? That I'm a fake? Others will think so. That's exactly what I was afraid of."

Tom dropped his eyes de-escalating the moment. Spoke in a low tone that had lost its edge. "There's no avoiding that now. All those in the church witnessed it, including a few I didn't recognize. Word will spread fast. We need to think carefully what to do. I need you to cooperate with me."

Paul agreed. "What do you want me to do?"

"For now, stay in residence and don't leave until we talk. Will you do that? No visitors. No phone calls."

"Okay."

"I need to think. Consult with the Provincial. I'll send up some food and come find you tonight." Tom escorted Paul out the side door across campus to his room.

After Tom left, Paul locked the door. Slumped on the bed. Then restless he got up and looked out the window.

I could sure use one of Ambrose's scotch shots. The church won't want this out. Hell, Tom doesn't want this out. I'll be forced into a cloister. I'll be studied and probed and challenged. No chance they'll decide I'm genuine. And genuine what? I don't even know myself. Jesus – God. Why're you doing this? What do you want from me?

After another two hours of fruitless internal debate there was a soft knock on his door.

"Paul, it's me, Tom."

Paul opened the door. Tom strode into the room, his lips tight and his eyes glaring. Closed the door behind him. "We've got a problem. Someone's already reported your conduct to Bauer." Tom sat on a chair and handed Paul a copy of an email.

"Fr. Paul Pennington is to submit himself tomorrow at St. Gudrun's Hospital for observation and evaluation. An appointment for admission has been made."

"I was able to discuss the situation briefly with the Provincial," Tom said, "but only after Bauer had already gotten to him. The Provincial agrees that a course of examination is the correct one. If there's a divine cause it must be evaluated, verified." Tom hesitated. "Will you go willingly?"

"Do I have a choice?

"Don't you want to know?"

"I've had enough of hospitals, doctors, and quacks treating me like I'm a mystery to be solved, or a charlatan."

Tom's voice was strained. "I'm sorry. I'm fighting a rearguard action. We've lost control of the situation."

The sting in his voice reminded Paul this might have been avoided or mitigated had he trusted Tom earlier. How to salvage the situation? Keep Bauer from interfering?

"Does it have to be Gudrun's? My neurologist is at Harborview. Couldn't I go there?"

"This isn't about neurology. Something that potentially bears on faith requires a Catholic Hospital, Catholic personnel. In any event, I've no choice. If you refuse, well, there'd be serious consequences."

Paul rose from the bed, turned away to peer out through the dormer window. There it is, the hammer, obey or leave. The church raised me, taught me, gave me a home, profession and faith. Leave it all for a secular life? I can't believe the purpose in all this is exile.

"I'll go. But I want to visit Marcellus and talk to my doctor first. Then I'll check myself in."

Tom rose, looked relieved. He put a friendly hand on Paul's shoulder. "I was staggered by what happened. After forty years the mass was alive to me tonight. For a moment I felt I was there at the first mass, hearing Jesus's words." Tom looked as if he wanted to express something more that he couldn't put into words, then left.

Paul locked the door, left messages for Rabia and Marcellus, then spent a sleepless night.

* * *

Next morning, he left early to walk to Mt. Olives Monastery. Marcellus was waiting for him in her room.

"Paul, you look exhausted."

"I've little time. You were there Marcellus. Tell me what you saw."

Her fierce eyes riveted on Paul as though it helped her to remember. "During the climax of the mass you produced a light – from your head. It wasn't just a light, it was alive. It wavered and flowed and pulsed. It was like a halo at first, but then grew into a shining cloud surrounding you and the altar. Eventually it dissipated."

She released Paul from her eyes and spoke looking into the distance over his shoulder out the window. "It was a deeply spiritual moment. I know it. Felt it."

"Marcellus, I don't have much time to explain. I need your help. What you saw was the aura state. I didn't mean it to happen, but I can't control it. I can't reach Dr. Rabia Habib at Harborview, the neurologist who's been helping me. I've been ordered to submit for clinical evaluation at St. Gudrun's. I'm worried about who'll be directing my evaluation. I don't want to be locked up in a mental institution for the rest of my life."

"You've got good reason to be worried." Marcellus picked up the nearly finished afghan. Her crochet hook flew with a vengeance. She snagged it on a loop and roughly pulled it apart. She put down the afghan and jabbed the crochet hook into the skein. "You're permitted a health advocate, especially in a case of suspected mental instability. Let me be yours. They can hardly deny me, a nun as well as a nurse. I have the training necessary to understand what they'll be doing. I'll have access to your medical records, tests, results, course of therapy. If I think anything unsafe or inappropriate is going on, I'll challenge it."

"I have to check in this morning."

"Then we'll go together."

24

"Hell is empty and all the devils are here." Shakespeare, The
Tempest

* * *

S t. Gudrun's Hospital looked like a fortress of concrete, a
study in gray. From the angle of the winter sun, the
windows reflected the hospital's external environment
of streets and cars, sidewalks and pedestrians, trees and sky, but
admitted nothing of the impenetrable interior. Patient admitting
was just as sterile, as though any warmth would be a frivolous
inefficiency.

The arrangement for Sister Marcellus to be Paul's health
advocate had been reluctantly agreed to as a condition of Paul's
consent to admission.

Over the next few days Paul was subjected to a plethora of
tests, physical and mental. Marcellus visited each day to assure
herself and Paul that the tests were reasonable and normal, and to
hear his concerns or complaints about treatment. She began to
notice that significant portions of his day were blank on his chart,
as though he was simply sitting around waiting. She brought him
his tablet to read and play some video games, and a deck of cards
to play solitaire. He was not allowed to interact with other
patients.

On Marcellus's fourth visit she found Paul sitting up in a hospital bed reading a paper instead of at the small table that had been provided.

Paul laid aside the paper. "Missed you yesterday."

"Missed me? I was here as usual. Don't you remember?" Marcellus said.

Paul frowned. "I don't."

Marcellus handed him a small bound book. "We talked about you keeping a journal. I brought one."

Paul placed it in his lap. His hands fidgeted with its cover, then shifted it to the side. Marcellus noticed his eyes looked dull and his hands shook.

"Dr. Rabia Habib called," said Marcellus. "Says she'll be dropping by Friday as soon as she gets back from her conference. And Tom says he'll be by this weekend."

Paul didn't respond.

"Why're you in bed?" Marcellus asked.

"I'm tired. They thought it would help me relax, rest."

"Why should you be tired? You seem to spend a lot of time waiting around. I can't believe they're so inefficient in scheduling your tests. Yesterday you didn't have anything scheduled at all. What did you do with yourself? It must be incredibly boring."

"It's boring. But they ran tests yesterday."

"It doesn't show on your chart. What sort of tests?" asked Marcellus.

"One was a functional MRI I think."

Marcellus re-examined his chart. "I wonder why that isn't recorded here? What did they tell you to do when in the fMRI?"

"They told me to pray." Paul sat up straighter. "I think they're trying to get me to reproduce the 'event' that happened on the altar."

"I need to find out why the fMRI isn't on your chart. And why you're so tired and don't remember me yesterday," Marcellus said.

At the nurses' station Marcellus asked why Paul's chart was incomplete. At first, she was informed that Paul was mistaken. After some persistence she was told to take it up with Paul's physician who'd left for the day. She called his cell and left a message but received no reply.

Marcellus arrived early the next day determined to confront the doctor. She didn't find Paul in his room. The duty nurse provided no information other than 'tests.' Yet nothing was shown on Paul's chart. As Marcellus considered causing a scene to get some attention, an orderly wheeled Paul into the room on a gurney and shifted him to the hospital bed.

Paul's physiognomy shocked Marcellus. He looked pale. A sheen of sweat covered his face. Damp hair stuck to his forehead that bore restraint marks. He opened his eyes, winced and then closed them. Mumbled something inaudible. A nurse entered, adjusted his monitors, inserted an IV, then left.

Marcellus was torn between confronting the nurse about Paul's condition and examining Paul herself.

"Paul. Paul. Can you talk to me? Please talk to me. It's Marcellus."

"Mmmrr ..."

Marcellus scanned his monitors. His blood pressure and pulse were elevated but he wasn't in danger. Something had been done to him. Why was he semi-conscious?

The duty nurse looked up in alarm at Marcellus baring down, her habit flying like brown sails.

"What's been done to Fr. Paul Pennington? I'm his health advocate. You've been keeping his treatments from me." Her eyes flashed. When angry Marcellus had the presence of a formidable woman. The habit accentuated her authority.

But it didn't get her far. The duty nurse stared up at her with a frozen face. "You will need to take this up with his physician."

"Where is he?" demanded Marcellus.

"I can't disclose that information," the nurse said.

Furious, Marcellus contacted Dr. Habib. Asked for her immediate help. They met at Harborview late that afternoon after Rabia arrived from the airport. Marcellus introduced herself and then launched into her concerns for Paul.

"Dr. Habib, I don't think they're running tests on Paul. I think they're destroying his mind. I'm his health advocate and they've kept his tests and results from me. He's confused and has significant memory loss. When I saw him this morning, he'd clearly deteriorated. I need someone who can get inside and find out what they're doing to him."

"I'm a consulting neurologist at St. Gudrun's. I'll find out what they're doing. "

* * *

That evening, white-coated with a stethoscope, Rabia entered St. Gudrun's armed with the legitimate excuse of seeing an existing patient.

When she found Paul's room he was lying on the bed, an image of exhaustion. The covers were disarrayed from thrashing, and his eyes dull and unfocussed. She studied the monitors and chart.

"Paul?" She held a hand, but he jerked it away, flailing his arms and legs as if to ward off an attack. She noted restraint marks on his arms and legs. His lips were dry and cracked.

"Paul. It's Rabia. Please look at me."

Paul did not respond.

The door opened, and a short, curly-haired, beak-nosed doctor hustled in. "Who're you? There're to be no visitors for this patient."

"I'm not a visitor. I'm Dr. Rabia Habib with the neurology department. I was told there was a patient here who requires my evaluation."

"You're mistaken. This patient is in my care and requires no additional evaluation. Please leave."

Rabia left. She accessed the hospital data base but Paul's medical information was blocked. Whatever they had given Marcellus was incomplete or fabricated.

"Hello, Sr. Marcellus? You're right. I think they may be giving Paul frequent high doses of electroconvulsive treatment, ECT. It can cause cognitive impairment and memory loss. They may be trying to force aura emergence or eradicate his ability to emit it. Has he told you about it?"

"I saw it. It happened at mass. There were several of us there. It was because of it that he was ordered to St. Gudrun's. We've got to get him out of there."

* * *

Later that night, Marcellus marshaled her forces in the lobby. An entourage of nuns from Mt. Olives Monastery, including one in a wheelchair, crowded around the nurses' station.

"Reverend Mother, I can't allow you to see the patient. Visiting hours are long over."

"I'm his health advocate and can see him at any time according to our agreement." Marcellus waved it in front of her face pointing out the relevant section on visitation rights. We're here for a vigil. Fr. Pennington seems to be much worse. We plan to pray a novena through the night for his speedy recovery. A Catholic hospital should not deny us the right to see Fr. Paul to provide direct spiritual assistance. Unless of course he's in a life-threatening situation. Is he?" Marcellus towered over the nurse like a heron ready to strike.

The nurse hesitated. "He's not in critical condition."

"Then as his health advocate I must insist."

"Very well. But please don't stray elsewhere in the hospital and be quiet."

With rosary beads clicking at their belts, Marcellus and her myrmidons made their way to Paul's room. Paul was either asleep or unconscious. Rabia, in nun's disguise, assessed his condition while the other nuns surrounded his bed blocking any views by the curious through the door window. He was stable. The sisters droned the rosary in low tones to cover any noise while Rabia unhooked the patient's IV, removed his ankle monitor and shoved it under a pillow. Once dressed in a nun's habit, they carefully lifted him into the wheelchair.

It was just past midnight. The sisters huddled around the wheelchair and decorously moved out of the room down the hall into the elevator. They just had to get out of the garage and they were free. No one bothered to count that there was one additional nun in the group. They wheeled Paul into the monastery van and pulled out of the garage, avoiding attention.

Soon they were back at Mt. Olives. They wheeled Paul into one of the patient rooms, removed the habit, and made him comfortable for the remainder of the night. The sisters took turns sitting with him in case he awoke in strange surroundings. Marcellus made sure she was there when he woke in the morning.

Paul stirred. Opened his eyes. "Where am I? Who're you?"

"Paul, don't you know me? You're in the Mt. Olives Monastery."

Paul passed his hand over his eyes and forehead. Moistened his lips. Looked around. His eyes cleared, focused. "Marcellus. How did I get here?"

"We brought you. How're you feeling?" Marcellus retrieved the quilt he'd kicked off and smoothed it over his bed.

"I don't know. Tired. Sore. Hungry."

"Hungry is a good sign. I'll get you some breakfast."

"I'd like to get up."

Marcellus helped him stand. Walk a few steps.

"Please, are my clothes here? I'd like to get out of this hospice dress and shave."

"We'll find something for you to wear. We have men's facilities down the hall."

Paul walked purposefully and steadily down the hall.

Marcellus organized her sisters to find Paul some clothes and fix him food. After calling Rabia she found Paul drinking coffee and munching granola and yogurt in the kitchen.

"I don't mean to be ungrateful. I don't remember much," said Paul.

By this time Rabia had arrived. She and Marcellus sat with Paul as he finished.

Rabia pulled out a tablet. "What's the last thing you remember?" Her fingers scampered over the keys.

"I remember being admitted to the hospital and assigned to a room."

"Is that all?" asked Marcellus. "That was six days ago."

"I lost six days?"

"When you're finished," said Rabia, "I'd like to check you out. We aren't sure what they did, but I think they were electro-shocking you. It's used as a treatment for depression and sometimes schizophrenia."

"But I don't have those."

"It could also be used to cause temporary or permanent amnesia, and possibly even other effects. You have memory loss. It's possible they were trying to 're-set' your brain."

Paul knocked over the remains of his coffee. "Jesus. Have they succeeded? I can't remember anything."

"It may come back to you. You still have your memories prior to admission. That's what counts. And you're safe here. There'll be no more 'treatments'." Rabia excused herself. "I have to get back to the hospital. See what kind of alarm your disappearance stirred up."

Paul turned to Marcellus. "I can't stay here."

"You can until you're fully recovered. We're a hospice. And while you aren't terminally ill, you're still not recovered. Besides, it'll be difficult for Bauer to dislodge you from a Catholic nursing facility without exposing his part in this business."

"But I may put you all in danger of archdiocesan sanction."

Marcellus snorted. "We don't care about that. And I doubt Bauer will be able to accomplish that in any case. We have our own protections. At least leave us nuns to work out our own problems. We're capable."

"I didn't mean to suggest otherwise. I just don't want to become a risk to you."

Marcellus wiped up the spilt coffee. "Let us take care of that. And I hope while you're here, you'll enlighten us about your gift."

25

"For there to be betrayal, there would have to have been trust first." *Suzanne Collins, The Hunger Games*

* * *

Marcellus parried all attempts by the church, order and university to have Paul removed from Mt. Olives Monastery. Even though Paul's memory of the hospital nightmare hadn't returned, his strength improved. He performed pastoral tasks for the nuns and helped with chores. But at some point he had to leave this safe haven. Then what?

His answer came in the person of Tom. They sat across from each other in the room where families mourned their departed ones. The nuns tried to make it homey and comforting. But the wallpaper exuded the pall of the dead, tears of lament, and the cloying scent of lilies.

Awkwardness replaced Tom's normal confidence. In the unfamiliar surroundings Paul saw him differently. During the twenty years Paul had known him, Tom had seemed an ageless strong pillar of the university. Now his hair grew scant and gray. Veins stood out on the backs of his hands threaded between blotches of brown skin pigment. His cheeks sagged slightly into vertical lines framing lips that had lost their fullness. Even his voice sounded thinner.

"I'm glad to see you looking better," Tom said.

Paul's fingers beat a tattoo on the arm of his chair then he suppressed a wry laugh. "No thanks to you and Bauer. At least I'm better off than the usual residents of this room."

"I'm sorry. I had no choice." Tom took a white handkerchief from his pocket and wiped it back and forth a few times across his lips as though trying to wipe away his words.

"You didn't even come to find out what they were doing to me in the hospital. If it hadn't been for Marcellus, God knows what state I'd be in now. Probably on the road to becoming a vegetable. Do you know what it's like having full days of memory gone? Obliterated. Like losing a piece of your soul."

Tom's eyes didn't meet Paul's for any length of time. He'd blink and then shift his gaze away over Paul's shoulder. "I kept in contact with your physician at Gudrun's. He said you were fine. Things were going well. That they were getting close to an explanation."

Paul laughed sardonically. "And you believed him?"

"I had no reason not to." Tom wiped his lips again. The tense atmosphere in the room was palpable.

"I was tortured. Helpless. Totally at their mercy. Can you understand how terrifying that is? You had to know Bauer was at the back of this."

The first sign of defensiveness sparked in Tom's eyes. "Knew? What I knew was that St. Gudrun's was a good hospital. And you gave me no time to develop a better plan because you hid this from me. You still haven't provided any adequate explanation of the phenomenon. I have to answer to the Provincial. So do you.

Paul glared. Excuses. Yeah, hide behind the Provincial.

Tom dug into his breast pocket and pulled out a long envelope. "I'm here to deliver this to you."

It bore the Provincial's insignia. Paul opened and read it with an anxious heart: a transfer to Provincial headquarters where further evaluation would be conducted under the auspices of the Jesuit Order.

Tom reverted to his diplomatic persuasive persona. "This is a reasonable solution, Paul. The Provincial will see you're properly treated."

"What about Bauer?"

"He agrees."

Paul threw it on the floor with a bitter laugh. "How can you both be on the same side?"

"We aren't. But this is bigger than us. If something preternatural is happening, then the order and the church have a stake. We must evaluate and determine its nature."

Tense silence arose between them again. Jesus, he talks about 'the phenomenon' as something disconnected from me.

As for Tom, Paul concluded that his priority was to cut his losses. Protect Ignatius by moving me to headquarters. Make me their problem. If he allowed me to be treated as a lab rat here, prisoner of an institution, how do I know it won't happen again? But if I don't comply, I'll be rejecting the church and the order. And then they'll reject me. Everything in his gut told Paul that compliance was the wrong thing to do regardless of the consequences. But imagination failed him to fathom the full magnitude of such a decision, and he was out of time. "I won't comply."

Paul watched Tom's face. Saw defeat and shame and remorse in succession cross his features. He seemed caught up in a difficult internal struggle for some time. He got up. Faced Paul.

"Then I have to ask you to leave the university."

26

"And it came to pass in the third year of the Desert War that Paul-Muad'Dib lay alone in the Cave of Birds beneath the kiswa hangings of an inner cell. And he lay as one dead, caught up in the revelation of the Water of Life, his being translated beyond the boundaries of time by the poison that gives life".
Dune by Frank Herbert

* * *

Early Saturday morning in the campus quiet, and with the sun still behind the eastern horizon, Paul returned to remove his belongings. He parked his old Subaru in the loading dock behind the priests' hall and entered it for the last time. Walked quietly. He didn't want any pseudo-heartfelt good-byes in the hallway.

He unlocked his door, walked in and looked around the room: white walls, desk, chair, wardrobe, rug rolled up against the wall, stripped bed where he'd laid his head for 20 years.

He crossed to the desk. Ran his hands along the back of the chair. Pulled it out. Sat down. He'd composed his lectures here. Wrote his academic papers here. Each item unloaded from its desk spoke to him of classes he'd no longer teach, students he'd never meet again. Pencils. Pens. A defunct cellphone battery. A charger to a tablet he no longer owned. Some paper for the printer. Sharpies. They all had no meaning now. Not worth keeping. They rattled and thunked as he threw them in the waste can.

He pushed his hair back from his forehead and moved to the bookcase. Here was the heart of his life: physics, theology, philosophy, poetry, classic novels. The tactile feel of a book compared to an online read was like the feel of a friend's hand versus viewing his picture. He laid them into a battered green trunk.

He'd prayed here. Had a few drinks with Ambrose here. Had his first aura experience here. But now the place echoed interior hollowness.

All he had in the world stood by the door in the trunk, and in a green and gray REI backpack. He'd never had a real home, not as a child, not as a student, not as a priest. Just empty spaces.

He opened the door to push his trunk and backpack into the hallway. The residence was silent, vacated by his now former colleagues who had purpose, things to do. Probably avoiding me. I'm an embarrassment. Did I ever know them? Ambrose? Tom? Did they know me?

He lifted the wooden crucifix off the wall that he'd won in a spelling bee as a boy and shoved it in his coat pocket, leaving the nail as the only evidence of his long sojourn. He closed and locked the window, and drew the stiff curtains releasing a pale dead moth that spiraled slowly in a parody of flight to the floor.

He took the room key from his pocket, the last talisman that showed he belonged here. This is it. After this I can't ever come back. He placed the key in the dead center of the desk, turned off the light, and closed the door – click – final – less personal than checking out of a hotel.

He drove to east Capitol Hill, parked on 15th, and walked to Volunteer Park. His mind was numb, nothing to do, nowhere to go, his insides Jello.

The black abyss inside gradually began taking shape as fear, loss, failure, regret. The pantheon of dark emotions expanded, swirling round and round, like figures on a merry-go-round, each astride a garishly colored horse with wild eyes and a teeth-baring grimace. Up and down – up and down– fear, anger, frustration, each cresting and descending to be displaced by another. Round and round – round and round, recycling decisions he'd made that got him here.

142

The problem wouldn't be solved this way. He wrenched his mind back to what to do now without profession, community, livelihood or home, all gone in one swift stroke.

Then the sky opened to one of those Seattle rains that embodies mourning; sky tears that soak a soul in sorrow. Rivulets ran down from Paul's hair into his eyes, around his nose, collected in the creases of his lips, dripped from his chin. Chilled, he rose. Pulled up his collar. Wiped his face with a handkerchief.

He returned to Mt. Olives. A novice hung up his wet coat and brought a towel. After drying off he knocked on Marcellus's door. She drew him in. Her subtle elegance and graceful movements reassured. Kind eyes searched his face.

"Paul, you look terrible." She gestured to a seat across from an aged nun.

He stayed standing.

"It's okay. Please meet the benefactress of Mt. Olives. You may call her Sister Magdala. You haven't seen her before because she doesn't live here." Marcellus poured them tea.

Paul sat. "But I have seen you before. You attended my disastrous mass."

"Extraordinary." Magdala's voice resonated, a contralto. Smile wrinkles etched her face. Veins and spots laced her hands, but her eyes gleamed at Paul with intelligence and vigor through gold wire-rimmed glasses.

"What's happened? You can be frank here," said Marcellus.

Paul chewed his lip. It was hard to get the words out, like if they remained unsaid, they could be changed, but once spoken they would become final. "I've been fired."

"Good God," whispered Marcellus. "Why?"

"I refused further evaluation of my condition by the church. What could they expect after the last disaster? No sane person would trust them with a second chance."

"What will you do now?"

He raised his hands in despair. "I need to find a job, a place to live, a purpose, how to be something other than a priest."

Magdala's eyes searched Paul's face. "Why? Understandable that you need a means to live. But you're still a priest. They haven't defrocked you."

Still a priest. For how long? The piebald cat jumped into Paul's lap and kneaded her paws on his legs. He flinched at her sharp claws and rolled her off. "Not yet."

Marcellus leaned back, frowning.. "You did the right thing to refuse them. What they did to you was barbaric. They subjected you to I don't know how many sessions of ECT – without anesthetic. They were probably trying to stimulate the aura state, so they could study it. They'd need you to be aware for that. You could have really been damaged or even had a heart attack. It's a mercy you can't remember."

"But I want to remember. I feel changed. An instability in my head, like small waves or vibrations felt deep in the right front side of my brain in the place where the pain starts before the aura emerges. It isn't pain, more like an itch. It's feels alive – not in the way I'm alive – but part of me physically and also something different."

Marcellus and Magdala glanced at each other.

"Your memory may return in time. Please stay with us," Marcellus said. "We'd be grateful if you'd share your experience with us."

Paul stared at his wet feet. "I don't know how to do that. It isn't something that I control and maybe no longer have. And I can't stay here."

Magdala's words came slowly. "You need a safe place while you fully recover, regroup, and process what you've been through. Bauer may not be through with you yet. I know him, too well. His tentacles reach all over the state and even the country through PXII."

Paul raised his head.

"We know of the organization," said Magdala, "and Bauer's their functionary in the Pacific Northwest. He has a few PXII minions here of his own. Tom and Ignatius have been a particular thorn in his side since he assumed his bishopric here. So has Mt. Olives. Our independence you see. I donated the land for the hospice to a foundation that supports Mt. Olives. Bauer doesn't control us anymore than he controls Ignatius. Anything or anyone that isn't under his control is a threat. But he dares not move against us. A hospice run by nuns. I'd like to see him try. We have our own protectors. And I'm one of them."

"But I left the order," Paul said. "And the church. How can I any longer be a threat?"

"Because of who you are," Magdala retorted. "What you can do. Don't you think he'd like to use that power? Control it? Or failing that eradicate it? There were others there that day. Witnesses to who you are and what you can do. They aren't going to easily forget, or have it explained away by Bauer as some chicanery. We could not only see the light that day, we felt its presence. And want to again."

Paul shook his head. "I need to remember."

"Stay with us until you do," Magdala said.

Marcellus agreed. "ECT patients sometimes do recover their lost memories, although they may be so terrible you don't want to. You may be blocking the memories because they're so painful. You need to be open to the memories to retrieve them. It helps if you're in a place that's completely safe and allows introspection."

"Bless you. Thanks for letting me stay here for a bit till I get a place, but there's something I have to do."

He donned his damp coat. Marcellus insisted on him taking one of her capacious umbrellas and gave him a key to the hospice.

Paul headed toward Broadway, Capitol Hill's main drag bristling with lights. The rain stopped, the clouds cleared, and out came a few stars that weren't overpowered by streetlights. Cars crept along booming low toned beats. A motley assortment of individuals strolled with earbuds for company to bars and bistros frenetic with Friday night revels. The animated atmosphere clashed with Paul's growing interiority as he approached Ignatius.

He'd determined never to come back here. But the Ignatius Chapel was a sanctuary. A place where he'd had a deep spiritual encounter even if he hadn't recognized it at the time. He entered. Moving by the font, he brushed the water surface with his fingertips, almost a caress. Genuflected.

He looked around at the pink-gray stone walls, sensing their ponderous weight. The skylight-windows admitted two watchful stars, eyes of the cosmos. Shadows crouched in the corners, under the pews and altar. The flicker of the single candle in the sanctuary lamp accentuated the darkness. The atmosphere felt tense with energy as though the air itself contained an unseen gravid density.

He approached the heart of the sanctuary, sat on the floor in the shadows, and began focusing his awareness. Many thoughts strove for attention as he dug deep: ego-preservation, aversion to pain, fear of what he couldn't remember, shame of weakness. He firmly and deliberately pushed them all aside, emptied his mind, centered his consciousness within that place in his brain that seemed different, where the internal shimmering like a low-level voltage from an electrode pulsed. He became still – silent – empty – open.

His heart rate slowed to soft gentle beats. Respiration quieted. All thoughts about himself, the world, God – noughted. Sensation left him. Suspended in nothingness he was no longer in the chapel.

He was in St. Gudrun's strapped to a gurney. Bolts of energy charged through his brain. Uncontrolled jerking of hands and feet and torso had him straining against restraints. Muscles contracted. Spasms and cramps. The taste of blood in his mouth. A muffled involuntary shriek.

And then he was hovering above himself. Watched his body's agony as the pulses of current wracked him multiple times. The resulting seizures lasted each about thirty seconds, and then after a brief pause, they charged him with current again. The muscles in his neck stood out like ropes. His heels dug into the gurney pad as he watched his body arch against the straps. The veins of his temples and hands stood out purple and pulsing. His breathing – desperate through his nose, since a mouth guard blocked his only other airway.

But he was free of it, like watching a hologram of himself. The doctors and nurses were shadows, the hospital walls became transparent. No pain. Bodiless and weightless.

His body on the gurney, the doctors and nurses, the hospital, people, the city – all faded away. He was bathed in light, waves of it. Then he was sucked through a tessellating tunnel of swirling color that went on into infinity.

Pure sounds cascaded in and around him, as much felt as heard. A basso profundo throbbed on the edge of perception. Mellow baritones in a range up through sopraninoes, tightly braided, resonated in a melodic prolonged tremolo. Intense joy moved Paul to laughter that sounded like a bell.

A presence, a dense center, rose like a swirling column of incandescent white fire. The great vortex of radiance swept him in, spun him down, pulled him as in a gravitational field toward the light center.

Stripped, he cowered in its radiance. Then falling – falling – into a light well. He descended. It drew him into the luminous abyss, unveiling and offering a super-consciousness joining.

Dazed, Paul wondered if he was still alive. No evidence of a having a body. Why am I still here? Why not just take me?

An answer arose in his consciousness, without words, but he understood.

Self-sacrifice – and freedom to choose

Damn my freedom.

Silence.

What am I choosing?

Catalysis

What?

The presence receded.

I choose.

It was like a blow felt in the deep intimate parts of his soul. He swooned. Cried out in angst and rapture, fire and thirst. Pain of joy, or joy of pain. It made no difference.

A community of infinite presences rose around him like a cluster of sparks, a union of consciousnesses like a great Volvox he'd once marveled at under a microscope – a sublime coupling with the center of super-consciousness. No dissolution, no oblivion of self, only completion and wholeness. But I can't reach the center. Can't join.

The light diminished with a sensation that he was whirling away from the center and the sparks.

I want to stay.

Was he going back or being sent? He became re-acquainted with limitation in space and time. His body disjointed, crude, weak. It was hard to return to the world. And a feeling within his consciousness was new. Like a current of energy inside his head had opened up, or a beam of light.

And the sparks? Individual bodiless auras?

And the center to which they were joined? They shared substance. The center appeared to be the seat of super-consciousness, to which all others were joined. Or from which they originated. A universal aura? The divine Aura?

Catalysis. I chose catalysis – to be catalyzed or to be a catalyst. The knowledge filled him both with exhilaration that he finally knew what was demanded of him, but also foreboding that he might fail.

He rose from the floor stiff and cold. Sat in a pew. Prayed. Tried to make some sense of it all. He had a gift. A direct divine experience he'd prayed for all his life. So why am I so sad?

It had been only half a choice. There remained the other half.

Still in a fog of awe and restless, he left the chapel and walked down Yesler to Sophia's. It was not quite midnight. His disordered feelings and thoughts revolved like a roulette wheel. Sophi raised her eyebrows at his order of a scotch. Then another.

She wiped tables and stacked chairs. When she got to Paul's, the last, she sat down.

"I know. It's closing time. Got to go."

She placed her hand on Paul's arm. "Something's wrong."

Paul stared at the table. Swirled the last of the scotch in the bottom of his glass. "I've been fired, turned out. I've no job, no home." Then with a mordant laugh, "And I've just been thrown out of heaven." He toasted the air.

Sophi's Felix the Cat clock ticked in concert with its pendulum tail. Then bonged 2:00 a.m. Sophi didn't move.

"I defied a directive from the Archbishop and the Provincial, and signed up for a divine mission." Paul swallowed the last of the scotch. "And that's that." He whacked down his empty glass.

Sophi squeezed Paul's arm. "That's what life's about, choices. Some work. Some don't. I'm sure you had good reasons."

"I don't know. Maybe. Mostly I'm just afraid of going back into that hospital. They hurt me." He pointed to his head. "Inside.

148

I haven't been the same since I got out. Not sure I'll ever be." He swirled the empty glass.

"Look at me. Paul. Please." Sophi took the empty glass from his hand and moved it aside out of reach. "You can feel sorry for yourself. Or take this opportunity to remake yourself. From what I've heard you have a great gift. Use it."

"Can't control it. Can't use it. Can't get rid of it. Sometimes I fear it. When I'm in it I never want to leave it."

"Then there's your direction. Where you have the deepest emotions – fear, love – that's where you should look. They'll point or nudge or drag you to the right path. You both fear and love this thing. So follow it. See where it leads. All your props are gone. You have to change. We aren't given gifts like these for ourselves. Think of all those great people I hear you talk about. Einstein, Teilhard, St. Paul. Think of Gandhi, Nelson Mandela, Martin Luther King. Think of Jesus. They all had great gifts. What would have happened if they'd never used them? Never shared them? Huh? You got to pull yourself together man. Get out of yourself. You've just had all the barnacles blasted off your boat. You're free to move."

Sophi was being about as sympathetic as a can opener. Paul got out his wallet to pay her.

She pushed it aside. "This night's on me."

27

"The two hardest tests on the spiritual road are the patience to wait for the right moment and the courage not to be disappointed with what we encounter."
Paulo Coelho, Veronika Decides to Die

* * *

The bell-towers of the cathedral emerged from behind trees with leaf buds glossy and greening up for spring bourgeoning. Terry Avenue daffodil and tulip bulbs, hidden like Easter eggs last fall, reached their finger-fronds for the sky. But the chancery, like a brick prison block secret behind curtained windows, clung to winter. Tom approached through a sad graveyard of planters and pots that held moldy flowers and brown mottled leaves from bygone summer.

Impatient with Bauer's games, Tom scaled the steps to the archbishop's entrance and walked straight into the inner sanctum. His taut face framed frosty eyes, and his usual genteel manner was absent. He leaned on his hands over Bauer's desk. "How could you do this? What did you do?"

Bauer sat back in his throne-like chair with both hands folded over his ample belly.

Tom's statements came in clipped bites. "I've just found out that you could've, or may in fact already have, damaged Fr. Pennington with unorthodox and dangerous treatments."

Bauer didn't flinch. "You exaggerate. St. Gudrun's has good doctors. They knew what was best for him."

Bauer's smug face triggered Tom into raising his voice. "Sr. Marcellus, his health advocate, was lied to. She and an independent neurologist witnessed he was in serious decline and could've died. He was fine when he agreed – voluntarily – to be admitted under your directive. When they took him back to Mt. Olives, I saw myself he was in a state of collapse."

"He's a sick man. Mentally ill," said Bauer. "All this bunk about auras. Seriously? You believe he's genuine? You surprise me, a Jesuit. He's a fraud, mentally unstable. We can't afford to have such people in the clergy."

Tom struggled to control his rising anger. "I don't know what his abilities are because I was too worried about what others like you would think if I took him seriously. Too worried about the fate of Ignatius. God forgive me that I abandoned him when he needed me most."

"Is this a confession?" Bauer cocked his head to one side and turned a gold ring around his right forefinger.

"I was complicit in his torture. He merited none of that."

Bauer grinned.

Tom, in cold fury, for a brief moment felt like striking him. Instead he stormed out and slammed the door.

The walk back to Ignatius gave Tom time to consider what, at this point, was the right thing to do. How to salvage Paul from the wreckage? Offer him a home within the order through an arranged sabbatical? Convince him to relocate? Missionary service? But the Provincial will insist on evaluation regardless. Paul must see that's necessary. He must be desperate to understand what's happening to him. But what reason does he have to trust me? Or anyone in the church?

By the time Tom arrived at Ignatius he was no further in resolving his questions or problems. Compunction made him anxious, like carrying around an unresolved seventh cord of music in the back of his brain, until a few days later when a truly horrific thought came to him. He called Magdala. They arranged to meet.

Air flowing in Tom's open window carried the scent of new green leaves, freshly mown grass, and rain. His chambers looked down on a stone square walled by lecture halls and labs, the main church, and the library. A sundial perched on a stone plinth that a patron had donated to the university long ago. Someone had hooked a sodden scarf on it that drooped down its side like a pink ponytail. The empty square looked uncongenial, forlorn. Students hurried through. Would soon be gone. Some for good. Others until fall term, returning like Capistrano swallows.

Tom fidgeted. He wasn't looking forward to Magdala's visit but he needed her. She would rebuke him – justifiably – for his lack of spine with Bauer's treatment of Paul, but she would understand his dilemma and anxiety. She'd always supported the university. Given large financial contributions. Fended off difficult politics. Helped maintain independence from the archdiocese as the last significant bastion of liberal Catholicism in the state.

He steeled himself at the knock on the door. "Magdala, please come in. Would you like coffee or tea?"

Her cane preceded her into the room. In a jet silk suit and with her gray hair swept up in a bun, she resembled his formidable primary school principal. She sat in one of the straight-backed chairs. Declined refreshment. Clasped hands in her lap. Pursed her lips and glared through her wire-rims.

Tom sat across from her. Her censorious face communicated better than words that this conversation wasn't to be softened with opening platitudes.

Magdala opened on the offense. "You made a mistake. You should never have placed Paul under Bauer's control. You could have gone through the order. Had him evaluated outside of Bauer's reach. You cared more about Bauer's retaliation than you did Paul. You could have asked for help. My help."

Tom didn't shrink from her gaze. "I've thought about it again and again and don't see how I could have acted differently. There was no time. Bauer heard about it and got to the Provincial before I did. Paul underwent some kind of preternatural event. If it wasn't faked, and I can't believe that of Paul, it had to be studied in a Catholic institution. Gudrun's was the only hospital in Seattle that could do this."

"Bauer gave all the directions, had all the communications. You didn't even visit Paul in the hospital to see how he was doing."

"I'm ashamed of that," Tom said. "No excuse. I thought he was in competent hands and I had a lot on my plate here."

"Competent? He was being tortured."

What could he say? There was no adequate response.

Magdala went mercilessly on. "I think you wanted to distance yourself from him. Are you that much of a coward?"

Her words stung. But she was largely right.

"I believe his experience to be genuine," said Magdala. "I felt it, didn't you? And it isn't the first he's had. Did you know that? The poor man's been trying to figure this out on his own."

"Why didn't he come to me? I'm supposed to care for the priests under my charge," Tom said.

"Because of fear of exactly what happened," said Magdala. "Your warnings about the problems he was causing the university. About Bauer and PXII and their threats? What would you have done? And now we've lost him."

"He's not lost," Tom said. "Not yet. If his ability is genuine, then it won't be thwarted." Tom turned toward Magdala and spoke carefully, reading her eyes. "There must be a reason this has happened, right here, right now."

Pregnant silence fell between them.

"You mean it's a sign that it's the 'proper time'?"

Tom sat on the edge of his seat facing her. "I've been thinking about it. Paul's preternatural phenomenon could be what John Paul I wrote about in his diary. What if Paul is the catalyst?"

Magdala's eyes opened into a wide stare. She took a few moments to digest the possibility and the consequences. "How can we find out? What exactly does John Paul's diary say?"

"It's been a long time since I read it. It's time I read it again."

"If true, then PXII will be after not just you, but Paul as well. You both need protection."

"But we have a defense," Tom said. "The Vatican documents are so serious they would take down Bauer and PXII if disclosed."

"I think it's time I saw these documents," said Magdala. "They'd have to be authenticated. Released in the proper way.

Charges filed. The reaction of the church will be swift. Self-protective. Harsh. Repercussions clear to the Vatican. You, Paul, Ignatius will be subject to extreme pressure, even danger." She smiled. "Maybe me too. I never could figure out why Pope Francis would have wanted the documents held in the first place?"

"I think I now know why," said Tom. "John Paul I had this spiritual gift and was murdered for it. Francis didn't want the next catalyst to be murdered as well before they could complete whatever task they had been given to perform. I think he knew that PXII's mission is to stamp out any emergence of this phenomenon. So he provided the ammunition when the next catalyst emerged to distract and disempower PXII."

"But he could have taken out PXII at any time. Why wait until now?"

"Exposing PXII and their satellites may have destroyed the organization, but their adherents would resurface somewhere else. They always do. The church is too attractive and effective a tool for amassing wealth and wielding power. As long as it is, it will never be impervious to infiltration by forces bent on using it for their own ends. Maybe there needed to be a contravening force before taking PXII down. Maybe that's the job of the catalyst."

Magdala took off her glasses and laid them in her lap. "I pray the catalyst has a much bigger role than just dealing with the likes of PXII. I'm sorry earlier that I called you a coward. The backlash will be severe."

"I was blind when I needed to see. You'll have to retrieve the documents. I'm certain I'm being watched. Then I'll need your help and the help of your network of high-placed friends."

Magdala's face assumed the grim but exalted look of a soldier going to battle. "Leave that to me. Paul needs to be warned."

"He will be."

28

"Woe to them that devise iniquity and work evil upon their beds! When the morning is light, they practice it ...."
Micah 2:1

* * *

Without speaking Bauer stabbed his finger toward a seat.

Herst positioned his large frame on the chair across the desk, set his pudgy hands on his thighs, and kept his eyes down.

Bauer found the big man irritating. His submissiveness, as though he might flinch when spoken to, added to Bauer's aggravation. "What progress have you made in finding the location of those documents? Geoffrey tells me you've nothing for us."

"I'm sorry sir. I've not been able to find them. The documents must have had the Vatican trace removed somehow, or be shielded, or the documents are not located at Ignatius."

Bauer stood, slamming his palms onto the desk. "That's not good enough."

Bauer strode around his desk and leaned over Herst who recoiled and shrunk even further into the chair like a tortoise into its shell.

Bauer shouted down at him. "Look at me."

Herst's pale moon face turned up at Bauer who was now looming over him.

"You – redouble – your – efforts – this – week. Find – their – location." The words jackhammered into Herst's brain. "You understand? Now get out."

After Herst left, Bauer buzzed for Geoffrey.

Geoffrey entered the room. "You wished to see me sir?"

Bauer jerked around to confront him. Then strode around his desk and relaxed back into his throne. "Sit down. I've some – work for you to do."

Geoffrey in his usual detached manner sat bolt upright in the chair reserved for supplicants awaiting instruction. His sandy hair tied back in a short pony-tail revealed a bland-featured smooth-shaven face, hard to recall when absent. Bauer often wondered how such a slight man could have been in a military special forces unit. Or how he got involved with PXII.

Bauer chose his words carefully so that he could in truth say he never said anything to Geoffrey that would be incriminating. "This renegade priest, Paul Pennington, continues to create problems. He's a fraud, of course. He's even ingratiated himself at Mt. Olives Monastery. This aura-thing is a hoax, manufactured."

Geoffrey nodded. "I can think of several ways to produce the effect."

"He must be discredited. Must be stopped." Bauer twisted his gold ring around his forefinger and looked intently at Geoffrey.

"Is that the work you have for me?"

Thank God things didn't need to be spelled out for Geoffrey. "Yes. And without it being traceable back to me, PXII, or the church. And I need that memory stick. Get it, whatever it takes."

"Understood sir. Is Herst also involved?"

Bauer snorted. "Absolutely not. He's not even a passable informant. I'll keep him out there as cover, but he can't be trusted with any of this assignment. You will work alone."

Geoffrey rose to leave.

"Geoffrey, what do you know about Herst? I don't understand why he's under PXII protection?"

Geoffrey turned toward Bauer. "I understand, sir, that Herst did some – work – for PXII in some hospital or other years ago

156

when he was a young chaplain. A patient there died under a suspicious circumstance that was never resolved. It was very convenient for Corelli."

Bauer raised his eyebrows. Well well.

* * *

MEDIA HEADLINE: Mars Bases in Conflict
EuroAm Mars base Eagle clashes with Russian Mars base Sputnik over territory and mineral rights. Allegedly the bases have only defensive weapons, however evidence ....

29

"The things we tell of can never be found by seeking, yet only seekers find it." Bayazid Bastami

* * *

Late spring was the low point in the year for scenery on Stevens Pass. The fluffy white snow expanses of deep winter gave way to dirty snow berms along the highway where winter debris concentrated in the melting process. Objects lost, forgotten, or thrown away emerged to pepper ditches with the *disjecta membra* from cars, amid roadkill that the crows hadn't got around to yet.

Paul's hands slipped around on the steering wheel. John's gentle old face was in the back of Paul's mind. I have to tell him myself, face to face.

When he pulled in John was outside splitting kindling. He laid aside his hatchet, wiped his hands on his shirt and greeted Paul with what should have been his usual bear hug if it hadn't felt so weak.

John pulled a bandanna from his pocket to wipe his face. "Wonderful you come to see me. You're the only two-legged company I get. Come on in. I was going to stop soon anyway for some grub. I've got a pot of homemade soup on the stove and some fresh biscuits I made this morning."

Paul's eyes followed John with affection as he bustled around the cabin, stoking the fire, placing out bowls, stirring the soup, slicing a slab of butter, making tea.

John looked a little thinner. His hands a little more palsied. He wheezed and was a little more out of breath than usual. His complexion resembled the color of a manila folder.

How will he take the news that I've abandoned everything he hoped for me. How to tell him?

Paul procrastinated by taking the opportunity before dark to trudge down to the river, misnamed Nason Creek. Only in the Pacific Northwest would such a large stream be called a 'creek'. The recent Chinook wind and resulting snowmelt had swelled it to the top of its banks. The melt had delivered large drift logs that lodged against the bridge piers. If the logjam didn't break free it could back up the river until it brought the whole bridge down. The river had been there before man's invasion. Which is the real blockage, the logs or the bridge? What've been the log jams in my life? Maybe the things I strove for have actually been impediments.

Dark came down like a curtain in the narrow canyon. He turned back toward the cabin, its lights a beacon. It was time to tell John.

Once again settled by the fire Paul asked, "How're you feeling? Sure you're all right up here? Can't be easy chopping and hauling wood, shoveling snow."

John said, "My heart's a bit dicky but the exercise is good for me. And I've got to die of something eventually." He laughed. "You haven't told me how you are."

Paul looked out on the family of Doug fir standing strong and straight around John's cabin, icons of strength and integrity. Inside their wood was red, like muscle. He took a deep breath. "I've been fired. I no longer live at Ignatius. In fact, I've left the church."

The only sound was the crackle of the fire. John looked dazed.

"Bauer found out about my aura and had me hospitalized. Their treatment ripped consciousness from my body. Something they did changed me inside." Paul turned his palms up and studied his hands for several moments, then curled them into fists. "I was given a choice to go back. I refused."

"I'm at a loss what to say." John's crinkly eyes blinked.

Paul walked over and put an arm around his shoulders. Squeezed him.

John pulled out a bandanna, wiped his eyes, blew his nose.

"What's hard is no longer being a priest," Paul whispered mostly to himself. "Strange now that I no longer am, I value it most."

John grasped Paul's arm. "You're still a priest. They can't take that from you. I know what it's like to be rejected by the church. But you aren't cut off from God. If they did this because they fear your gift – then – well, that's their failure. The church fears what it doesn't understand or control."

Spring heavy wet snow fell now so thick and fast it was like being suspended inside a cloud. Somewhere an overburdened or undermined tree fell and took out the power line. The cabin was pitched into blackness, except for the fire that had collapsed into coals. Neither of them moved.

"Paul, please hear me."

Silence.

"There's great freedom not being a part of the church, at least the church they've become," John said. "They've left the path of compassion and openness. They're too big and complacent to accept change from within. Sometimes it takes a crisis from the outside to wake up a sleeping giant."

Paul shivered. They needed more wood. He suited up to uncover the woodpile and load up the log carriers. John was right, but then he gets to stay up here spending his days in the trees, and snow, and the solitude of the mountains. Could I do that? My path is different. If I'm to be a catalyst, it must be from within a community to awaken it, even if I don't yet know how.

He built up the fire.

John lit a couple of kerosene lamps and pulled out the scotch. "Have you had another aura experience?"

"Yes, but not since reliving my ordeal at St. Gudrun's. What I learned in that intense experience – what I accepted – is that I'm to catalyze the latent auras within others. That's my purpose."

160

"Like you shared with me on your last visit?"

"More than that. I'm to awaken the aura in others. You and I, we shared my aura. A while back I succeeded in awakening the aura of another, a terminally ill woman before she died. I don't even know how. I can't believe random occurrences like that are the goal."

"Have you tried again?" asked John.

"No. But something they did changed me, in the area of my brain connected in some way to the locus of my aura. It feels like there's something alive or restless there, I mean something that is, but also isn't, me. Or a source of energy of some kind. I know that doesn't make sense, but I can't explain it better. It could have a role in aura transmission. When I awakened the aura of the dying woman, I felt like I lost energy."

"Why not try here? With me?"

Paul glanced at the old man. He deserves to have this gift, not me.

"I'm willing to try," Paul said. "I'm better at accessing it now but still not in control. I can't promise anything."

Paul cleared the table and turned down the kerosene lamps. The firelight silhouetted John, his white hair like a halo, his gnarled hands like old tree roots. They sat across from each other, then Paul said in a low tone, "I've found that interior silence is important."

Paul closed his eyes and breathed deeply and regularly. The flames crackled, hissed, and spit. Snow from time to time slid from the roof to thump the ground. Muted through the snow fall, the Burlington Northern whistle wailed through the railroad crossing a quarter mile away.

Still and straight they sat. Paul's inhalation reduced to a quarter as long as his exhalation.

After a while John breathed in the same cadence. They settled into a rhythm that eventually silenced thought and sensation.

Paul sensed it coming on unlike any time before. Not with pain, but with a tingling localized to a pinpoint in his brain. It magnified until he felt intensely conscious, as though waking from a dream. The pinpoint pulsed, sending out rhythmic waves of energy, light-energy that fanned out until its waves emerged.

For the first time he perceived the gold-blue halo spreading from his head and enveloping his upper torso.

John's eyes were closed, his face upturned. Paul clasped the sides of John's head with both hands. Paul's waves of light energy flowed through his fingers and penetrated John as before, but this time, to Paul's surprise, his consciousness expanded to include John's.

John didn't open his eyes, but a silent gasp escaped his lips, and then a smile stole across his face.

John's consciousness was calm, silent. Paul perceived a small spark of light. He infused it with waves of his light-energy. His fingertips felt a slight tremor wash through John. The spark absorbed the energy and grew into an ember, then into a glow that emerged as light.

Paul dropped his hands. John's aura was crystal white. Both of them were enveloped in the double-aura light. They communicated. Not with words. Emotions? He wasn't sure. John was so open. Am I that open?

Yes, you are

Am I? Who am I? Pictures of his past swam up into his consciousness. His mother, a pair of hands, arms and eyes; soft, comforting, then gone. Can I forgive her? My father, a complete unknown. Can I forgive him for leaving mom and me? Never loved. Can I forgive them?

I love you

Grateful. I've been so angry. Forgive?

You have been forgiven

Even for anger at God?

Even that

Paul's aura connection with John waned. He came fully out. Tears had dried on his face. His hands were clenched and his knuckles white. His spine that had been as straight as a lance now softened as he relaxed. But he dared not move further.

John was still in full aura, John's own aura. It shimmered silver-white, an extension of his unruly white hair. Paul sat with him, filled with love of the old man, feeling fully forgiven of the bitterness he'd carried for decades. Grateful to be able to have given something back to someone who had given so much to him.

Paul prayed, 'I thank you Lord with all my heart; I sing praise to you before the gods....'

It was almost an hour before John's light faded and he returned to normal consciousness. He blinked like an owl and gasped. Took and held both of Paul's hands, speechless.

Paul squeezed his old friend's hands. "Thanks for your kind forgiving words. They mean a lot to me."

"What words?"

Startled, Paul dropped John's hands. Looking off into the distance over John's shoulder, realization of what happened stole over him. And so he didn't hear John's gratitude.

30

"When the heart weeps for what it has lost, the spirit laughs for what it has found." Anonymous Sufi Aphorism

* * *

Green Lake was beginning to show signs of spring. Clouds of midges emerged from its depths to find mates. Rainier daffodils unfurled in neat ice-yellow patches. Male mallards, like prissy plump butlers with ungainly gait, pursued females.

Nic had welcomed Paul to live at the abbey after convincing him that it would be an act of kindness to have another human being rattling around the big barn of a place.

The view out the open window of Paul's room was pastoral: lake, grass, flowers, trees. Still living in a garret but lighter, airier. His soul quieter, a new beginning.

After unpacking his few things away into the closet and drawers he tried out the threadbare slider-rocker, then lay on the quilt-topped bed. The mirror over the dresser revealed his transformation: clear calm eyes, smooth brow, soft lips, the demeaner of a new man.

Over the past several months his life had changed completely. Feared psychosis transmuted into a supernatural gift. Repression at Ignatius transformed into free expression at Tahoma College. The oppressive impersonal priest residence exchanged for a welcoming intimate home at the abbey. Superficial colleagues of the order and university replaced with authentic friends. And a new purpose in life.

Tonight there was to be a small celebration. He felt like a kid at his own birthday party.

"Are you finding everything you need?" Nic leaned on the doorframe. Glasses that magnified his eyes, and eyebrows that jutted up his broad brow, made his face look owl-like. "This old room will be happier to have an occupant. It's been empty for many years."

"I feel at home here already. You're generous to share the abbey with me."

"Nonsense. No one else would live here with a gruff old dog like me. I'm the one who's grateful." Nic's eyes twinkled with amusement. "And just to show you, I've picked up several bottles of an excellent Bordeaux. You've sloughed off the old skin and put on the new man. Will you be coming down soon? I want to sample some of the wine, and I don't like to drink alone."

Paul laughed. He trailed Nic downstairs and through the hallway toward the heady odors wafting out of the kitchen.

Dishes ranged from middle eastern falafels, hummus, curries, kebabs, pita, and babaghanoush; to Italian and French cheeses, tapenades redolent with garlic, apples and grapes, bruschetta of tomatoes and basil, and spicy salamis with peppers. Someone had picked a flamboyant bouquet of flowers from the garden and placed them on the table, their scent blending with the other exotic aromas. Paul's stomach rumbled.

Rabia and Isaac were preparing fresh strawberries. Paul mused that he'd known her for less than a year, but he felt that he knew her better than anyone except John. And she knew him, with all his flaws and regrets, and didn't pull away. Her hands were red with berry juice. She bantered with Isaac.

Paul reached around her, grabbed a strawberry and put it in his mouth. Its essence roused his taste buds; pleasantly stimulated his saliva glands. The taste of spring.

Nic handed him a glass of the Bordeaux and they sat watching Rabia's prosaic, graceful movements mixed with Isaac's comical ones – getting in the way, sampling the wares, his yarmulke in danger of falling into the fruit bowl.

The door to the kitchen was wide open for the fresh breeze to circulate and access for the arrivals. Paul, with no skill at kitchen tasks, stayed out of the way by tucking into a corner to sit on a large sack of rice. Jesse, David and Ali arrived about the same time as Phillips. Despite the roominess of the rectory, everyone wanted to be in the kitchen. Expansive though it was, it became crowded and noisy, the sound of convivial souls meeting, helping, talking, laughing.

Nic wore something that at one time might have been called a smoking jacket of deep burgundy brocade, with black velvet lapels a bit frayed. Rabia's apron covered a saffron sarong matched with leather sandals tooled with small dragonflies. Isaac was all in black even on the unseasonably warm day.

Someone put on some lively klezmer music. Traffic from the kitchen to the dining table was brisk. Paul marshalled extra chairs to the long table. The homey sounds of bottle corks popping, and glasses and plates clinking, called them to the table. As they all sat down, Paul smiled up at the image on the ceiling of the agape feast they mirrored. Isaac blessed the bread and wine before they began. Two hours of laughing, eating, drinking, and joking commenced.

The evening was a welcome respite and celebration marking a new beginning. The antics of Nic; the good-natured contests between Isaac and Jesse – the old Jewish traditions against the new; the music; feminine wit; outstanding food; and a little too much wine he had to confess; all contributed to a cheery expansive contentment as he climbed the stairs to his room. The entire evening, he hadn't once looked back in regret, or forward to an uncertain future.

He found his book of psalms, lit a candle, cut the lights, settled in the rocker and leafed through to find one on gratitude. Out of the pages a card fluttered to the floor. He couldn't believe his eyes. How did it get here? He didn't want to pick it up. There, like the Ace of Spades, on its face was the garish insignia of PXII. He stared at it for several moments, then picked it up, burned it in the candle flame, and crumbled the ashes in his fist.

31

"The body is always in time, the spirit is always timeless, and the psyche is an amphibious creature compelled by the laws of man's being to associate itself to some extent with its body, but capable, if it so desires, of experiencing and being identified with its spirit and, through its spirit, with the divine...."
Aldous Huxley

"We are not human beings having a spiritual experience; we are spiritual beings having a human experience."
Pierre Teilhard de Chardin

* * *

As spring warmed toward summer Paul discovered Tahoma College, where he now taught, to be a dream. He hadn't before fathomed the benefits of teaching at a secular college. No one monitored his lectures for compliance with orthodox dogma. He was free to explore all sources of science and spirituality with his students. Be open and honest with his opinions. Fellow professors were collegial. No one appeared to be harboring academic secrets fearful of discovery. No spies for the archbishop.

His first class was studying the interface between science and spirituality. Clues weren't only buried in scriptures and biology, but cosmology and physics as well. Today he would be covering a difficult theory much debated over the last few decades.

"Spiritual history going back 6000 years and continuing today holds that the universe is not random," Paul lectured. "Some scientists have come to the same conclusion. Einstein believed the universe to be non-random and stable, which was a basis for his General Theory of Relativity. He added lambda (Λ), the cosmological constant, to his equation to make the universe stable. The design or plan for the non-random universe as we know it has been called 'inflation', 'implicate order', 'divine consciousness', or 'energy-verse'. It organized the outcome of the Big Bang in order for the universe to exist. I'm going to use the term 'template' for this going forward."

Sasha interrupted, "But I thought Einstein said his Λ was wrong. It was a fudge factor?"

"True, but later discoveries about dark energy and dark matter, and Big Bang microwave data, showed that Λ was necessary to make the theory comply with what was observed. A sort of balance between a static universe and a completely unstable one. So, it seems Einstein was right even when he thought he was wrong. Now that's genius."

A soft laugh went around the room.

"This template continues to act today because it exists in pre-space, outside of space-time and not limited by laws of our physical universe. Scientists describe the template for the universe like a template for a hologram. The universe exists in the template and also in the template's expression – the hologram – simultaneously. The former creates the latter.

"The implication for man is that we also exist in both simultaneously. We have a spiritual 'body' within the template, and a physical one within the universe. When we die it's only our physical body of matter and energy in space-time that dies. Our spirit continues within the template where we have always been and always will be, the law of conservation of consciousness if you will. As physical entities tied to our senses, we've not been able, except some rare individuals, to access the divine-consciousness since it's a non-physical realm beyond space-time. But as evolution has proceeded from energy, to matter, to life, to consciousness, we're poised for the final stage of evolution to spirit, the final step in the creation of the pneumasphere...."

168

While Paul enjoyed teaching he missed the pastoral side of being a priest. Since his escape from St. Gudrun's, Bauer had removed his faculties within the diocese. He didn't mind so much not hearing confessions or performing other sacramental duties. But ever since the disaster on the feast of St. Paul, the mass meant much more to him. He had tapped into a spiritual well-spring. Paul occasionally celebrated mass alone in his room. He knew Nic wouldn't care, but he still felt a little furtive about it until Nic insisted he use the vacant church.

Rabia, Nic, Isaac, Phillips and Paul continued to meet, exploring the properties of the aura. Tonight, they sat around the library table at the abbey listening to Rabia. She was finally, after several months of persistence, able to obtain copies of the medical records on Paul the hospital was required to keep. They revealed that Paul's brain waves had changed during and following the ECT treatments. And certain sectors of his brain were hyper-active. With this new information, they wanted to revisit details of what he'd experienced.

Paul found it difficult to recount; the experience was still so raw. He glanced around the room. The keenness in Phillip's eyes was matched in the faces of the others. Only Rabia looked away into unspoken territory.

"I was strapped to a gurney and wheeled into a room, a tiled cell with no windows. Nurses moved me onto a heavily padded rubbery table, fitted me with restraints and strapped a wire contraption to my head. I asked what they were doing. They said the doctor would explain and then inserted a mouth guard. When the doctor arrived, he explained nothing, and I couldn't talk. He wheeled some kind of large monitor behind my head that I couldn't see. I heard clicking of connections being made."

Paul chewed his lip. Took a sip of wine. Set down his glass. Rubbed his hands up and down on his thighs. Shuddered.

"Then bolts of electricity shot through my head. The pain was beyond a ten out of ten. It reminded me of my first experiences with the aura, only worse. My body was not my own. It arched, jerked, trembled, spasmed, and cramped uncontrollably. The table under me shook. From my throat I heard a muffled involuntary scream. And then it was over. My body went slack –

sunk onto the table. I was exhausted. My mind that had been a cacophony of thoughts, emotions and sensations in a kaleidoscope of visions and feelings, was – blank."

Paul looked at his feet.

"And then it started again… and again… and again." I couldn't fight it. I couldn't flee."

A barely audible intake of breath went around the room.

"And then I was hovering, watching myself. But I was free of it – no pain. Suspended in light. Conscious outside my body. I thought I was dead. Peace. No fear."

Paul sipped his wine. Looked each of the group in the eye. "That's where I encountered it. There's a light presence, I think it's a universal Aura. It presented as a vast dense center that offered joining. It was from this presence that I understood why I have this – gift. I'm to catalyze the auras of others, like I did with John."

No one broke the silence in the room.

Paul sighed and looked off into the distance. "Next thing I knew I was aware of my body, back in my hospital room hooked to a bunch of monitors and an IV."

The recollection was painful, not just physically. He'd been helpless. Dominated by something malevolent. "They repeated this over a couple of days I guess. I had difficulty remembering things. I didn't recall Marcellus visiting me. My sense of time and sequencing of events seemed disjointed."

Nic spoke. "Perhaps they were trying to force aura emanation. Did they succeed?"

"I don't know what they observed."

Phillips had been uncharacteristically quiet during Rabia's and Paul's revelations, his normal nervous energy turned inward. Even his mustache that frequently quivered like rabbit whiskers was still. His piercing eyes had a far-away look until he nodded his head and rejoined the conversation.

"I find it intriguing how you describe your reaction. Neither able to fight or flee, and the out-of-body experience you characterize as peace, no fear. Could the amygdala be involved?"

"What's that?" Paul asked.

"The amygdala are two almond-shaped small organs in the brain that regulate fear and compassion – involved in emotional learning and interpersonal attunement – underlie empathy and social connectedness," said Phillips.

"You may be right," Nic said. "And the amygdala can be influenced by association or behavior. Functional MRI data show that Buddhist monks during meditation can modulate their amygdala. The amygdala also creates a pathway for transpathy, the transference of an emotion one to another, or whole groups. It's theorized that it happens through a simulated shared body state."

"When you could neither fight nor flee, your amygdala took – sorry to sound so anthropomorphic – the only other option to respond to your state of danger," Phillips said, "and projected consciousness out of your body." He sat back in his chair studying Paul's face.

Then it was like a curtain going up on a play. They all started talking at once. Paul got lost in the technical jargon about neurotransmitters, premotor cortex, stria terminalis, glutaminergic neurons. But part of what they were discussing sounded familiar. Like the part about the 'other' we see or hear becomes the 'other self' in our minds. That sharing someone else's emotions recruits brain regions involved in producing similar emotions. This was the aura sharing experience. He'd shared his deepest feelings with Rabia, and she communicated back, helping him modify his emotions.

With this new insight, he looked up at her. She was the only one besides Paul not deeply engaged in the conversation of the group. Her eyes appeared unfocussed and her face intent, deep in thought. Paul was about to cross the room to her when Phillips rounded on him with a question.

"You said you somehow were able to awaken John's aura. How did you do that?" The room silenced again.

"I don't know. We were meditating facing each other. More than any time before my aura felt alive. It was sort of vibrating, throwing off energy that then emerged and penetrated him. But this time I was in his consciousness. I received impressions of his thoughts and emotions but without language. Very like I did with

171

the dying Russian woman. It's hard to describe because that requires language. John had a small shimmering bright dot or spark within a matrix of some sort. I directed aura-energy to the spot of light, and I felt a force go out of me. His aura then expanded and emerged."

Phillips looked Rabia. "Has this been your experience?"

Startled out of her thoughts, she took a few moments to respond. "I haven't had an out-of-body experience as Paul describes. My experience of sharing auras has been limited to my father and Paul, people who already had awakened auras. But I've thought for some time that transpathy is involved. I think focus on the amygdala is the right direction given that the experience is deeply emotional, deeply personal." She dropped eye contact with the group, then rose and left the room.

Paul's eyes followed her. We're the only two here who've experienced the aura. The only ones for whom this discussion isn't just academic. It appears to be distressing her, as it does me. They can't understand how revealing it is; how transparent it makes us; how vulnerable. We've never considered the risks involved.

"If it is associated with the amygdala," continued Phillips, "that would explain how it could evolve along with the brain's evolution."

Paul refocused on their discussion which didn't ring true with his intuition about the experience, with the connection to universal Aura. "I don't think that's how it works."

They all turned toward him.

"Genes, neurons, lobes in the brain – they're physical. Made from matter. The aura isn't. So it couldn't have evolved through physical means."

"Then you don't think consciousness is physical?" Isaac asked.

"I think consciousness could be like lichen, some of both," answered Paul. "Lichen are part algae and part fungi, two different types of life forms fused together as different as plant and animal. Consciousness could be like that, a fusion of the physical and spiritual. The physical part evolves through the laws of evolution but not the spiritual part."

172

Isaac asked, "Then how would the spiritual part evolve?"

"I don't think it does," Paul said. "I think it's always been here. We've had to evolve from inanimate matter, through the biosphere and noosphere to this point. The physical part of consciousness has to evolve the capability to access in ourselves the spiritual part of consciousness, or the aura. It is this that joins with the universal Aura in super-consciousness."

"From the Big Bang to this." Isaac raised his glass. "Almost fourteen billion years. God is patient."

"Paul, do you think you could do this with another – awaken their aura?" asked Phillips.

"I don't know. John and I've been close for many years. We trust each other. He must've been ready. Open. No negative emotions. He's a humble selfless man."

"But you tell us that's your purpose. How do you intend to go about it?" asked Nic.

"John told me I need to learn from it – from the aura itself. I don't think I'll find understanding from analyses but from experience."

Isaacs's eyes shone. "But wouldn't it have to be experience with another?"

32

"He was despised and forsaken of men,
A man of sorrows and acquainted with grief..."
Isaiah 53:3

* * *

Paul stood in Tom's chambers staring out the window. He'd returned to meet at Tom's urgent request, although what they had to meet about Paul couldn't fathom. He'd never felt so betrayed. Tom moved around doing something behind him, but Paul didn't notice or care.

Ignatius, once familiar, felt alien. Images floated in and out of his mind of his time here – lectures, students, the chapel, his garret room, the watery-well staircase, the smell of the library. Ignatius was also the place of spying, betrayal, dark secrets, a disastrous mass that sent him to St. Gudrun's, abandonment by his superior and order, and a forced choice to leave this world.

"Paul. Please. Sit down."

Paul ignored him.

"Thanks for coming," said Tom. "I know you had good reason not to."

Paul stood with his back to Tom.

"I didn't treat you as a brother here. Didn't give you support when you needed it most." Tom walked around to Paul's side. Stared out the window with him. "I'm sorry. Please forgive me."

Paul asked, "What do you expect me to say? You had your reasons."

Tom shoved his hands in his pockets. "My reasons were only excuses."

A blue bottle fly bumbled around the window trying to escape, oblivious of the glass barrier. Like the barrier between Tom and me. "I forgive you because I must. But I don't think we have much more to say to one another right now." He cracked open the window for the fly to escape.

Tom sat down. A distant claxon marked the change of classes. Tom's wall pendulum clock chimed the hour.

"I wanted to fathom the phenomenon itself," said Tom, "without considering what that meant to you. I thought only about the consequences to Ignatius. Of what the order had on our hands. I've talked with Marcellus and Magdala several times. You could've been irretrievably damaged or killed at St. Gudrun's. For God's sake, I supported Bauer forcing you there. And then when you escaped, instead of helping you, I was the messenger to return you to church control. I've been sickened with myself ever since."

Paul turned around to confront Tom. Someone Paul had always revered. Someone who had been strong and flexible like a fine steel sword. A defender. But now Tom was tired with conflicting priorities and limits like everyone else. Like me.

"Don't be too hard on yourself. I could've refused to go to Gudrun's. But I chose to remain loyal to the church, though it was undeserving of my loyalty. Either way, it didn't matter. In the end I didn't escape sanction. How could I stay after that?"

"I wish I could undo that. Please come back here. Live at Ignatius again."

Really? He can't be serious. "Why? I've built myself a new life. Found freedom I'd never known existed. There's nothing for me here. And I'd only exacerbate conflict between you and Bauer."

The pinched frown on Tom's face made Paul question what was behind this belated attempt at reconciliation.

"I want you to come back here because you're in danger," Tom said. "We both are."

Paul would have considered this uncharacteristically melodramatic but for the expression of anxiety on Tom's face.

Tom had never been fearful. A respectful distain was more in his line when it came to the church.

"From what? I left the church. I'm just a disgruntled former priest, a freakshow," Paul said. "How're you a threat?"

"Remember last fall when I told you Jesuits took some documents from the Vatican after Francis died? The documents provide evidence of PXII crimes, and they also include a portion of Pope John Paul I's diary."

Tom moved to his desk and took out a sheet of paper and handed it to Paul.

"What you hold is an excerpt from a translation I made of John Paul I's diary," said Tom. "The diary describes a phenomenon such as you possess – and a need for a catalyst. The last person we know of that PXII identified as a catalyst, Pope John Paul I, was murdered." A Jesuit in Sao Paulo – my friend – who held the only other copy of these documents was tortured and murdered. They're searching for these documents to destroy evidence of their crimes – and to find the catalyst.

Paul left the window. Sat down. Read the paper.

"...light from my head emerged and enveloped me like a nimbus. Within the light I was intensely conscious and perceived I was within an immense cloud of light with a nucleus. I joined with this essence of light. Energy, like a sustained static charge, flowed into and through me. I felt like a radio antenna. Without touching him the energy flowed through the light into the novice. Then I was within his consciousness. In the darkness of his consciousness I saw a faint spark vibrating, but at low energy like mine before awakening. The energy channeling through me stimulated his spark and the vibrating increased until we achieved alignment and harmonized. The energy channeling through my body was almost too much to endure. Then his dormant spirit ignited, and his nimbus emerged.

It is clear to me from several such experiences that awakening the light in another requires a catalyst. It does not or cannot apparently be generated initially on one's own, as indeed mine was not."

176

The church bells rang for evening mass. A few footsteps passed Tom's door and then the building became silent.

"You think I'm the catalyst."

"Are you?"

Paul knew, better than Tom, that he was. But would PXII kill him? And Tom?

He put down the paper. His mind blanked. He was conscious only of a weightiness behind his solar plexus and bitterness that he was not going to survive this. It didn't immediately terrify him, but instead made him feel desperate that he would fail yet still pay the ultimate price. Just another catalyst down through the ages who had been too slow or too ignorant to perform his mission.

Tom broke the silence. "That's why I want you to come back to Ignatius. It will be safer for you here. Seattle isn't Rome or Sao Paulo, but I do fear what PXII is capable of. I intend to reveal the Vatican documents, at least those dealing with PXII crimes. That will take them down and reduce the threat."

"Do they know you have them? That they're here?" Paul realized that Tom could hide the documents. But there was no place that Paul could hide that he could not be found. Especially if he was to perform his mission.

"I don't know. I've kept them hidden off campus. I found Ambrose poking around here a while back. Asking questions about my time at the Vatican and departure. Asking about documents and safe storage. Bauer placed him here to snoop. Then there was the attack on me and the search of my chambers."

"Why not just publish them?"

"They are being retrieved to be authenticated. The worst outcome would be premature disclosure and have them disproved or disputed without resolution. These are grave offenses. They'll need to be purged through both church and civil courts. But we must be sure of what we're doing, the evidence iron clad. If the case is proved it will mean the end of PXII, but more seriously the end of P13."

"That would be chaos."

"A crooked bone must be broken to mend straight," Tom said. "A cleansing fire purifies and makes supple hardened materials to remold. PXII has been obsessed with the prophecies of La

Sallette, Fatima, Akita, and Huaraz that are supposed to predict the ascension of an Anti-Christ into St Peter's Chair. The Vatican documents will point the finger straight at P13 as that person. It's what PXII and P13 fear."

"My returning here can only focus more unwanted attention on you and Ignatius," Paul said. "They may suspect but they don't know I'm the catalyst. Nor do you. The safest thing I can do is to keep distant. We both need to be careful and the farther apart the better. Besides, we Jesuits were founded as soldiers of Christ. Perhaps it's time we are again."

33

"The wound is the place where the Light enters you ...
You have to keep breaking your heart until it opens...
There is a voice that doesn't use words. Listen...." Rumi

* * *

John had to come to Seattle for a cardiology appointment. Paul arranged for him to stay at the abbey as more comfortable than a hotel. Paul and Nic sat with him in the kitchen.

"How've you been getting on?" Paul asked. "I hope this appointment isn't about something serious."

"Just routine." He turned to Nic. Smiled over his first cup of coffee of the day. "Thanks for letting me stay here."

As Nic and John were becoming acquainted, Paul observed how much older John looked in this setting. The skin hung loose on his face. His cheek bones protruded just below spiderweb crinkle lines around his eyes. A perceptible stoop to his spine. Small waves in his coffee transmitted the tremors from his gnarled chalky hands.

They finished their coffees. Nic excused himself to work in the library until time for mass.

Since his move-in, Nic had convinced Paul to celebrate mass on a regular basis in the vacant church connected to the abbey. He'd drawn a following, first from curious neighbors, then from some of his students, a few street people, and lately some regular church goers who couldn't stomach the ultra-conservative preaching at their parish pulpits. It broke Bauer's strictures against him but Paul didn't care.

"Would you like to concelebrate mass with me?" Paul asked John.

John placed his hand on Paul's arm. "I'd like that very much. It's been a long time since I've celebrated mass in a real church. And with you."

They walked across to the church. Paul readied the altar with a white tablecloth. Placed the bread and wine gifts at the church entrance on a small table. Then he put out chairs facing the altar and around the walls.

John had his old thread worn stole around his neck and was shuffling around, hesitant where to stand.

"How about you presiding, and I'll serve like old times?" Paul said.

John smiled. "I'd like that."

The congregation wandered in, a motley group. Some came in sweats and flip flops with unruly hair. Others dressed in Seattle-casual attire, smart but comfortable. There were children, old men and women, but mostly young adults, with interesting hair styles and colors, tattoos, and jewelry or hardware depending on your point of view. They settled in, filled the chairs, milled around the back. Paul was pleased to see that Rabia and Nic had come.

The mass began. John's weak voice stilled the crowd straining to hear him. Paul read the scriptural passages chosen from Revelations and St. John, and gave the homily. It was clear from the behaviors and responses that some of the attendees were long time Catholics and recognized the ritual. But most did not. They listened and watched, even chatted in whispers among themselves.

When it came time for the blessing of the bread and wine, Paul retrieved them from bearers who brought them from the table at the entrance of the church. He placed the basket of bread and carafe of wine before John who continued with the consecration. He broke the bread, ate a piece himself and passed the basket to Paul.

Meanwhile John took the carafe and poured some into a goblet. He held it, said the blessing, took a mouthful and closed his eyes. Paul watched him patiently for the hand off. But John's eyes shot open with a grimace of pain and horror.

"No," he rasped. His palsied hands dropped the goblet, spilling wine down his chest. It bounced on the floor and rolled under the altar. He grabbed for the altar with his left hand and with the other swept the crystal carafe holding the remainder of the wine onto the floor where it broke into a myriad of shards splashing a crimson pool. He arched backwards grabbing his chest, then collapsed on the floor dragging the altar cloth with him.

Paul reached for the goblet, then grabbed for the carafe, and finally lunged for John as he stumbled and crumbled to the ground. Paul knelt in the broken glass and wine cradling John's head.

"John? John."

John coughed several times then subsided into stillness. His rheumy eyes gazed into Paul's, then dulled.

Paul, dazed, paralyzed, eventually realized others were moving about him. Nic and Rabia performed CPR. Someone close by called 911. Soon sirens wailed. Medics arrived. Took over. Strapped John to a gurney. Hustled him into an ambulance and were gone. Paul mechanically got towels and wiped up the spilt wine, like John's blood.

Rabia knelt down and put her arm around him.

Paul continued to wipe the floor like an automaton. "He's the only father I ever had."

* * *

Rabia drove Paul to Harborview with a heavy heart. She knew John to be dead but until Paul heard it pronounced at the hospital she didn't speculate. Paul sat there with a blank visage and fixed eyes.

She parked in her stall and guided Paul to the emergency room. Gave him a handful of tissues. Paul couldn't sit or stand still. He kept checking his watch and the emergency room door. The wait wasn't long before a doctor Rabia knew came out with the inevitable news – dead on arrival, looks like a heart attack.

Paul sunk down on the nearest couch and withdrew into a painful private world.

The doctor took Rabia aside out of earshot. "Do you know anything about the patient's medical history? Does he have a heart condition?"

While talking Rabia kept her eyes on Paul. "I don't know for sure. I just met him. But Paul mentioned he has a heart condition. Takes heart medications. He came here for a cardiology appointment. I can find out where for you."

"I'm trying to determine whether to order an autopsy. An elderly man with a heart condition collapsing in a crowd from a heart attack isn't unusual."

Rabia barely listened. She could see Paul's heaving shoulders from where she was standing. "I'm sure you're right. Excuse me please."

She approached Paul, took him by the hand, raised him up, and steered him to the hospital chapel. He was as biddable as a child. She closed the door, settled him on a floor cushion, and sat across from him. She held his head in her hands, transpathed hope and love, and shared his grief.

She awakened her aura, wrapped it around him, hovered, then as across a permeable membrane, passed through.

Paul was lost in anguish, another of life's great losses. But he allowed the great cauterizing flame in. Allowed Rabia in. Together they experienced loss, the losses of both their lifetimes. Family. Friends. Child?

34

"Both light and shadow are the dances of love." Rumi

* * *

In the nightmarish days following John's death, Paul didn't teach. Seldom ate. Couldn't pray or sleep. All he could hold on to was Rabia's compassion and the great gift of sharing her aura in the hospital chapel. During their first aura-sharing several months ago she'd opened him to love, but it was an all-embracing love of humanity, the good earth, and God. Now in Paul's grief he found that he loved her. The love of an individual selfless soul. No matter how much suffering he experienced he was exultant and whole when they shared consciousness. As John had said, *charmolypi.*

But he wasn't prepared for such a complication. Forbidden love for a priest. Am I still a priest?

And what about Rabia? What does she feel? There are parts of her that are closed off from me and I've never intruded into those places. But there's no mistaking her deep caring, enough to risk exposure. Of what?

A relationship with her?

* * *

Several weeks later, still raw from John's passing, Paul crossed to the abbey church to pray and meditate. The purple martins had already ceded airspace to little brown myotis bats that roosted in the church bell tower. Paul loved their mouse ears and tinny clicking sounds darting through the columns of midges wafting over in the evening from Green Lake into the garden.

He found Rabia seated on a couple of meditation rugs. Periodically Rabia would come to the abbey to meditate, sometimes joined by Nic and Paul. But Nic was at a conference for a few days. She was alone.

"May I join you?"

She opened her eyes and smiled, nodded.

Paul pulled plush meditation rugs from the trunk near the door and arranged them facing her. Then he sat down and started deep rhythmic breathing. Soon they breathed in unison. Paul felt a crescendo of wave energy stimulate his aura. The waves grew in intensity, amplifying his aura until it billowed from his body. Without opening his eyes, he sensed Rabia's aura hovering close. Their auras expanded until they merged. Then they were inside each other's consciousness.

Warmth. Wholeness. Love. He experienced her joy of connection. But something was different. Her aura, that had been largely gold, contained rays of dark blue radiating from a place deep within her consciousness.

He could see her without opening his eyes, not imagined but a real vision. Jet lashes of gossamer silk framed her shining eyes with pupils like pools of night; a nose like Queen Nefertiti's; rose petal lips; her elfin face framed by black lush hair; the barely perceptible pulse of her throat from the beat of her heart hidden beneath a creamy sarong. One naked shoulder of mocha skin curved into her right arm, lithe and lovely, then down to fairy-fine hands and fingers. Bare feet peeked out from the edge of her sarong, the soles as pink as a baby's. From her body came the scent of jasmine.

A spike of love and yearning that was not his own penetrated Paul. He answered in kind. His hands cupped the sides of her face, then slid down her neck to rest there.

Rabia stretched her neck and pressed against his fingers. Then entwined her hands with his. He uncurled and kissed each of her fingertips and then lightly brushed them along his face. His left hand stroked down to her exposed right shoulder.

She leaned into his touch.

He kissed the crease into her armpit and felt her shudder. Then he took her by both shoulders and laid her down on the meditation rugs. He lay beside her propped up on one elbow and stroked her face, neck, shoulder and arms until he leaned down and gently kissed her.

She kissed back, her lips warm and wet.

Both in full aura, Paul felt an ecstatic charge from her lips travel down his spine through his loins to the soles of his feet. Her fingertips traced a trail of titillating sparks down his face. The follicles of his hair tingled.

His fingers shifted the sarong from her other shoulder. Her small nipples pushed up against the creamy cloth. He brushed the sarong down to uncover breasts that were like small firm mounds of chocolate mousse with cherry nipples. He kissed them then cupped her breasts in each hand. So smooth. So soft.

She breathed heavily and arched her back pressing against his palms.

He undid the buttons of his shirt and took it off. Lowered down until his chest hairs brushed her breasts. Her entire aura now pulsed slow and steady. He synchronized with it as he penetrated deeper into her consciousness. He wanted to experience every part of her. To become one.

As he swam deeper the blue rays of her aura became darker and more concentrated at her core. He followed them, parting through layers of love and compassion, then vulnerability and sadness, and finally reached hot darkness.

Rabia stiffened. In that instant guilt and shame pierced Paul's consciousness searing him like a burning brand. Confused and anxious, he retreated from Rabia's consciousness, rolled aside from her body and sat up.

Rabia's aura extinguished. She sat up breathing hard and quaking on her mat. Turned away from him. Wrapped herself in the sarong. Stumbled to her feet and hurried away trembling and crying.

Paul's aura collapsed. Too bewildered and mortified he just sat there in the darkness watching her retreating figure. Emotionally exhausted he put on his shirt and laid his back on the cool floor.

Stared at the ceiling. He loved her. Knew she loved him. What happened? What did I do? Am I like Merlin? Denied earthly love for a higher purpose?

He grimaced as he recalled an old Jewish aphorism. Lay Yahweh's words on your chest so that when your heart breaks the words will sink in. What words are sinking into my heart now? Love? All I feel is rejection. All I've ever felt.

I didn't choose this sacrifice.

He lay there until his shame and anger dulled into despair. Drifted back to his boyhood. Six years old. Playing in a backyard with a dog. White with black spots. Spooky jumped in his lap, licked his face. He hugged the pup. Laughed. Rolled with it in the grass. Scratched its tummy. It squirmed joyfully in his arms. More laughter. Got licked again.

Then a whistle from a taller older boy. Spooky ignored it. The older boy strode across the lawn. Jerked the pup away. Said, "Not yours. Not for you."

35

"One cannot help but be in awe when he contemplates the mysteries of eternity, of life, of the marvelous structure of reality. It is enough if one tries merely to comprehend a little of this mystery every day. Never lose a holy curiosity."
Albert Einstein

* * *

In the aftermath of losing John and his anguished experience with Rabia, Paul spent his time teaching. Or at Mt. Olives attending to the spiritual needs of the dying. Or sequestered in his room contemplating the means to be a catalyst. He fought against spiraling down into depression. Why has anyone I've ever loved rejected me, or died?

He diverted these dark unproductive thoughts into curiosity about his condition. He studied the page of the diary. Matched it against his experience. And a theory began to take shape. He asked Nic to convene the abbey group. They all attended except Rabia.

After the usual preliminaries, like ants waving and touching their antennas with each other, Paul became impatient. "I've learned that Pope John Paul I emitted an aura. He left a description behind in his diary that's been kept secret for over 80 years. He wrote about his experience back when he was Bishop Albino Luciani." Paul pulled notes from his pocket. Read the statement from the diary in a rush of words. Then looked up eagerly at the group.

Nic frowned and pinched his eyebrows. Phillips stared across the room as though he would discover the answer to the riddle written on the far wall. Isaac smiled with a far-away gaze as if reliving a stimulating experience.

"I think we've overlooked something important about my experience at Gudrun's," Paul said. "We were looking for the aura seat in brain anatomy or chemistry. Maybe we should be looking for energy – neural oscillations – brain waves."

Phillips snapped to attention. "You described a seizure. One so powerful that your consciousness was ejected from your body. Seizures create terrific brain waves."

"You're on to something," Nic said. "There was a study several years ago at the University of Wisconsin. Gamma waves produced by Buddhist monks were measured during meditation. The monks were able to produce gamma waves of extremely high amplitude that had long-range gamma synchronicity. They're the highest gamma waves recorded in humans to date – except during seizure."

"What are gamma waves?" Paul asked. He'd studied gamma radiation, but this was obviously very different.

"Gamma waves are produced by neurons in the brain," Nic continued, "by individual neurons or by ensembles of neurons firing together if synchronized – called 'gamma synchrony'. They range from 30-100 Hz. Enough neurons sufficiently synchronized produce macro-waves observable by EEG. Producing and synchronizing gamma waves is trainable. In the same University of Wisconsin study students with minimal training in meditation were able to improve and increase their gamma synchrony after only a few weeks. Some studies suggest that gamma synchrony amounts to a conscious experience."

Phillips joined in. "Gamma waves have been shown to activate the insular cortex and almost all sub-nuclei of the amygdaloid complex." Phillips picked up his tablet and started rapidly writing, consulting at points the page from the diary.

"You remember we theorized from your experience that the amygdala must be involved?" said Nic. "That it might be the locus of an individual's aura? Or it could be associated with the insular cortex – that is if it's associated with a physical brain structure at all. But given the emotions and euphoria you've experienced in the aural state, I have to believe they're part of the puzzle."

"How could this explain transmission from one person to another?" Paul asked.

Phillips had been scribbling furiously. Now he was virtually quivering with suppressed energy, but he spoke in an awe-filled whisper. "It could go something like this," and handed round his tablet.

>*Skilled meditation*
> *activates neurons*
> *produces gamma waves*
> *produces gamma synchrony*
> *activates the insular cortex and amygdala*
> *produces a transcendental state*
> *stimulates and emits aura (highest synchronic state)*
> *accesses, converts and conducts universal Aura/super-consciousness energy in gamma waves (his radio antenna analogy)*
> *transmission of gamma wave state to novice (transpathy)*
> *activates novice's insular cortex and amygdala*
> *novice's aura activation*
> *achieves highest gamma synchronic state*
> *shares consciousness.*

"Bozhe moi," whispered Nic as he handed the tablet to Isaac. "I think you've got it."

"Maybe that's where the term 'brainstorm' comes from," Isaac said as he handed the tablet to Paul.

Paul studied the equation. In a flash the pieces of his experience focused and came together. Synchronous energy creates aura activation; the speed of energy distorts time; neuron synapses unable to sustain such energy bursts create pain; brain structures through meditation learn to avoid pain and mediate euphoria; but the last piece had eluded him until now. Brain waves – gamma waves – if strong enough leave the brain and can be shared with another and moderate the gamma waves of another. And the light?

"But then what does that make the Aura? It's not matter. And I can't believe it's gamma waves or any kind of energy. You determined that the light has no signature. No frequency, amplitude, or phase. Yet it's in the visible spectrum. We see it. How can this be?"

"You're trying to make this all rational. About physics. About neurology. It isn't," Isaac said. "Maybe the aura is a deific substrate or milieu for communicating with us mortals from beyond space and time into space and time. Maybe we just need to leave it at being a *mysterium tremendum.*

Paul hardly listened. Where can I try this? I need people like John, open, empty, selfless. Then he sat back and smiled. Mt. Olives houses a whole community of them.

36

"...(W)e are no more than conscious particles. Awaiting us is a center of higher order..." Teilhard de Chardin

* * *

Paul spent several hours every evening at Mt. Olives training nuns in the type of meditation that he was taught by Rabia that leads to hyper-consciousness. He frequently shared his own aura so they became familiar with the sensations. They were quick to learn. The Benedictine Rule based on prayer and contemplation in community had prepared them well in mindfulness. Humility and detachment were a necessity in the hospice. The selfless service to others in their last extremity prepared them to be empty.

Paul recruited Rabia to help with their instruction and practice. But he felt awkward around her, and she avoided being alone with him.

Marcellus and Magdala had the most difficulty. Years of church politics, fund raising, and responsibility for the operation of Mt. Olives were impediments to the necessary mental state. Magdala confessed she was too old, wealthy, controlling, and not even a real nun, to hope for enlightenment. But she nevertheless participated.

It took two months for Paul to penetrate the consciousness of one of the novices and catalyze her aura. After that at almost every session one or more of the nuns awakened. Paul got better at it. He knew where to seek and how to energize. The nuns shared their own experiences and practiced collectively between Paul's visits. Finally, nuns began sharing their auras with the hospice patients, transpathing calm, joy, divine presence, dispelling fears of death.

Families of the hospice patients came to hear about and then experience the Mt. Olive's unique gift to the dying. Their gratitude poured out in financial and community support. Some of the most grateful were influential in Seattle and Magdala secured them as champions.

Paul had less success with Nic, Phillips and Isaac. While they progressed in meditation technique, their analytical bias prevented them from the detachment necessary to achieve emptiness. Rabia, while proficient at teaching technique and sharing her aura with others, was unable to awaken anyone's own aura. Paul sensed her deepening disquiet, and several times considered approaching her. But to teach her how to awaken others would require sharing each other's auras, and he doubted she would risk that again.

One evening at Mt. Olives Rabia waited for him in the hallway next to the empty 'lying-in-state' room. She drew him in and shut the door.

Paul slumped against the wall. Catalysis sapped energy that was often in short supply at the end of a day of lectures. He looked at Rabia, then controlled his feelings. They hadn't been alone together since his ill-fated attempt at intimacy. *Something important must be driving her to seek me out like this.*

She sat down. Paul sat across the room from her, curious what she needed of him, hoping that he could provide it.

"Paul," she started, folding her hands in her lap and focusing on them.

She kept her eyes down, smoothed the soft silky sarong, folded her hands again, then finally looked up her eyes resolute. "How do you catalyze the aura of another?"

Her deep brown eyes, like two dark tunnels, peered back at him with hope, but also with fear. He wanted to follow those eyes, the pathway to her soul. But she had a secret place there, a dark place, where he wasn't welcome.

He realized their roles had reversed. Was this hard for her? It's hard for me. What does she really need? He'd known too many penitents to not recognize the symptoms of deep emotional distress within the soul.

"I will teach you what I know, as you taught me. It will require us sharing auras as we have in the past. Are you ready for this?"

Rabia's eyes darted from side to side, then she trained them again on her folded hands. Her lips quivered.

"Rabia," Paul leaned forward and whispered, "what's wrong? I want to help you. There's nothing you can tell me that will change how I feel about you. I love you. Please let me help you."

Her face looked to him like that of a frightened child. She shook her head, rose, opened the door, stepped through and closed it behind her.

Paul sat there. Heart heavy. Body leaden. Spirit deadened.

37

"Ideas stand in the corner and laugh while we fight over them."
Marty Rubin

* * *

From Mt. Olives word spread. The monastery received an invitation from St. Jude's to speak about the nun's work to their congregation. Marcellus was inclined to decline but Magdala felt strongly otherwise. "Paul should go. It's his mission. He's done great things for the poor souls in our hospice. It's time he shared his gift with others."

Paul didn't feel the same.

Magdala was insistent. "Paul, you must. What do you think God gave you this gift for?"

"But I'm not good at preaching. My homilies aren't very inspired. And it isn't as though I am going to be able to awaken anyone. They aren't ready." His excuse sounded lame in his own ears.

"Nonsense. You're a great teacher. Think of it as a lecture and the audience as students. Think of getting them prepared."

The invitation was accepted and Paul, after he got through it, didn't feel that badly. More invitations trickled in and then grew until at least once a week he was hosted by someone wanting to know about his gift, skeptics and believers alike.

* * *

MEDIA HEADLINE: Glowing halo engulfs audience of maverick priest.

Attendees insist they witnessed a disenfranchised priest glow a halo that spread across the congregation.

Earlier today Paul Pennington, former Jesuit priest, was guest speaker at St. Jude's Catholic Church where he taught about meditation and the aura, an alleged visible manifestation of super-consciousness. During his presentation it was reported he emitted an aura, seen as a halo around his head that subsequently expanded to flow over the entire congregation. Attendees spoke in eloquent words of bliss and transcendental states. Witnesses report the phenomenon lasted about twenty minutes. Mr. Pennington refused comment when asked by ....

* * *

MEDIA HEADLINE: Halo or hooey?

Congregation claims a halo appeared above renegade priest and then like magic set all aglow....

The story was picked up by Tonight Show host Janey Fallon and within twenty minutes became the number one trending story in the nation. The BBC took notice and ran with the story reminiscent of the 15th century sighting of the Lady of Guadalupe surrounded by a full body glow.

* * *

Paul hated the notoriety. It complicated his teaching duties at Tahoma. Students came to packed classes that were closed to registration and stood in any available space. The college requested Paul teach a new class on meditation. Between his college duties, sessions at Mt. Olives, and speaking engagements at increasingly larger venues around Seattle, he had time for little else.

The abbey group enlarged to include some of the family members of the hospice patients, and a few students and professors known to Paul, Nic, Isaac and Phillips. Nic's home became too small for the group to meet so he moved the sessions to the abbey church.

* * *

MEDIA HEADLINE: Super Consciousness or super cult – nearly a million Americans now follow disgraced priest from Seattle.

Paul Pennington, a former Jesuit priest who once taught at Ignatius University, is drawing crowds of converts to his new spiritual movement. Atheists, Jews, Christians, Muslims, Buddhists and others are flocking to see and hear him. He allegedly produces a visible aura he shares with others. The phenomenon is described as the visible result of super-consciousness. Attempts to interview Paul Pennington were refused.

* * *

MEDIA HEADLINE: Archbishop warns of hoax and sacrilege

A mass at Abbey Church presided over by Paul Pennington is deemed a fraud and sacrilege by Archbishop Bauer today in a prepared statement. He further states that the alleged aural display at these events is a hoax produced by special light effects and the alleged euphoria through hypnotic techniques and drugged wine. He prohibits all Catholics and warns all good Christians to avoid contact with the Abbey Church and Mr. Pennington, or any of his followers.

KPOR interviewed several attendees who have experienced the aura and they say otherwise. Several families of patients at Mt. Olives hospice told us confidentially that the experience is genuine and helped their suffering relatives die peaceful deaths.

Fr. Tom Bradbury, Chancellor of Ignatius University where Mr. Pennington once taught, when reached by our correspondent, could neither affirm nor deny Pennington's ability or experience. He said Paul Pennington was a good teacher while at Ignatius. When asked why he was fired, Fr. Bradbury responded that it was more about church politics than Paul's religious theories or abilities. He would not further elaborate.

Archbishop Bauer labels both Paul Pennington and Chancellor Tom Bradbury radicals who are part of the Jesuit Order and not under the direct control of the Archdiocese. He further states that Pope Pius XIII expelled Fr. Bradbury from the Vatican before his return to Ignatius. Since then some valuables have been missing from the papal chambers.

* * *

Over the months that followed it became evident that Paul and the abbey were the target of the conservative media. Paul endured labels of charlatan, disgruntled ex-priest, and the anti-Christ. The abbey was branded a media light show that hoodwinked the simple-minded and dangerous to the gullible. It was claimed that followers were mostly minorities, moral deviants, and hysterics who mingled together in meditation. Even Mt. Olives came in for allegations of fraudulent treatment of hospice patients so as to extract increased contributions from clients and families.

Despite the negative media, attendance grew at the abbey for meditation sessions and for mass. Nic became concerned about possible violence from the hostile opposition. During sessions hecklers blocked the sidewalk in front of the abbey. Some were peaceful, handing out pamphlets detailing the blasphemies they felt were being committed by those visiting the abbey. But others openly jeered, and occasionally threw refuse. Nic had a fence erected around the property that acquired foul and threatening graffiti.

Paul's abbey friends had become targets on their own. Phillips found himself within his professional community indignantly defending the abbey as a legitimate center for meditation. Nic experienced outright derision at the university.

"We need to do something to defend ourselves," Nic said in a meeting at the abbey.

"Why?" Isaac asked. "They can't hurt us with untruths. Truth will out."

"They can hurt us," Nic said. "They're harassing us professionally, as well as those who come here for help. If this movement is to survive, we need to do something other than turn the other cheek."

"Going on the offense would be the wrong thing to do," Isaac said. "You need to get your story out there. The truth."

"How do I do that?" Paul asked. "Bauer appears to have a lock on most of the media."

"You could give an interview to one of the more neutral news agencies. Give them a scoop," Isaac said.

"But what do I say? They'll think I'm a fraud."

"Approach it as one of your lectures. Be factual, specific, give details, true accounts that can be verified by other sources, like from Mount Olives and St. Jude's," Isaac said.

The national news media picked up and ran Paul's interview. But it only served to deepen the controversy, and embolden the detractors, quacks and manipulators. And then came something unexpected. Paul was not alone.

* * *

MEDIA HEADLINE: Another halo glows and grows hope for new age of bliss

More documented events of super-consciousness are proving a Seattle priest and his legion of followers are right.

Yesterday in Delhi at a local shrine a woman has been reported as producing an aura. The phenomenon witnessed by over 100 people allegedly lasted for 18 minutes after which the woman collapsed and was taken to a hospital. This follows a similar event involving a man reported last month in Bhutan. No identities have been released and the state of ....

38

"Do not stray into the neighborhood of despair
For there are hopes: they are real, they exist
Do not go in the direction of darkness —
I tell you: suns exist." Rumi

* * *

Paul sat in his room preparing university class lectures in fits and starts between interruptions. It didn't matter if he tried working in his Tahoma office, or here at the abbey, the seekers found him. Since the interview he had been invited to numerous churches, auditoriums, synagogues, community halls, and once even a movie theater. Sharing his aura with large groups exhausted him. It sucked his energy until he pulled out to avoid collapse. But these mass events resulted in no aura awakenings. Frustrated and desperate, Paul's sense of urgency grew. When would PXII make their move?

Late that evening Paul approached the Ignatius chapel with unease. Ambrose, after no contact for several months, had asked to meet Paul. In the still air the reflection pond mirrored the inverted shadows of the surrounding landscape punctuated with stars. The chapel had been the ground zero for many of Paul's most transformative experiences. A place of refuge and discovery. But tonight, Paul's skin prickled as he entered.

Ambrose was already seated in an end pew off the middle aisle. The sanctuary lamp cast Ambrose into silhouette, his head down, face veiled in darkness.

Paul slid in and sat in stillness beside him.

Ambrose's right-hand pinched and pulled at his pant leg over and over. He was obviously wrestling with something.

The chapel ignited Paul's memories. Prayers. Appeals. A visitation that overwhelmed him that he'd denied. Life would be so different if ....

"Thanks for coming." Ambrose fidgeted and then firmly clasped both hands together in his lap, inhaled deeply, sighed and began speaking while staring at his shoes. "I've been troubled. You need to know – you deserve to know – Bauer had me watching you. Giving him reports while you were at Ignatius. I'm sorry."

Ambrose turned to Paul in appeal. The reflected flame of the red sanctuary lamp danced in Ambrose's eyes, as though some devilish spirit lurked there.

"I know he objected to my teaching," Paul said. "And my – unique ability. But I'm gone. Bauer was hard to deal with. I'm actually better off. So don't beat yourself up about it."

"Not just you but anything he could use against Ignatius."

"You're still spying for him?"

Ambrose winced. Then frowned at Paul. "You Jesuits. You question, test, doubt, debate. I can't escape it. I'm surrounded all day by books and files. Lots of time on my hands. I started reading them. Then I saw – saw what you can do. I can't escape wondering – worrying – about what's right." He turned away to stare at the altar and started pinching and pulling his pant leg again.

"Please. It's okay," Paul said.

"There's more." Ambrose crossed his arms, hugged himself, rocked back against the pew. "When I was a seminarian there were several of us preparing for ordination. One a very charismatic man, a zealot. A member of the Society of Saint Pius XII. They're...."

"I know who they are."

Ambrose's headed jerked around to face Paul. "Then you'll know they're very persuasive. Very forceful. Certain about their direction. I was drawn in – became a member."

"Are you still?"

"Once inside there's no going back. They've been working a long time to elect one of their own and succeeded in Pope Pius 13. They believe the prophecies of La Sallette, Fatima, Akita, and Huaraz about the coming of the anti-Christ to usurp the papacy. Not the published accounts but those that remain suppressed in the Vatican. They'll stop at nothing to secure the next papal election. They believe you're undermining their control."

"Really? I no longer have any interest in the church. Why're the prophecies repressed? What do they say?"

"I'm not privy to them but I'm told that P13, and most popes before him, believed they'd be misinterpreted by the masses. Used to lead the faithful astray. PXII believes that's what you're doing. They're watching you now more than ever. They think you're a fake and want to know how the aura-thing is done. You're already drawing a following away from the church. They want to stop you before you become powerful."

"Me? Powerful?"

"Well, then your movement. Bauer interrogates me about you. Please stop, or go away, hide."

"It wouldn't work. I didn't choose this path. It chose me. I was struck down by it, helpless like my namesake."

Paul felt sorry for Ambrose. He wanted to do the right thing. But he'd lost or had driven out of him the ability to reason out for himself what that was. "Do you think that PXII is doing the right thing?" Paul asked.

"I don't know who's right, who to believe. Are you sure you're right?"

"Ambrose, it isn't about being right. It's about doing good. 'By their fruits you shall know them.' Ask yourself who around you is compassionate, strives for unity, seeks truth, and works for the progressive advancement of mankind? And who generates fear, division, controls the beliefs and conscience of others with threats of damnation, wants mankind to turn back the clock a thousand years?"

"But the church ...."

"Ambrose, the word 'church' in the original Greek was *ecclesia*. It translates 'assembly' – not an edifice, not an organization, but a gathering of people, the people of God. All of them. Not just the clergy. When I left the church, I was devastated. But I soon discovered I'm still part of the divine *ecclesia*. There were times when the church was the *ecclesia* of God on earth, but it's not now. I'm free. I haven't lost – only gained."

Paul studied Ambrose who now had his head in his hands and was trembling, or silently sobbing, Paul couldn't be sure. He put his hand on Ambrose's shoulder. "It's okay. I'm okay. You followed your conscience."

Ambrose sniffed, wiped his face with a handkerchief and look at Paul. "Will you hear my confession?"

Paul asked, "Why don't you ask someone at Ignatius, or at the Chancery?"

"I can't go to them. I can't have what I've done be known by them or anyone. It's something I did for PXII many years ago. I've not had a good confession since then. Please."

"And you trust me?"

"Yes."

"Go ahead."

"Bless me father for I have sinned ..."

Paul tried not to let the shock show on his face. Ambrose was clearly suffering. Had suffered since he was a young man. All because he'd turned over his conscience to the custody of an organization. Too weak to rebel. Paul couldn't think of any penance worthy of the act, or that Ambrose would be capable of accomplishing, except to pray.

"My God, Ambrose, this's been eating at your soul for decades. Even though there were no consequences to anyone else except you and the victim, you should've taken responsibility. Even if it would have put your life in danger. Then or now."

"I know. I was afraid. Am afraid." Ambrose trembled. "I've prayed for guidance. What's the right thing to do? All I could think of was to confess to you. Please. Tell me what do to."

Paul wasn't prepared for this, but he couldn't leave Ambrose without hope. "You should continue to pray. Have no further contact with PXII. Stay away from Bauer as much as you can. Leave the priesthood if you have to. You might find it a relief." And then almost as an afterthought, "And find a life somewhere you can save from evil."

"Thank you." Ambrose's voice sounded dull, tired. His big hulk slumped down in the pew, then heaved onto his knees. He mumbled an act of contrition.

"Your confession is safe with me, and if I still have any power or grace to give you absolution, I give it."

39

"Let yourself by killed by him: is he not the water of life?
Never, ever, grow bitter: he is the friend and kills gently..."
Rumi

* * *

Spring quarter's end was in sight. Students showed up for class more regularly and crammed for final exams. Paul tasted summer just around the corner. Tahoma's grounds bloomed in a cacophony of wildflower colors in landscaping that didn't rely so much on trimmed hedges, regal roses and formal flower beds. Trees lacked the dignity of full maturity. Grasscrete served instead of lawn.

Paul hated his growing fame but came to appreciate that it conferred authority. He'd made the transition from having to buttress his theories and opinions with the support and data of others, to one who knows and speaks with the authenticity that comes from demonstrable personal experience. He used his talent for teaching to lay the ground for understanding and embracing the aura experience when it manifested within mankind. His lectures became increasingly popular and so were moved to a larger lecture hall.

"The universe or geosphere began about13.8 billion years ago. Life or the biosphere began about 4 billion years ago. The genus Homo appeared about two million years ago. There's evidence that human consciousness was well established about 40,000 years ago based on symbolic communication. Since then we've become a thinking, communicating, mass of individuals, unifying when necessary for survival. In the last century our human mass has covered the earth, wired together by technology that extends our abilities to communicate and unravel the secrets of our universe.

"The timeline for our evolution has been accelerating since the Big Bang. Are we as a human species through evolving? Leading scientists and mystics say not. Some posit there's at least one more stage for human evolution – to spirit – in a pneumasphere. This is also my own belief."

At this the crowded lecture hall became still.

"What is the pneumasphere? It's comprised of consciousness, many consciousnesses in unity, and a connection to super-consciousness. Christians call this the Holy Spirit. In Jewish Old Testament scriptures she is termed Wisdom. In Native American spirituality she is termed the Great Spirit. By the Greeks she is known as Sophia. She's the connective tissue between the universe and the theosphere. The pneumasphere is the human preparation to join the theosphere, the final step in our evolution. I believe at that point all the stages – geosphere, biosphere, noosphere, pneumasphere –will be jettisoned when no longer needed like stages in rocket flights that propel us into space. While not all will think so, this should be a very hopeful if not ecstatic future for mankind."

As Paul left the building he was accosted by a group of young men and women who shouted at him.

"Anti-Christ. Heretic. Satan." They threw raw eggs at him until he was dripping in yellow and clear slime. Many of his students rushed to his defense but the offenders fled.

He cleaned himself off in the nearest restroom and headed back to the abbey for the evening. He found Nic surrounded by tomes in the library. Paul left him undisturbed in favor of much needed sleep.

A few hours after midnight, a blast shook Paul's bed and compressed his eardrums, followed by a second explosion. Shaken, confused, awakened from deep sleep, he wasn't sure for a moment what was reality. Dazed, he read the clock, 2:42. Then he heard sounds of cracking, breaking, and falling masonry. He flung off his bed sheets and ran barefoot downstairs toward the noise coming from the side of the rectory next to the church to encounter broken glass and rubble. Acrid smoke filled the rectory from the direction of Nic's room making breathing difficult.

Paul coughed and shouted. "Nic, Nic, can you hear me? Are you in there? Nic." he shouted louder. More coughing. The smoke took both his voice and breath away. He ran for his cellphone, called 911, grabbed a wool blanket, wrapped it around him, jammed his feet in Nic's garden boots and headed back toward Nic's door. "Nic. Nic," he yelled again. The growing roar of flames was the only reply. No access that way.

He ran outside to where Nic's bedroom window should have been. Horrified, he saw a gaping hole belching flames. Across the garden the church was a holocaust, blazes reaching through the roof lighting the night sky. The onion dome had been completely blown off.

Sirens howled and engines roared onto the scene. Paul stood shaken and paralyzed. Figures in yellow suits and hard hats poured from the engines. Connected hoses. Unloaded ladders. Grabbed hatchets. One of them approached.

"Do you live here? Is there anyone in there?"

Paul had to pull his eyes from the inferno to even notice the man. "Yes, Nic. He sleeps in that room," pointing.

The man disappeared for a few moments then returned to ask Paul questions, but Paul had few answers. "I don't know how it started. A big double explosion woke me up."

He shook uncontrollably. A kindly person led him away to a vehicle that seemed to be the organizational hub of the firefight. Wrapped him in a blanket. Gave him something to drink.

Radios squawked. Bullhorns shouted. More sirens approached. Paul became aware he was sitting on the curb across the street. Many figures moved purposefully in choreographed movement subduing the conflagration. Several firefighters pulled a swathed figure through the flames. Medics converged in a flurry of activity and then loaded the figure into a Medic 1 van that immediately pulled away and was gone, its siren at full cry.

He realized he didn't even know Nic's fate. Alive? Dead?

He stumbled toward the man who appeared in charge. "Chief, please. Nic? How is he?"

"He's just been taken to Harborview. That's all I know. Are you all right?"

How to respond to that? I've never been all right he wanted to shriek at him. He took a couple of quavery breaths. "Yeah, I'm okay, but please. I need to get to the hospital." He called Rabia en route.

* * *

By the time Nic was pronounced dead Rabia had already slipped away. Paul found her in the hospital chapel seated on the floor alone, where he'd sat not long-ago. A faint weak aura almost entirely blue enveloped her head. He sat beside her saying nothing, not daring to touch her.

Paul closed his eyes. He longed to hold her, but would she cringe at my touch? What can I say? My fault. It should've been me. I brought danger to the abbey.

And Nic? His toothy smile, jutting eyebrows, bushy beard, quick laughter – Paul's soul cried out in a groundswell of grief. I should've left the abbey, never exposed Nic or anyone else to such risk. Tom warned me. Why didn't I listen. I'm a danger to anyone around me. They're trying to kill me...kill me.... The melodramatic words ricocheted around in his mind like a bullet in a boxcar but were less real than Nic's death.

Nic had been a second father to Rabia. Paul had always found Rabia to be psychically strong with reserves to carry others. Now waves of grief poured from her. Without a family of her own, his death left her utterly alone.

Paul, amidst his own grief and guilt, and with Rabia's rejection still raw in his soul, felt helpless. He took one of her hands and placed it in both of his. She didn't pull away. He focused deeper, silenced all his own pain, own thoughts, concentrating only on Rabia. He listened until he heard her. She was keening inside, not just for Nic but for her father Kabir, her mother, her brothers, and another life. He could do nothing but sit with her, share her desolation without questions. Through wave after wave of loss, guilt, and shame, he accepted her, absorbed her dark emotions. But he would not intrude on her core of black shadow.

He placed one arm around her shoulders. She showed no sign of awareness of his touch, until long after when she laid her head on his chest.

He sat through the remainder of the night stroking her hair and sharing their grief until Rabia's aura faded and she slumped exhausted into his lap.

40

"My decline you have seen, now discover my soaring ascent.
Would setting cause any harm to the sun or moon?
To you, my death seems a setting, but really it is dawn". Rumi

* * *

The abbey church and rectory were burnt hollows in a landscape of mud, acrid rubble, and broken glass. The beautiful lush garden was no more. The two willows like charred toothpicks poked accusingly at the sky.

They'd missed their intended target. The guilt dragged on Paul like being shackled to the dead man. This can never happen again. Then a terrifying thought came to him. I was supposed to have celebrated mass that day. What if John was murdered? Poisoned. They never did an autopsy.

John had willed his cabin to Paul. He resolved to leave Seattle immediately.

The driveway to the cabin was still muddy from the melted snow. The woodpile had fallen down. Polypore mushrooms covered the logs hastening the return to their earthy origin.

The key slid in the door lock and turned smoothly. Memories poured out of the door like vapor. Paul crossed the threshold into the chilly interior. The cabin's unique scent blended from smoky log fires, kerosene, and John's pipe was tainted by a hint of stale must.

The *refugeo* was still. The small noises that made the cabin alive to Paul – the crackling fire, John's creaking rocker, the bubbling of the teakettle, snow shedding off the roof, or rain beating down hard or softly pattering, the wind scratching tree-fingers against the windows – all were silent.

He built a fire in the stone fireplace and stood gazing down into it leaning on the mantlepiece. He told himself it was the smoke from the flames that caused his eyes to smart. He made tea and lowered into John's creaky chair, slowly rocking. Sitting in the lap of a specter, an adult cradle. Forgive me, John.

Nic, who'd welcomed him into his home. Made him laugh with good food, good wine, good friends. So generous. And now Nic was gone too.

And Rabia. Their relationship had subsided into embarrassed silence. Love that can't be. She carries a burden that I didn't respect and have added to.

My 'mission'? Dear God, you should have chosen a less feeble instrument.

The full impact of his losses and failures churned inside. The worst headaches of his aural episodes were more bearable than this pounding penetrating pain. He abruptly got up, leaving the empty chair to continue rocking as though occupied by John's ghost. He opened the cabinet where John kept his liquor and poured himself a large scotch. Cold, he wrapped himself in a blanket and huddled on the floor facing the fire. Hot flames flickered across his face. Deep within the fire, coals glowed red-orange like hot lava rock. A spark flew out to burn a pinhole in the blanket. It smelled like burning hair before it went out. Paul closed his eyes.

Dear God, help me.

His prayer faded away into silence. Drained of emotion and empty of sensation he hardly noticed its approach. To surrender in the fiery crucible of oblivion was all he wanted.

Weightless, Paul fell, kept falling into waves of liquid light. Bodiless, he drifted out of time. Wave upon wave crested and fell carrying him along toward the center.

Invisibly tethered to the nucleus of this same field danced an infinity of sparks, orbiting, spinning, oscillating. They overflowed with energy. Shimmered, glinted, flashed, at times shooting off like small comets, sometimes straight through the center and back. If bliss could take shape, this would be it.

The center was difficult to perceive. It gave the impression of vast density without a visible boundary. Yet it presented a smooth iridescent surface that seemed to flow in phantasmagoric shapes. Space around it shone. Space within it vibrated. It was evident why communication from the center was difficult to decipher. So might a sun communicate with an electron, powerful and felt without being understood.

Paul was halted at the perimeter, unable to approach, like Aesop's bat caught between two worlds. He'd never been able to go beyond this horizon for fear of loss of self. Now he welcomed it.

I surrender.

Paul had the odd sensation of letting go of the earth like letting go of a helium balloon. Saw it float away. Or am I the one who's floating away?

As he approached the center, he sensed its embrace. As pure spirit he withstood the painful joy of union that would have been death in physical form. But no oblivion. Instead, ultimate completion.

Paul recognized the sparks as a communion of consciousnesses, bodies sloughed off like a snakeskin or molted feathers, leaving a pure aural core for conjoining. Here the Law of Conservation of Consciousness reached its apex. Here in the template were the essence of John and Nic, along with all the creative and good in mankind since the dawn of humanity. They've always been here and always will be, outside of space and time.

And so am I.

Yes

What must I do?

Trust

41

"Sorrow trembles down my spirit's way –
Uncomplaining, dark as night she seems."
Rainier Maria Rilke

* * *

Harborview felt leaden. While many died here, Rabia hadn't known any of them personally, not until now. Nic's body was still in the morgue awaiting autopsy. She couldn't think about that. To her he wasn't yet a body, a thing.

Rabia hadn't felt so alone since she was a young girl in Syria. She'd blocked out the painful memories of her life cratering there until Fakhruddin and Ibrahim found her. Now the trauma of her childhood had returned. She'd learned from her building manager that they had been at her apartment building.

Tired after a full day, Rabia had her keys already in hand as she approached her door. That morning when she'd left her apartment, she'd taken two long strands of her hair and draped them individually over the door before closing and locking it. She shone the small flashlight on her keychain at the top of the door. Neither strand was there.

What to do? Call the building manager? Call the police? Walking away seemed the wisest course. She returned to her car and drove to Mt. Olives.

Rabia sat in the window seat in Marcellus's room. The piebald cat joined her. She stroked its back as it arched to her fingers.

"A while back my uncle came to the hospital with Ibrahim, my husband." Rabia nervously glanced at Marcellus.

Marcellus's eyebrows raised, then softened to concern. "I didn't know you were married."

Rabia's eyes focused into the distance. "It was a forced marriage – in Syria – when I was ten, a year after my father died."

Marcellus's inhaled sharply.

"Child marriages are not unheard of in the Middle East. But it was a terrible marriage, cruel. I ran away." Rabia stopped, a catch in her throat. Images of Ibrahim, his family, her virtual imprisonment, the beatings – the long-buried memories resurfaced with a vengeance. "I came to America a Sufi refugee. I thought I'd escaped. While the war went on, my uncle was unable to obtain a visa to the U.S. But now, after all this time, he came to find me. He demanded I return to my husband. I declined. So he brought Ibrahim here. Uncle says I've shamed both families. We had a confrontation. I hoped that would be the end of it. Then today they somehow got into my apartment building. I've been worried about something like this happening for a while. I don't know how it will end since they won't take 'no' for an answer."

"Can't you get a divorce?"

"It wouldn't matter. It would need to go through an Islamic court, and it won't go well." Rabia swallowed. "I'm Sufi, as was my father. Conservative Muslims consider Sufis heretics. My father was murdered for his beliefs. Then I became the responsibility of my uncle. Then of my husband. I was beaten again and again. I tried to run away but was always dragged back." Rabia shuddered and paused long before continuing. "I became pregnant."

Marcellus rose, crossed the room and sat beside Rabia. Placed an arm around her.

"Even that didn't stop the beatings." Rabia shivered. "I lost the baby."

Marcellus hugged her and rocked her in her arms as Rabia heaved and sobbed.

"I feel so much guilt. If I'd been an obedient wife, hadn't run away, the baby might have lived."

"You can't think that. You were a child. You were forced by people who didn't love you into a marriage that resulted in what amounts to rape. You might've died. Forgive yourself. We all must go on from where we are."

Pent up horror, shame and remorse locked away for thirty years were released in a torrent.

Marcellus eased Rabia's head onto her breast and stroked her hair. Crooned soothing prayers of forgiveness, compassion and healing; poetry of love and beauty; words of oneness and eternity.

Eventually the words seeped in and Rabia breathed evenly. She swallowed, sat up and brushed back wet tendrils of her hair. Took the tissues Marcellus offered and wiped her face. Blew her nose. "I thought I'd escaped all this when I came to America. But there's no escape."

"What do you think they'll do?" asked Marcellus.

"I can't imagine my uncle seriously harming me. But he's a conservative Muslim. Such men expect to have absolute control over the women in their families. I know in his own mind my uncle thinks he's doing the right thing. But would he do violence? He beat me when I was young, but I can't say if he would now. Ibrahim? He's a radical Islamic fundamentalist. I know from experience that he's violent. He frightens me."

"Be cautious. There've been cases even here in the U.S. of Muslim women facing violence from their own families, even honor killings. Why don't you move in here for a while as a precaution? I'd feel better if you were in a place with people around you who know and care about you. Besides, an onsite doctor would be a blessing for Mt. Olives."

"Thank you. Hopefully it won't be for long. My uncle and Ibrahim can't stay here indefinitely."

"True, but that may precipitate action."

42

"Let me not pray to be sheltered from dangers,
But to be fearless in facing them.
Let me not beg for the stilling of my pain,
But for the heart to conquer it."
Rabindranath Tagore

* * *

Tom regained consciousness with a dark bag over his head. His arms, legs, and torso were tied to a chair. The air felt dank and chill and stank of mold. He heard no sound. He kept absolutely still hoping to give the impression that he was still unconscious.

"Time to wake up," said a smooth alto voice.

Ice water drenched Tom's face.

"Where is it?"

Silence.

"I have no time for subtleties," said the voice.

Something hard, like a metal pipe, hit Tom's right shin so hard he cried out and nearly passed out from the pain. He was sure his tibia was broken.

"Now that you know I mean business, where is it?"

Through the haze of pain Tom thought the voice vaguely familiar.

"We already have Garcia's copy. We know what it says. It's been destroyed. I'm waiting."

Whack came down the rod on Tom's left shin. He screamed. He must have passed out because the next thing he knew more ice water was poured over his head.

"Your running out of time," said the voice.

"You'll never find it if you kill me," said Tom.

The metal rod slammed into his face. Shards of broken teeth floated in blood in his mouth.

"We didn't find it at Ignatius. Did you give it to someone? Paul? It talks about Paul doesn't it. The catalyst," he laughed.

Tom finally placed the voice. "You're Bauer's assistant." Tom struggled to speak through bleeding lips.

"Bauer. He's a stooge. Tell me where it is so we can end this."

"You're just going to kill me so why should I?" whispered Tom spitting out blood and bits of teeth.

"Because I can make that quick and painless, or excruciating. Your choice."

Tom heard a snick, then a noise like something blowing hard. The bag was whipped off his head. Geoffrey held a blow torch in one hand.

43

"He was a warrior and mystic, ogre and saint, ... less than a god, more than a man. There is no measuring Paul Muad'Dib's motives by ordinary standards. In the moment of his triumph, he saw the death prepared for him, yet he accepted the treachery."
Frank Herbert's Dune

* * *

The prognosis was grim. Tom had been left for dead below the windows of his burning chambers. Both his legs were broken. He had burns over most of his body and suffered head injuries.

Knowing this still didn't prepare Paul for what he encountered when he was admitted to the room. Most of Tom's head was swathed, leaving slits for his eyes, nostrils, and swollen and split lips. He was on oxygen. His right hand and arm were wrapped in gauze. His left arm, mostly unharmed, lay naked on top of the sheet that covered the rest of the wreck of his body. Other than the labored rising and falling of his chest, Tom didn't move.

Paul sat down next to him. "Tom, can you hear me? It's Paul."

Nothing changed. The monitors on the wall behind him glowed and blinked but told him nothing.

"Tom." Paul observed the barest quiver of Tom's lips and a slight increase in his respiration. The forefinger on his left hand twitched, might have beckoned. Paul bent low to hear, but Tom's lips would not form words.

Only one way to communicate with him now. Paul closed his eyes and focused inward. Emptied his thoughts of anything besides Tom. Paul's consciousness penetrated to confront pain, exhaustion, anguish and remorse.

"Tom. You're forgiven. Absolved."

Unfinished. Something was unfinished. Tom mentally fought to communicate. The sense of urgency increased.

"Magdala? You want me to warn Magdala".

Paul perceived a lessening of tension. Tom was weak, losing the battle, in terrible pain. He found the touchstone of Tom's aura. Infused it with energy to expand and emerge. As it grew stronger and more vibrant Tom's physical life force commensurately declined.

Thank you. Bless you.

Paul stayed until Tom's aura detached, a whispery translucent silver that rose like fog off a lake at dawn. The monitors flat-lined.

"Go in peace." Paul blessed him.

* * *

Paul burst in. "Tom's dead."

Both women whirled around.

"Oh my God." whispered Marcellus.

Magdala turned white. Her lips quivered.

"He was tortured. The Ignatius fire was not what killed him. We were able to communicate as he was dying. He urgently wanted to warn you, Magdala. Why?" asked Paul.

Magdala pursed her lips. Sat down. Removed her glasses. "Do you know about the Vatican Documents?"

Paul nodded.

"Well I have them. I made copies for a group of attorneys who are preparing a case to file charges against PXII. But poor Tom. PXII is responsible for this." Magdala's eyes flashed. "I have no doubt they torched Tom and his rooms to destroy all knowledge of the memory stick."

"Burning Tom's room was an act of desperation to cover their tracks," said Paul. "They couldn't be sure the memory stick was there. I don't believe PXII will stop until they are absolutely sure they're safe. Tom was worried about you. You'd better act fast. And you'd better get protection."

"Charges will be filed any day now," Magdala said. "After that I won't need protection. But you do. You're in danger as long as PXII still functions. Tom's hope was that once PXII and P13 were exposed, they wouldn't have time to worry about you. But I'm not so sure. There are zealots within PXII who are motivated less by power than belief in prophecies about anti-Christs and catalysts."

Paul turned to the window, chewed his lip, looked out at the Cascade Mountains with the sun shining off their snowy peaks. "I still have a duty to perform, and I don't know how long I've got. I need a big venue that will accommodate thousands and I need it soon." He turned to Magdala. "Can you help me?"

"There's the Gorge," said Magdala. "It seats 27,000. It'll cost a fortune but I think I can manage it, and the owner owes me a favor." Magdala's eyes glittered at Paul. "What do you intend to do?"

"Attempt a massive aura awakening."

Marcellus caught her breath.

Magdala frowned. "You'll be an easy target."

"If PXII survives, I'm as good as dead anyway. I may have this one chance to complete my mission before they take me out."

"Could you manage that many? Initiates I mean?" asked Marcellus.

"I've never tried such a large number. The energy drain will be enormous. But I'm running out of time. I have to try, and I have to trust."

Marcellus hugged him.

Magdala crossed herself.

44

"'You wanted me to die,' said Achilles quietly.
'I expected you to solve your own problems,' said
Suriyawong.'"
Orson Scott Card, Shadow Puppets

* * *

Archbishop Bauer read the story he had put out from the Chancery.

MEDIA HEADLINE: Archbishop connects death of Ignatius Chancellor to recent controversy
A statement released today by the Archdiocese Chancery expressed shock and sorrow at the death of Fr. Tom Bradbury, Chancellor of St. Ignatius University. St. Ignatius has been involved in a recent controversy regarding Paul Pennington who formerly taught there. Mr. Pennington was also involved in the fire and death at the home of Dr. Nicolas Novgorod where Mr. Pennington had been staying and making the center of a new-age religious movement. Archbishop Bauer issued a statement last month condemning Pennington's new movement as fraud, and warned of grave spiritual consequence to anyone ....

He cancelled all appointments, held all calls, and hunkered down in his office. He pinched and rubbed his nose. Things hadn't gone well. Officially he had no knowledge of how the deaths of Fr. John O'Malley, some Russian doctor, and Fr. Tom Bradbury occurred. But *sub rosa* he was furious and anxious about how they did. Too messy.

I never really trusted Geoffrey. Am I safe? And I still don't have the documents. What if Geoffrey's wrong and they weren't in Tom's room? And Pennington free. Corelli will brand me with this.

His private cell beeped. An unfamiliar voice addressed him.

"Bauer, I have the documents you've been searching for. The ones Fr. Tom Bradbury took from the Vatican. The ones you had him killed for. I know what they say."

"Who is this?"

"You don't need to know."

"What do you want?"

"To purge the church of vermin." Then the call dropped.

Bauer sat still as a stone gargoyle on his throne-chair. Adrenaline shot through him and his heart rate mounted. Muscles, unaccustomed to use, tensed. His world closed in around him to a single thought. Escape. He steadied himself with a couple of deep breaths. I can't afford to show fear.

Bauer made the call he was hoping never to have to make. "Things have not gone according to plan here. Serious consequences are developing that could point to us."

Bauer rubbed his forehead as he listened to the reply. His upper lip trembled. His brows narrowed to a squint. His mouth twisted into a grimace of bared teeth and his eyes bulged. Then he exploded. "What d'you mean sole liability? We're in this together. You can't simply walk away, you must take some responsibility... they have the documents ... ... I could transfer ...."

The call dropped. He set aside his mobile and pressed fists into his temples. They can't do this to me. Must think this through carefully. I still have friends, powerful friends in the Vatican. People who owe me. He reached for his cellphone again.

* * *

Later that evening, after a meal and a bottle of wine, Bauer felt somewhat mollified. Help was promised that would leave no trace. Assurances of Geoffrey's trustworthiness were given. All Bauer had to do was to hold hard and await further instructions that would be forthcoming. He enjoyed a cream de menthe to settle his nerves, climbed in his four-poster, and with difficulty finally read himself to sleep.

Shortly after midnight Bauer's eyes blinked opened to Stygian darkness. Something woke him. Maddening, since it'd been so hard to get to sleep. A figure moved furtively.

"Who's there?" He rolled over and switched on his reading lamp.

"You." He sat up in bed, his eyes glaring. "Why are you sneaking around my room in the middle of the night?"

The figure approached the bed, a finger to his lips.

"Speak man," Bauer said. "Why are you here? What are you doing? I've told you never ...."

The figure pulled a revolver from his pocket.

45

"All the false notions of myself that once caused fear, pain
Have turned to ash as I neared God.
What has risen from the tangled web of thought and sinew
Now shines with jubilation through the eyes of angels
And screams from the guts of Infinite existence Itself."
   Hafiz, The Gift

* * *

It was ten in the evening. Rabia headed for the hospital garage absent-mindedly jingling her keys. She planned to drive through the night to be at the Gorge to support Paul the next evening. Marcellus had a room in Yakima where she could get some rest.

The heavy metal door to the cavernous garage slammed behind her. Shadows dominated the space. Odd noises from the building's mechanical systems reverberated in the featureless landscape, along with her own clipped staccato steps. She noticed a large laundry van parked next to her car making it difficult to get in the driver's side. Why park here so close when the whole garage was available?

Its side door slid open. A dark hand reached out.

She turned away and dashed back toward the entrance to the hospital, fumbling for her cell as she ran. But before she could key in the emergency code, strong arms grabbed her bodily and a hand clapped over her mouth. She tried to twist out of his grasp but was dragged to the van and thrown into the back on the floor.

In the scuffle she lost a shoe and dropped her cell that slid under the van.

She tried to scream. Ibrahim hit her hard, twice. Blood oozed into her mouth. His fists punched breath from her. He threw her to the floor face down banging her head on the metal. When she struggled, he hit her again until he had her gagged, and her hands and legs tied. Then he got into the driver's seat and started the ignition. Rabia, barely conscious, felt the van back up then drive forward out of the garage. A venomous flower of fear unfurled in her heart.

They must have driven for some miles, at first turning and stopping occasionally, but after about half an hour the vehicle continued with few interruptions.

Ibrahim occasionally looked back from the driver's seat. Clenched his fist at her. His anger came out in shouts and snarls. It was like being caged with a wild carnivore.

"Allah the Sustainer, the Merciful. Help me," she silently prayed over and over again like a mantra.

The van slowed, pulled off a paved road and onto a rough track. It bumped and jolted along and then stopped. Ibrahim opened the sliding door and stood in front of her as she lay prone. He pulled her into a kneeling position facing him. His face was a hard mask, frozen in a stony determined grimace, barely recognizable. His voice flat, with a thick accent, recited a verdict.

"You have shamed me and my family for the last time." He slapped her face back and forth. Then he eased a knife out of his jacket.

He berated Rabia, marching around in front of her brandishing the knife, recounting how she had wronged him, working himself up into a frenzy. Rabia on her knees didn't listen. About to die, she closed her eyes and focused on inner stillness and silence and a prayer: "I will give up all fears, all doubts, all anxieties, all thoughts of weakness. I have placed myself under the guidance of an All-Powerful Being. Do with me what you will."

Here was to be the end of all the horror and sorrow and shame that had haunted her since her father's death. The confrontations with Fakruhhdin and Ibrahim clearly showed there was nothing she could have done as a young girl to refuse the marriage or prevent the death of her child. And what kind of life would the child have had with this man as a father? In infinite compassion Allah had taken her child to himself. With a wan smile of compassion toward herself her aura emerged blazing, complete, silver-gold.

Ibrahim stopped his diatribe. Rabia didn't move. She looked steadily into Ibrahim's eyes, right through to his weakness. Consumed by male ego there was no place for him to go when confronted with feminine divinity. With wide eyes he approached her and lightly touched her arm, then recoiled as from a flame.

Ibrahim threw his knife on the ground. Jerked Rabia out of the van. Got behind the wheel and sped off.

Rabia landed on her face. She spat blood and dirt from her mouth. Then rolled over to the knife and used it to cut through her bonds. It wasn't easy and took quite a while, but she eventually freed herself. She wiped grime and grass from her face. Brushed off her damp and dirty clothes. With only one shoe it was going to be slow going. She didn't know where she was, but it didn't matter. She was alive, breathing, seeing, feeling.

Dawn eased into the sky in pastel watercolors.

Her fears were gone. Ibrahim wouldn't be back. Uncle wouldn't be back. They have no hold over me. But more importantly, the experience had burned away the guilt burden of her past.

A new woman, she looked around. She was standing on a bluff overlooking the industrial area of south Seattle. Instead of seeing the sordid flattened grass specked with her blood, or the muddy path with the imprint of her body, or even the ugly manufacturing structures below, the earth spread out whole and good under the sun's rays.

She followed the track that led back to a road. Walked barefoot as on a pilgrimage, oblivious of the stones under her feet. Gratitude upwelled in a litany. "Blessed be Allah the All Merciful, the All Compassionate, the Sustainer ...."

46

"It is the time of union,
It is the time of vision,
It is the time of resurrection,
It is the time of grace,
It is the time of generosity,
The treasure of gifts has arrived.
The brilliance of the sea has flashed forth.
The dawn of blessing has arisen ..." Rumi

* * *

Ambrose saw the news before he left the Yakima hotel for the Gorge. His coffee cooled as his stomach burned, and blood drained from his face.

MEDIA HEADLINE: Another tragedy for local Catholics with the death of Seattle's Archbishop Bauer just three days after Ignatius Chancellor's death.

Earlier today Archbishop Bauer of St. Luke's Cathedral was found dead in his home on Capitol Hill. The staff who found the body hanging in his bedroom are unwilling to provide further comment. Police are investigating. Archbishop Bauer came to Seattle five years ago from Chicago, after an incident involving a scandal at the Vatican Bank and his ....

* * *

MEDIA HEADLINE: Popes John Paul I and Francis I deaths revealed to be murders

Charges were filed today in Rome against members of the Vatican regarding the alleged murders of two former popes. Vatican officials repudiate the allegations as ridiculous and irresponsible ....

* * *

"What of me?" Ambrose's narrow world closed in around him. Tom had given him a home. Now Tom was dead. Bauer sent him here. Now Bauer was dead. PXII had protected him. Now they had big challenges that didn't include him. The more he read the clearer it became that PXII's actions were not justified in the name of God. Yet he'd believed. Followed. Sinned for them. Wasted his life for them. Tears of anger and anguish brimmed in his eyes. He wiped them away with the back of his hand.

Why go to the Gorge now? But then where else would I go? At least I can see Paul. He forgave me. An ember of hope flickered in his heart.

* * *

The amphitheater filled slowly in the cream and sapphire twilight. The night portended to be a clear one of stars with no moon. The surrounding hills glowed in the muted colors of ginger, plum and russets of fall. Warmed by the late afternoon sun, the scent of wild sage and thyme effused from the scrub brush for miles around. Rock columns from eons past exposed by river and wind stood to attention, silent sentinels to the human stage. White-throated swifts from the cliffs swooped to catch the last of their prey before the sun died.

Ambrose had never been to such a place. He didn't enter the large open-air amphitheater, at least yet, but watched those who did: a few priests, nuns, and monks; others in scarves, hijabs, and yarmulkes; several in saffron robes; some oddities with tattoos, chains and outlandish hair, or no hair with painted scalps. The throng streamed in. Then he saw someone he recognized, tall,

227

gaunt, in a black robe and cowl. The figure nodded slightly toward him as he entered, his eagle eyes and spidery hands unmistakable even in the concealing garb.

Why is he here? The amphitheater continued to fill but Ambrose decided to remain outside keeping his distance.

A few stragglers jostled in and took the remaining seats. The sun dipped below the canyon walls. A hush fell over the crowd. Stars and planets began to pierce the heavens with sharp purity, magnified through the atmospheric lens as though the whole universe bent low to witness the proceedings.

A slender man like a grub steadily crawled up a promontory just outside the amphitheater high enough to overlook the stage. The man, clad in the same dun colors as the ground he traversed, had a backpack and moved stealthily between sagebrush and clumps of balsam root. He frequently scanned 360 degrees around. Ambrose watched from behind a stunted pine. The man finally crested the hill and hunkered down. He unpacked his backpack and started assembling something. Ambrose caught a glint in the last faint rays of the setting sun.

* * *

All of Paul's anxiety about this night coalesced into tension that tasted like a sour apple. It was building, crawling up the back of his neck, pooling in his stomach. He needed strength, all his psychic energy and focus to bring it off. Can I do it? I may not get another chance. Trust. He said it over and over like a mantrum.

Someone said, "It's time. You're on."

Paul didn't move.

"Paul?"

Paul stepped onto the stage. He arrived at a straight-backed chair he'd requested instead of a podium. Finally, inexorably, he raised his eyes to the thousands of faces. Like a sea of grain, they fanned out below him and up the sides of the bowl. In his mind, the crowd formed an impersonal unit that made it easier to douse the burning tension in his gut. Marcellus, Magdala, Phillips,

Isaac, and Jesse sat in what would have been the orchestra pit if there'd been one. Where was Rabia?

He shuffled his feet and wiped his face with a blue bandanna. The small microphone got in his way. Every time he fidgeted it projected a rasping sound to the audience.

He prayed silently. I don't trust myself to do this. But I must do it. So I'm trusting You.

"Good people. Many of you have come a long way to be here. Some curious. Some skeptical. But most of you I sense are here because something is missing in your lives. Or you experience persistent alienation that seeks connection, wholeness. Or you suffer from a lack of hope, a lack of something to live for. Perhaps you perceive something just on the verge of awareness that causes restlessness or even a drive to find resolution, but don't know what it is. Or it may be the greatest unknown, the last frontier, death."

* * *

Death. Tom's dead. Bauer's dead. I'm afraid to die. A failure at everything. Chose the wrong side. Coward. My whole life a regret, wasted. No going back. The incessant voice inside Ambrose went on, hammering away at his conscience, turning on him. He clung to the scrub pine.

* * *

Paul continued with his introduction. "I would ask you to consider these as spiritual questions. They can't be answered by the intellect or rational thought. That doesn't mean however, that those who seek such answers are irrational. Some of the greatest seekers have been our greatest scientists, who've seen an ineffable consciousness behind the universe that we can never know through physics, cosmology or biology. The mystics down through the ages had a glimpse and pointed the way toward the Light."

* * *

Ambrose gulped air to calm down, wiped his face with the back of his hand. He continued to observe Geoffrey and a chill slithered up his spine. The incessant voice started up again, taunting and disdainful. Run away. You'll be caught, *blamed.* You *betrayed* Tom. Tom's *dead,* dead because of *you.* Bauer's *dead.* Now who'll protect you?

Ambrose recognized the voice now. It was his mother's. *You're nothing but a pathetic, feeble, useless fool.* The words dripped like acid into his soul. He rocked from one foot to the other. Shook his head. Put his hands over his ears. Then sighted Geoffrey again. He was setting up a small tripod.

After a brief hesitation Ambrose moved from behind the tree and quietly circled around the back of the hill where Geoffrey perched. Climbing, keeping as low a profile as possible, Ambrose reached the top, just as Geoffrey lowered to his stomach and propped himself up on his elbows behind the tripod. Startled by Ambrose's approach, Geoffrey rolled over and pointed a rifle at him.

"What the hell are you doing here, you fat fool?" Geoffrey hissed.

Ambrose stopped.

"I don't need or want you here," Geoffrey said. "Between you and Bauer this situation has been botched. Got out of control. You're endangering my mission. Get out of here." He rolled back onto his elbows, fitted the rifle to the tripod and sighted down its scope.

* * *

"Everyone has an aura. What you experience tonight will depend on you. You must be willing to be open and to surrender your ego to awaken your aura. Through your aura you are joined to each other and to the eternal super-consciousness. The great gift of this unity is that we are no longer alone but are complete and whole beings with all beings – forever."

Paul closed his eyes.

Many in the amphitheater stood.

* * *

Now. Do it now. The cowled figure practically levitated on his toes to watch.

* * *

Ambrose breathed heavily. Geoffrey ignored him and focused on his aim. Quickly and quietly for such a big man, Ambrose jumped on Geoffrey and flattened him onto the ground. Ambrose's knees dug deep into Geoffrey's thorax, the rifle pinioned underneath his body. He felt some of Geoffrey's ribs break and his chest collapse. The force expelled the air from Geoffrey's lungs in a blend of a cough, a mute scream, and a wheeze.

Ambrose heard a muffled snap. Geoffrey's right arm folded under him at an odd angle. He kicked his legs trying to roll Ambrose off, but Ambrose wrapped beefy arms around Geoffrey's slim chest in a crushing hug and continued pressing him hard into the ground. Geoffrey couldn't move. Couldn't breathe. He lay still. Ambrose held him under his full weight and didn't get up for a long while.

Crickets sang a dirge in the thickets nearby. Ambrose smelled the desert incense of sagebrush and wild thyme. Golden-brown paper-thin dead cottonwood leaves blew over and caught around the two men, wreathing them in decay.

Geoffrey's still body felt shrunken, like a broken doll. Ambrose softened his hold and struggled up. Geoffrey made no sound. Didn't move. Ambrose left him face down splayed on the ground, and unhurriedly walked down the backside of the hill into the darkness.

* * *

Behind the diamond arc of the Milky Way, the sky by now was so black as to be a void; the night thick, close, and expectant. The wind died. Grasshoppers hushed still and silent. The assembly collectively held its breath. Minutes passed.

Paul's head started to shimmer. The shimmer grew to a glow. The glow expanded to emerge from his whole body. As it extended, arcs of light issued from his head and chest, shot up into the air like jets of gold-silver flame, then curved around down to the ground. The arcs rose higher like a fountain spewing light sprays into the night that threw off curtains of light in blues, greens, yellows, purples, and reds at the highest point. The curtains wavered and pulsated, spiraled and wrapped into streams; curled around the arcs; feathered off only to reappear even stronger.

The intake of breathes from the audience at the spectacle was a long collective aspiration. Necks craned back to take in the full sky. Some climbed on their seats to get closer to the phenomenon.

Paul emptied himself and surrendered to the torrents of energy pouring through him from the Aura. A barrage of emotions broke in on him from the crowd: wonder, fear, adoration, envy, elation, shame; all jumbled in a cacophony of sensations and passions.

Paul's body shook and shone as the Aura-light burst from him. Every cell in his body vibrated. He gasped. His knees buckled. His heart beat so hard and fast it felt as though it would erupt from his chest.

I can't ... I'm sorry ... the light wavered, faltered. He staggered and grabbed for the chair. Hunched over.

Then Rabia, in full aura, entered the stage, a triumphant radiant blaze of silver-platinum light. She crossed to Paul and took his hands. He straightened up to face her. The light strengthened, grew more animated. Jets of multi-colored sparks showered from them to drench the onlookers. Eventually the light grew so pervasive and intense that the black void and stars were blotted out by its incandescent radiance.

The spirals and sparks flowed over and through the amphitheater, one by one penetrating the audience. Paul pushed catalyzation. It became a chain reaction. Now others in the audience moaned or rocked or keened through the transcendent experience as the Aura took them. Awakened them.

The Aura-light enveloped the entire amphitheater. Thousands became one, sharing in super-consciousness.

* * *

The Aura flowed over, caressed and pierced the cowled figure. He shook. Every fiber of his being throbbed. Though he closed his eyes, the light softly penetrated his optic nerve and flowed like milk down into his consciousness. He grasped the sides of his head. Fought to close his mind to the alien thing. Its tentacles pulled him in along with those near. Snatches of consciousness from those around him intruded, and he feared his own thoughts would escape, become transparent, lose control. This cannot be. What if this proliferates? It will undermine everything we've built. Political alliances exposed. Manipulation of enemies revealed. Financial networks bared.

With a violent effort he pushed through the enraptured crowd to the exit, his robes flapping in the night breeze like an overgrown carrion crow.

* * *

Paul was unaware of Rabia's body. He was aware of her only within the Aura. Her darkness was gone. The two became one and whole, a single consciousness in two beings fused into a column of light, one in love and passion.

* * *

A dense presence distills from the light. Paul-Rabia turns toward the presence, as a sunflower to the sun. The presence pulls like a gravity field toward a vast cloud of encircling glints of light. Waves of immense bliss penetrate Paul-Rabia in the joining as the couple transforms into sparks of celestial fire.

* * *

The crowd fell silent. Paul-Rabia's form could not now be seen. They had become pure light, so intense as to be a column of silver-white-gold flame that towered up from the stage at least 300 feet. Spirals and sparks showered and saturated the ecstatic audience-initiates and whirled off into the atmosphere like spawn to traverse the earth and enkindle prepared souls. The initiates gaped at the column of Paul-Rabia fire as it levitated into the sky to join the stars.

And the Pneumasphere was born.

* * *

Book of Wisdom – 7:22-8:1
 Wisdom is spirit ...
 She is an Aura of the might of God
 A pure effusion of the glory of the Almighty ...
 She is the refulgence of eternal light
 The spotless mirror of the power of God,
 The image of his goodness ...
 And passing into holy souls from age to age,
 She produces friends of God ...
 She is fairer than the sun,
 Surpasses every constellation of the stars ....

Pneumasphere

Pneumasphere